MURDEROUS SPIRIT

By

Geoff Loftus

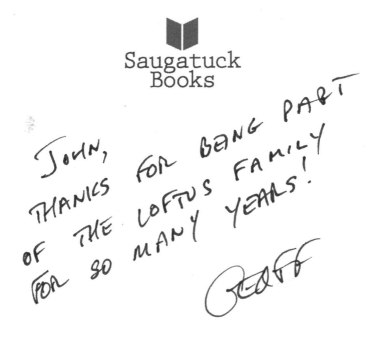

Saugatuck
Books

JOHN,
THANKS FOR BEING PART
OF THE LOFTUS FAMILY
FOR SO MANY YEARS!

Geoff

For information, please contact info@geoffloftus.com.

Murderous Spirit is a work of fiction. Any resemblance to actual people is unintentional and coincidental. While a serious attempt has been made to portray the details and geography of the New York metropolitan area accurately, the needs of the story may have driven me to exercise poetic license, even with some actual places and buildings. I hope the reader will excuse this.

Cover designed by Keri Knutson.

Published by Saugatuck Books.

For Margy
Who is the answer to my prayers each
and every day

And

Thanks to
Charles Dickens for "A Christmas Carol"
Philip K. Dick for "Adjustment Team" and
George Nolfi for "The Adjustment Bureau"

1

It was my fault that my wife was murdered. Right on the front steps of our home. I was shot, too, and almost killed. I deserved it. Maggie did not.

We were walking home from a movie. A romantic comedy. Maggie thought it was fun; I hated it. But I was in such a foul mood those days that I could have gone to a double feature of *Casablanca* and *Play It Again, Sam* and hated them both. No matter what I saw or did, I would have hated it, because I hated myself.

I was a U.S. Marshal, and I had accepted a bribe. There you have it: the unvarnished ugliness at the core of my being. Despite years of service with the Marshals and before that in the U.S. Army Special Forces, I had taken money from some loathsome criminals who planned to kill other loathsome criminals who happened to be in the Marshal Service's witness protection program.

Please don't think I jumped up and said, sure, I'll take your money. I wasn't that easy. Like a lot of veterans returning from Afghanistan or Iraq, I suffered from PTSD. And like a lot of us, I had a hard time admitting that I had a problem and seeking help for it. Instead of therapy, I drank. I drank a lot. I hung out in bars that cater to Federal agents of all sorts: DEA, FBI, Treasury, and Marshals.

Just as there are bars for Feds, there are bars for cops and for bad guys. Both the good guys and the bad guys are aware of this. It makes it easier for law enforcement to find suspects in bad-guy bars. At the same time, it's easy for the criminal element to identify those in law enforcement who might be approachable regarding bribery—odds are that at least one federal agent who gets soused on a regular basis is susceptible to an offer of easy money. And since I was avoiding therapy, which was bitterly ironic since my wife *was* a therapist, I self-medicated with booze in the same place most nights: Dugan's Pub. Instead of going home to Maggie, I told her I was working late on a case. I often did work late, and she believed me. Now that I think about it, she probably was pretending to believe me. It was a lie of convenience that we shared. If I was honest with myself—something that was difficult in the extreme—I had to admit she had tried to help me. Suggestions that we go for long walks, where there would be nothing to do but admire the scenery and . . . talk. Suggestions that we drive into the country and admire the scenery and . . . talk. Suggestions that we spend the evening at home, listening to music and . . . talking. Maggie had a mischievous sense of humor and a great line in flirtation, but heaven forbid we should just . . . talk. For crying out loud, she was a *therapist*. She was a caring and concerned person, and she would have figured

7

out what a mess I was. I couldn't have that.

Well, the first few times Dommy G approached me about passing information to him, I waved him off with an obscenity or two. Dommy G was short for Dominick Something, but nobody used his actual last name because of his "family" connections. The scuttlebutt was that the G stood for garrote, which he was rumored to have used on occasion. Dommy was tall with wavy, dark hair slicked back over his ears, shirts that he never bothered to button up as far as he should so that long curly chest hairs spilled into view, and a gold Rolex that clunked on the bar whenever he leaned on it. He wasn't just a piece of mob muscle, at the same time, he wasn't capo material. Dominick was smart enough to know he was a mid-level thug. Regardless of his mob status, I didn't report him to my supervisors, which is what you're supposed to do when criminals attempt to bribe you. He continued to proposition me to do him a favor while he did me a favor: "Come on," Dominick said, "you hate protecting scumbags like me. So give me the information I want, and I'll eliminate a couple of them for you. Less work for you." My cursing must have been losing its effectiveness because he repeated his offer again and again.

One night, I pushed my $20 bill across the bar, and the bartender pointed in Dominick's direction and said, "He's buying."

I should have left the $20 and paid for my own drinks. Told Dominick where to go. And informed my superiors.

Instead fate intervened and pushed me farther in the wrong direction: Maggie was accepted into a prestigious program at New York University. We weren't poor, but graduate work in psychology at NYU doesn't come cheap. Some *pecunia ex machina* would be very handy, especially since the deadline for payment was soon. I rationalized that it was okay to accept the bribe—I didn't work in witness protection so I couldn't actually deliver the information and betray the Marshal Service. Oh sure, I occasionally delivered the witness protection subjects—many of them criminals—to a handler. But the path to their actual ultimate destination, their newfound lives of comfort and security, had several steps. I was just a way station in the process. But after delivery, I hadn't a clue what happened to them—it was impossible for me to give the mobsters what they wanted. So, if I took the bribe, I'd just be stealing from some very bad people. Didn't seem particularly immoral to me.

The elephant in this particular room of my drunken head was that Dominick and company wouldn't appreciate being ripped off by me. But I dismissed these fears. I'd survived war in Afghanistan; a couple of mobsters didn't frighten me. Besides, were they really stupid enough to risk the inevitable manhunt that would follow the whacking of a law-enforcement officer?

The deal was $50,000 up front with another $50,000 when I handed over the information. One night I met

Dominick a couple of blocks from my usual bar. He handed me a plain white shopping bag with a shoe box inside and said, "Here's a pair of the loafers we were talking about: 12½ D, right? Let me know if they don't fit. Be sure to call me." He walked off without another word.

The bag felt heavier than a pair of shoes. $50,000 in $100s is a bit bulky. I felt very pleased with myself for having earned that much money by lying to criminals. Very pleased. For about five minutes. Then it hit me that I had dishonored everything I had ever stood for as a Marshal and a soldier and a husband—everything my wife believed about me.

I couldn't live with myself or with my wife, who cared so much about others she had become a therapist. Whose sense of humor was sly and surprising. Who had brown hair, blue eyes, and a small scar over her left eye from a childhood fall from her bike. Maggie was disproportionately self-conscious about that little scar. She shouldn't have worried: it was barely noticeable. She was beautiful.

After the movie, we had walked along West 76th Street, heading west away from Columbus Avenue and toward our home on the third-floor of a brownstone. The June night was pleasantly warm, a light breeze rustled the leaves, and we were both dressed for the weather: Maggie was wearing a light yellow T-shirt, mine was a dark blue, and khaki shorts. Her legs were much prettier than mine. We had strolled down the sidewalk hand in hand. It had taken every bit of mental fortitude I possessed not to yank mine from hers—it was beyond me why she would want to hold my hand. Yes, the hand I'd taken the bribe with.

It had also been impossible to enjoy a stroll on a wonderful June evening with my wife when I was spending most of my mental energy scanning every doorway and window and rooftop, wondering if someone was about to kill me. I had been stupid and immoral enough to take money from criminal scum, and reneging on my deal with the scum left me in a state of fear. Not to mention the phone call I had received earlier that day: I picked up the phone and said, "Hello." A man's voice replied, "Well? We're waiting."

As we had climbed the stoop to our building, Maggie released my hand and fished in her purse for her keys. There was a noise, like the tearing of a piece of paper, and in a fraction of a second, something smashed into my right shoulder and slammed me against the door frame. As I fell, another something hit my leg.

There was a distant sound of footsteps pounding away, slowly fading out of hearing.

I lay on my back, sprawled on the landing at the top of the stoop, breathing hard. I touched my shoulder and felt a jagged tear in my shirt and skin. My fingers came away covered in blood. I gazed up and realized the glass in the door was broken.

Where was Maggie? I slowly rolled to my stomach

until I could see down the stoop. She was crumpled at the bottom, her legs on the sidewalk, her torso on the steps, all of her covered in blood. Her head lay on one of the stone steps, her face toward me, her eyes wide open and sightless. I tried to call her name but couldn't collect enough breath to make a sound.

She couldn't be dead, she couldn't. The bullets were meant for me—I had taken the bribe but never delivered. This was payback for me. What had I done to my Maggie? My breathing was more strained as I pushed myself over the edge of the landing and down the steps. Every nerve in my body screamed with pain. I rolled down the last steps and came to an uncontrolled stop with my head in her lap. She didn't move. I reached out and took her hand, gave it a gentle squeeze. Nothing. I whispered her name. No answer.

The sound of sirens filled the air, and I blacked out.

*   *   *

My beautiful wife did not deserve to be murdered.

It took months for me to recover physically. I only remembered being shot twice, but it was four times. Lost a lot of blood, but nothing vital was damaged. Still, not what you'd call a good time.

When you've been shot in what looks like a professional hit attempt, the Marshals Service is remarkably understanding about your taking long-term disability. All you need is the right kind of note from your doctor—and four bullets passing through your body makes it very easy to get the right kind of note.

I spent the next five years on disability, not working, angry with God, feeling sorry for myself, and justifying the worst behavior I was capable of. I supplemented my disability income with a bit of detective work from time to time: I found cheating spouses, did half-assed security consulting (and sometimes industrial sabotage) for businesses that were too small or too cheap to hire someone good, and occasionally collected debts that were not legal obligations. Maggie would have been extremely disappointed in me, but then again, I'd been disappointed in myself ever since I took the bribe. There was no way in hell that I could justify taking money from very disreputable people for illegal behavior. Even though I hadn't delivered—I never had access to the witness protection information I was supposedly selling—that didn't make me any less guilty for accepting a bribe from human slime.

My failure to deliver on the bribe was the most probable reason someone had fired eight times at Maggie and me. Probably with a refurbished M21 sniper rifle with sound suppressor. At least that's what the ballistic evidence pointed to. The gun was never found. I was hit in the shoulder—that bullet went through me and smashed the front door window—in the ribs, puncturing my right lung, and twice in my right leg. Maggie was hit three times, twice in the chest and once in her left arm. The last bullet ricocheted off the stone stoop into the night. Neither it nor the weapon were ever found.

Given the type of weapon and the quality of the shooting, the killing was considered a hit directed at me, with Maggie as collateral damage. Like most law-enforcement agencies, the Marshals Service will move heaven and earth to find someone who attempts to kill one of their own. And the Service did exactly that on my behalf. But since I wasn't going to give myself up and tell them about the bribe—getting shot and losing my wife seemed like sufficient punishment to me—the investigators had no motive. No physical evidence except the bullet fragments. No suspects. Maggie's and my case went into the unsolved files where it probably would have stayed forever.

Fortunately, justice was meted out. By a random piece of luck, Dominick Gianetti, the guy who had bribed me—and been enraged by my failure to give him the info he was paying for—was killed barely a week after Maggie was murdered. I was still in the hospital. If only he had been shot *before* she was. His death didn't make things right regarding Maggie. Nothing would ever make that right. Or so I thought.

The fifth anniversary of her death found me still living in our apartment, now mine, which had stayed the same since she had died. Our living room had cream-colored walls and a lot of naturally finished wood furniture: bookshelves along the wall by the door, a couple of Woodstock recliners, and a couch, upholstered in a maroon-rust herringbone pattern. The bay window overlooked 76th Street. The brick fireplace had been unused since, well . . . you get the idea. The living room ended in a large counter that marked the beginning of the kitchen. A tiny hallway ran toward the back of the apartment where the bathroom and bedroom were. The whole place could have used fresh paint. Not to mention a fresh attitude on the part of the tenant.

I handled the anniversary with my usual aplomb. I started drinking around noon, which probably doesn't sound *too* unreasonable until I mention that I got up at about 11:45 A.M. I had gone into the bathroom, swallowed two aspirin, and stared at myself in the mirror. I'm six foot two, and the mirror wasn't set high enough for me to see the top of my head. But I knew my hair was sandy brown with a few streaks of gray. Bloodshot blue eyes over unshaven cheeks. Not a pretty picture. I had exited the bathroom and walked a few steps into the tiny kitchen where, to quote Johnny Cash, ". . . the beer I had for breakfast wasn't bad, so I had one more for dessert." To ensure it was a truly nutritious breakfast, I ate a couple of pieces of dry toast with the beers.

When I got seriously hungry in the middle of the afternoon, I left the apartment, walked down the stoop where Maggie had died, and went west to a deli on Broadway, where I bought a roast beef on rye sandwich with a little mayo and a bit of black pepper. A small bag of potato chips and a six pack of beer completed the meal. I went home and ignored the spot at the bottom of the front steps where my wife had bled to death. Safely inside my apartment, I ate my food and drank my beer while channel-surfing between sports and news. I didn't really give a damn what was on TV, but I wanted the noise to block out my mulish, drunken self-pity.

In the early evening, I switched from Budweiser to Johnny Walker Black and had Chinese food delivered. Probably Kung Pao Chicken, but by then I was disgustingly drunk, and I don't remember. At some point in the middle of a weather report on some channel or another, I passed out on my couch.

Maggie woke me up. I heard her softly calling my name. My eyelids were so heavy I could barely open them. I blinked, expecting to see an empty apartment, believing that her voice was a dream. But she was standing a few feet away from me.

"Jack," she whispered, "I need to talk to you."

She was in the same light-yellow T-shirt and khaki shorts she had died in, but there was no blood. And she was surrounded by a warm glow, almost as if her body were in a halo.

"Jack, are you awake?"

"Maggie?"

"I'm here."

"You can't be. It's just not possible. Not. Possible. NOT." I pushed myself off the couch and took a half-step toward her. She stepped back the same distance, her halo moving with her. "Are you . . . are you . . . I'm sorry, but you're . . . dead. Is this a dream?"

"No. I'm really here. We're really talking."

I shook my head—a truly terrible idea when you've had as much to drink as I had in the last twenty-four hours. "I've been drunk before . . . even had some hallucinations, but this . . . this is the worst. No, best—it's good to see you, to talk to you, even if you're not real. I've missed you so much."

"I miss you, too."

I didn't know what to say. Should I offer her a drink or a seat? Ask her how she was? "I, uh . . . well . . . I . . ."

She cut me off, "I hate what you've become. You're more than this."

"Sorry, but I'm not trying to impress a hallucination—"

"Stop that," she interrupted me. "You're throwing your life away. You're capable of more."

"Says the ghost. Or the hallucination. Take your pick."

"You're drunk, but I am not a hallucination. I'm here to help you become what you're supposed to be."

I collapsed back onto the couch. "Oh, geez. I don't think I need my drunken subconscious delivering a self-help lecture. Forget it. Not interested. Get lost."

"I thought you missed me."

"I do, but you're not really you . . . you're not really

the one I miss." I paused and tried to consider the meaning of what I had said. "Did that make sense?"

"Yes." She was sad and disappointed, and for a fraction of a second, I wanted to take her in my arms and comfort her. But only for a tiny speck of time—you can't comfort an alcohol-created hallucination. And my head hurt so badly I wasn't sure I could take her in my arms.

Maggie paced a few steps toward the bay window overlooking 76th Street then came back to face me. "Please don't drink for the next twenty-four hours."

"Why? What difference will twenty-four hours make?"

"Please? I'll come back tomorrow night, come back when you're capable of understanding that I'm really here and not an alcoholic hallucination."

"You are the damnedest dream I've ever had."

"If you love me, don't drink, and I'll return tomorrow."

And she was gone.

Maggie didn't fade away, and she didn't pop invisibly out of sight. She just . . . disappeared.

"Holy shit," I muttered. "That was a doozy." I stood up and staggered to the little kitchen where my bottle of Johnny Walker sat on the counter. I grabbed a clean glass out of the cabinet above, picked up the scotch, and was going to pour myself a glass when Maggie's words echoed, "Please don't drink for the next twenty-four hours. Please?"

I stared at the spot on the living room floor where my hallucination had been. Why the hell should I not drink for a hallucination?

But I couldn't bring myself to pour. I put the bottle back on the counter, the glass back in the cabinet, went to the bathroom to wash up, and then, finally, blissfully to bed.

*　　*　　*

The day after the fifth anniversary of Maggie's death was the first really good day I'd had in the five years since we were shot. I woke up at a reasonable hour, showered, shaved, dressed in clean jeans and a gray Fordham T-shirt, walked to a diner on Columbus Avenue, and had bacon and eggs. I even drank a glass of orange juice, my first without vodka in years. I walked all through Central Park, enjoying the smell of the grass and the beautiful park scenery, framed by the towering buildings along Fifth Avenue and Central Park West.

I couldn't begin to understand why I was in such a good mood, filled with a sense of promise. It was as if I had a hot date. Was I eagerly anticipating seeing Maggie again? As that thought hit me—and it hit me like a hammer coming down squarely on a nail—I stopped and swayed in the middle of the pathway around the Park's Great Lawn. I took a deep breath. What the hell was the matter with me? Could I really be looking forward to a repeat performance of the drunken dream I'd had last night? But without the aid of alcohol?

19

I dumped myself onto the nearest park bench. What a pathetic loser. Getting all pumped up about seeing a woman who'd been dead for five years. Why? What was motivating this joy? I stared at the trees on the far side of the Great Lawn without really seeing them. I had no idea how long I sat there, staring without seeing. Eventually, I realized the reason I was happy *was* the thought of seeing Maggie again.

Hallucination or not, last night was the best moment of the last five years of my life.

Hallucination or not, Maggie was absolutely right: I was throwing my life away. And now I was hoping my dead wife would return and save me from myself. I laughed at the idea that my life was such a mess that my best hope was an appearance by my wife the ghost.

After spending hours walking around the park, I went to my gym and worked out—the one good habit I'd maintained since Maggie's death. To be completely honest, all the physical exertion helped with my anger. Although I don't know how the gym equipment remained intact after I used it. Showered and freshly dressed, I went home with a pizza and Diet Coke for dinner.

When I walked up the front stoop, instead of making a conscious effort to look away from the spot where Maggie had died, my eyes on the top of the steps and the front door. I practically bounded up to my apartment and ate three slices of my pizza. I wrapped the leftover pizza in aluminum foil and shoved it in the freezer.

Cleaned the apartment. I can't tell you how long it had been since I cleaned the place, but after a couple of hours, it was spotless. All the bookshelves had been dusted, the dishes washed, the floors vacuumed, and the bathroom scrubbed and shiny. I even changed the sheets on the bed, not because I was crazy enough to think I'd be entertaining company, but because when you're cleaning from top to bottom, well, you change the sheets.

After that burst of activity, I didn't know what to do with myself. I watched the Yankees on television, and after the game ended in a New York victory, I watched *Casablanca*. I'd probably seen it a dozen times, but it was still fantastic for me. Poor Rick, pining away for Ilse, and then his life turns around when he takes on the Nazis. He doesn't get the girl, but he does find himself.

I finished *Casablanca* a few minutes after midnight. I don't remember drifting off to sleep on the couch. Maggie woke me up, softly calling my name. She was smiling when I opened my eyes.

"You didn't drink today."

"I wanted to see you again." I sat up.

"You believe in me now. I'm not just a drunken dream?"

"Maybe you're a symptom of some kind of mental break, I don't know." I found it impossible to believe she was really there, standing in my living room in her halo, but there she was, complete with pretty blue eyes and the little scar over her left eyebrow. I was incredibly happy to see her. "I'm glad you're here, whatever you are. I've missed you."

"I know, but you can't use me as an excuse for what you've become."

"You're disappointed in me . . . "

"Of course I'm disappointed. The man I loved was someone I wanted to have a family with—now you're a . . . " her voice faded, unable to finish.

"A bum? A guy who drinks too much? Who's throwing his life away running errands for people on the wrong side of the law?"

"Yes."

I took a deep breath and confessed, "That started before you died."

"You took a bribe."

"Yes."

"Why? Why would you do such a thing?"

"I don't really know." To tell the truth, I did know. But I wasn't capable of being honest with myself, and I certainly wasn't capable of being honest with Maggie, regardless of her current plane of existence.

"That's not good enough," she said.

I couldn't look into her eyes; I lowered my gaze and stared at the floor.

"Why did you do it?" she asked.

"I've asked myself that a thousand times, and I still

don't have a good answer." I paused to swallow and then take a deep breath. "I . . . I saw too many awful things in Afghanistan. Maybe I was suffering from PTSD, I don't know. And . . . I was angry that we had fertility problems, . . . I was ticked off with my bosses, I hated the mob guys I was escorting into witness protection. And since I had no intention of passing on the info the bribe was paying for, I didn't feel like it was as horrible as it was."

"That's all rationalizing," she said gently.

I nodded. "I was angry and felt sorry for myself because of the war, and because of our issues, and my work . . . my drinking . . . I acted out. It was an angry, terrible thing to do. It was an incredibly stupid thing to do—I'm . . . sorry." I paused, trying to collect myself. "I got you killed, I never . . . " I swallowed hard a couple of times. "I'm so sorry," I muttered through my tears.

Maggie took a step closer but stopped short of touching me. "You didn't kill me. You are not the evil person who murdered me. You made a very bad choice, but someone else killed me."

I wiped the tears from my cheeks.

"You volunteered to serve your country, and you served well. You won a Silver Star and a Purple Heart. But those medals weren't enough when you came home and needed help to adjust. You buried your feelings and joined the Marshals and that meant you could continue to serve. But you never got any help. When we met and fell for each other, it was wonderful for both of us. I saw how funny you are, how caring. But the happiness of early romance masked a lot of your issues. Eventually, even with our love, your problems were still there. Because we were close, I couldn't see what you needed and do anything to help you. And, since you didn't get help, you acted out. You made a horrible choice. But you're not a bad man, and you didn't kill me. Do you hear me?" she asked.

"Yes."

"I still love you. That's why I'm here. I love you too much to watch you waste your life. I interceded on your behalf and got you a chance to turn your life around."

"What the hell are you talking about?"

She smiled again. "Hell has nothing to do with it. I'm talking about a second chance. Do you want it? Do you want to redeem yourself?"

"I don't know . . . I'm . . . "

"Are you kidding me?" her voice was sharp and her eyes flashed angrily. That was my Maggie. "Are you crazy?" (A question I was asking myself every thirty or forty seconds as I talked with this ghost or hallucination or whatever she was.) "You have a chance to turn everything around, and you're not sure you want it! Do you have any idea how many people there are who wish they had this chance?" She paused, looking at me to see if her words had any effect. "Well? Do you want to redeem yourself?"

"I . . . guess so. I mean . . . yes, I do."

She waited for a moment, obviously hoping I'd say more. "Don't you want to know what you have to do?"

"Sure, of course. What do I have to do?"

"Help others. Make things right for them. You've been wallowing in self-pity for five years when you could have been focused on helping others."

"Geez, don't hold back."

"It's true, and that is *your* fault."

I took a deep breath. "Okay, you're right. Whom do I help and how do I help them?"

"Don't drink again for the next twenty-four hours. Tomorrow night you'll be visited by Harry. He'll tell you what to do."

"Harry? Who the hell is Harry? Maybe I should ask, what the hell is Harry?"

"He'll be your . . . ," Maggie hesitated, searching for the right word, ". . . guide. He'll explain what you need to do for your second chance."

"Oh." I was afraid to ask what I had to ask, "What about you? Will I see you again?"

She whispered, "I don't know."

I took a step toward her, but she maintained her distance from me. "Seeing you is the best thing that's happened to me in five years."

She smiled again, but her face was sad. "You have no idea."

"Please, please come again."

"I will if I can."

And she was gone. I sat on the couch, put my head in my hands, and wept.

*   *   *

The next day was long and dry. Long because I didn't have the hope of seeing Maggie again, and dry because she had asked me to stay away from alcohol. To my surprise, I discovered it wasn't a problem to go a day or two without a drink. In addition to not drinking, I didn't take a bit of work I was offered that day. One of my contacts had asked me to "collect a debt" down on Wall Street. Some financial whiz kid had gotten in over his head snorting cocaine and losing money in private poker games—the kind of games where the buy-in was $10,000 and where nobody left having won or lost only $10,000. If I collected the $200,000 debt for my employer, I'd collect for myself, too—a 10% fee, tax free. But I had declined the job and let the $20,000 go to someone else.

While I frittered away my day in righteous fashion waiting to meet Harry, other people were up to no good. I would discover what had happened later.

*   *   *

MANHATTAN, WALL STREET AREA: THE YOUNG MAN APPEARED OLDER THAN HE WAS. HIS FACE WAS LINED AND WEATHERED, as if it were a still solid but old Adirondack chair that had been left outside for too many years. He was wearing a dark-gray suit, not new, not fashionable, not particularly noticeable for any reason. His shoes were black dress shoes, well-worn but with a shine. The only thing about him that seemed fresh and crisp was his black leather brief case.

He walked south from the subway stop at Fulton Street to one of the shorter, older buildings near Wall Street. He was on Broadway, two blocks north of a shiny, black-glass skyscraper with that was taller than any other building in the financial district except the new towers at 1 and 4 World Trade Center. Among other businesses, this skyscraper housed the global headquarters of Dwayne, Horner & Metaxis.

The young man peered down Broadway at the black skyscraper then entered the shorter building that was his destination. The lobby's décor was that of an old movie about business. There was a marble floor, desperately in need of polishing, and painted walls that had grown dingy since the last fresh paint had been applied. The two security guards behind the desk could have used some polishing, too, or at least freshly ironed uniforms. Both men were aging badly, with cheap haircuts and bad shaves.

Despite their unimpressive visages, they were quick enough to ask the young man for his identification, which he produced. They watched carefully as he opened the briefcase to show them the laptop inside.

"Could you boot that up, please?" said the shorter guard.

Without removing it from the foam cut-out, the young man opened the lid of the laptop, pushed a button, and it hummed to life. The guard looked at the computer and nodded, "Thanks."

The young man closed the laptop and then his briefcase. The guard gave him a small plastic basket, which the young man filled with his watch, some keys and a few coins. There was nothing impatient about his movements; nothing happy or energized, either. His face was expressionless, his posture upright; his movements slow and smooth. He stepped through the metal detector. No alarms.

"Thank you," the guard said.

"You're welcome," the young man replied, his voice flat and without affect. He collected his watch, keys, coins, and briefcase and took the elevator to the fifth floor. He walked slowly down the corridor, switching his briefcase from one hand to the other as he pulled on clear-latex gloves, and let himself into an office with one of his keys. The office was empty with the exception of a few wood armchairs and a couple of plain, wooden tables. The pale beige walls needed fresh paint and large, old windows needed replacement. The man draped his suit jacket over a chair and pulled a table over to a window, opened it, then used a cloth handkerchief to wipe down the table and window—even though he was wearing gloves. The handkerchief went back into a jacket pocket. He opened the briefcase and pulled the laptop from its foam cut-out. Under the laptop, in deeper cut-outs, were the parts of a sniper rifle. The young man began to assemble the weapon.

For the first time, there was a microscopic display of emotion. His lips were tight, almost a smile. His movements as he fitted together the weapon were much quicker and more fluid than they had been in the lobby. Finishing the assembly, the young man checked the rifle's action and glanced through the telescopic sight.

He reached back into the briefcase, pulled out a small metal bipod, opened it, and placed it on the table. He set the rifle onto the mount and pointed the weapon out the window. The young man bent to the telescopic sight and scanned the sidewalk in front of the skyscraper that housed Dwayne, Horner & Metaxis five hundred feet away.

On Broadway, in front of the black tower, a chauffeur-driven, black Mercedes S65 AMG sedan came to a stop. Edmond Garner stepped from the Mercedes and walked toward the tower. Garner was the kind of man who dominated almost everyone and everything around him. He had the chiseled features of a male model. His gray hair was brushed straight back from his face, and not a single hair dared be out of place. He wore custom-made Italian suits and shoes, the crispest white shirts imaginable, and gorgeous silk ties that cost more than his lowest paid employees made in a week. He had taken Dwayne, Horner & Metaxis from a profitable but small player in the investment banking industry into an international colossus. As a result, he'd been high on the Forbes 400 list of the richest men in the world for more than a decade.

The young man watched as Garner walked toward the entrance of the building. The young man was not impressed by the costly elegance of Garner's car or clothes and did not care about his immense personal wealth. To the young man, Garner was merely the object of a plan of action. A plan that would end with extreme brutality. The young man focused the telescopic sight on Garner's stern profile. The young man's right forefinger wrapped around the trigger.

Garner was only about ten feet from the front door when he pitched forward, his face slamming into the sidewalk. People entering the building stopped at the noise of his body pounding onto the sidewalk, and a few of them began to move toward Garner to help when there was a dull thudding noise as something hit the fallen body.

One of the onlookers shouted, "Oh my God, he's been shot!" and everyone scattered, getting as far away as they could. A number of people pulled out cell phones and dialed 9-1-1.

In the fifth-floor office, the young man disassembled his rifle as carefully as he had put two bullets into Garner. He felt satisfaction at a successful job. No guilt at killing another human being. Nothing. He realized that his loved ones would be horrified by what he had done, but he couldn't afford to feel any horror—he pushed those thoughts away. He placed the rifle's pieces into the foam cut-outs that lined his briefcase. Then the laptop went in. He checked the floor, found the ejected shells from his rifle, picked them up, and peeled off his gloves around the shells. He tucked the balled up gloves in his pants pocket. He took his suit jacket off the back of a chair, put it on, adjusted his tie, picked up the briefcase, and calmly left the office—using his handkerchief to open and close the door.

By the time he reached the sidewalk, there were police vehicles and an ambulance in front of Dwayne, Horner & Metaxis. Still showing no emotion, the young man walked uptown, away from the scene of the shooting. When he reached the IRT subway stop at Fulton Street, he went down to the platform and took the 4 Train uptown to Grand Central. He exited the subway station and took the escalator up to Grand Central Terminal, with its grand hall and gold constellations against a blue-green sky on the ceiling. He left Grand Central and walked west along 42nd Street then south on Fifth Avenue. Opposite him stood the elaborate entrance to the New York Public Library's main branch, guarded by carved lions on either side of the broad stairway leading up to the doors. He crossed Fifth Avenue toward the library and casually flicked the balled up gloves toward a sewer grate. The gloves bounced into the darkness below street level.

The young man never hesitated or paused. At the corner of 40th Street, he headed west again, past the library and Bryant Park toward Sixth Avenue. He ignored all the people enjoying eating and drinking under the trees of the park. His attention was focused on his path and nothing else. When he reached Sixth Avenue, he turned north and headed uptown, past the back side of Rockefeller Center and the front of Radio City Music Hall. He continued to ignore everything but his own movement. When he reached Central Park South, he crossed the street, walked into the park about a quarter of a mile, and . . . disappeared into the woods.

*　　　*　　　*

I didn't know Edmond Garner. But his murder was the big story on the local news on television that night. I couldn't speak to whether or not he'd done something that created a motive for his being killed, but it seemed bizarre that an investment banker had been the victim of an assassination. Sure, lots of people made grim jokes about killing bankers in the wake of the Great Recession of 2007-2009, but as far as I knew, Garner's murder was the first time it had happened.

I thought about the word "first" while mulling over the killing. Was this the first time it had happened, or was I so drunk until a couple of days ago that I had missed an earlier Wall Street killing? I considered another possibility with the word "first"—if Garner's was the first of its kind, would it be the last? Was his the first in a series of assassinations of Wall Streeters? And what difference did it make to me, anyway? I didn't know any titans of finance, and I certainly wouldn't be asked to help the NYPD investigate.

I defrosted and ate a couple of slices of my leftover pizza, while watching *Chinatown* and wondering at the tragic outcome: The hero, Jack Nicholson's J.J. Gittes, loses the woman he's trying to help, and one of the other characters says, "Forget it, Jake. It's Chinatown." A phrase that said "this is an impossible situation, you've lost, and you need to move on." I channel-surfed a bit and fell asleep on the couch as I waited for Harry to make an appearance. At least, I think I fell asleep. . . .

I found myself standing on a beach, the waves breaking below me and then rushing up the sand toward my bare feet but stopping inches short of my toes. The sun was setting and the sky was red with a beautiful, end-of-day glow. It made me think of the old adage: Red sky at night—sailor's delight. Looking around, I realized two things: I didn't know where I was and I didn't know the black man standing next to me. He was tall, slender, and wearing a well-cut, light-gray suit and a dark blue tie. His dark skin was without wrinkles and stretched smoothly from his cheekbones to his solid jawline. He could have been anywhere from twenty-five to forty years old.

"Do I know you?" I asked.

"I'm Harry," he said. His voice was deep and firm. "Your wife told you I was coming."

"I'm—"

He interrupted me, saying, "Jack Tyrrell."

I grunted in response.

"I know almost everything about you," he continued.

"*Really*?" I packed as much sarcasm into the short word as was possible.

"Yes. For example: I know when, where, and how you were shot and how Maggie died."

"*What*?" I spun around, looking at the red evening sky and then back at him. I struggled with the possibility contained in his words. "Are you serious? Did you witness her killing?"

"Yes, in a way," Harry said quietly.

His soft, steady tone was unnerving. "What does that mean?" I repeated in shock.

"It means, 'Yes,' I am completely aware how she was killed, how you almost died in the same incident, and your feelings of guilt."

His calm demeanor and large, unblinking brown eyes made me angry. Or maybe it was his pronouncement that he knew about Maggie's death and my guilt. I gazed out to sea and watched the ocean toss wave after wave onto the sand. How could I be on the beach? How could I hear the surf and smell the salty air? I had fallen asleep on my couch—how could I be here? I was struck by a thought so overpowering I couldn't believe it.

"Are you . . ." it was impossible to say the words, but I tried again, "are you . . . ?"

"No. But I work for Him."

"Are you taking me somewhere?"

"No, I'm going to *send* you somewhere."

"Where?"

"Wherever the Chairman wants you to go."

"The Chairman . . . ? Is he . . . ?" I couldn't phrase my question. Instead, I timidly pointed toward the sky.

"Yes." Harry nodded. "I work for Him. I'm your Supervisor."

I found it hard to breathe. I walked around in a small circle, ignoring the tide line and the surf coming over my feet. "You work for . . . Him? And . . . I work for you?"

"We—you and I—both work for the Chairman. I'll be the one conveying His plan to you."

"Do I get to meet the Chairman at some point?"

"Everyone meets the Chairman eventually."

"Could I . . . could you tell me what His plan for me is?"

"You're going to right wrongs."

"Excuse me?"

"Have you ever read *A Christmas Carol* by Charles Dickens?"

"I saw the movie. The one with Alistair Sim. Does that count?"

"Yes. Do you recall what the ghost of Jacob Marley says to Scrooge?"

"Something about three spirits, Ghost of Christmas Past, Ghost of —"

"Yes, but before that, Scrooge is shocked at Marley's suffering. He doesn't think it fair. Scrooge says: 'But you were always a good man of business, Jacob,' and Marley's ghost becomes very upset and shouts: 'Business! Mankind was my business. The common welfare was my business; charity, mercy, forbearance, and benevolence, were, all, my business.'"

I was breathing even harder now, "Are you telling me that mankind is my business?"

"It's the Chairman's, mine, yours, everyone's—it's the only true business there is."

"And now my job in this business is to right wrongs?"

"Yes. Jacob Marley also tells Scrooge that 'It is required of every man that the spirit within him should walk abroad among his fellowmen, and travel far and wide; and if that spirit goes not forth in life, it is condemned to do so after death.' "

"But I'm not dead . . . am I?"

"No, you're alive. Maggie interceded with the Chairman to give you this chance before you die."

"Why didn't the Chairman give me this chance before taking Maggie?"

"He did."

I stopped walking in a circle. "What the hell does that mean? Are you saying I had this chance and I blew it?"

Harry replied evenly, "The Chairman has given you

many chances."

"Have you come to me before?"

"No. But some of my colleagues have. The Chairman doesn't give up easily—even when dealing with someone as obstinate as you."

"Why didn't He make me see the light?"

"That's not how it works. We all have free will; we all choose how we live. You chose not to recognize my colleagues, and you chose not to listen to their messages."

"Do I have a choice now?" I asked bitterly. "Can I choose not to work for the Chairman? Are there other options?"

"Yes, you can choose. You can always choose. Your options are: Work for the Chairman or continue to live a miserable life."

I scanned the almost-dark sky and the phosphorescent surf rushing over the sand. "If this is my miserable life, I choose this."

"This isn't your life. Your life is empty, lonely, corrupt. You take no action to help anyone. You do nothing, but wait and brood. You haven't got the slightest sense of the Chairman's presence."

"So, if my choice is to live this way, I die and go to hell?" I asked bitterly.

"Yes, if you choose to continue your life as you have."

I pounced on this: "In that case, is it really fair that

hell is one of my choices?"

"The Chairman is always fair. And your choice is fair, because it's *your* choice. Have you ever read *The Great Divorce* by C.S. Lewis?"

"What the hell is this, an English-lit class?"

For the first time in our conversation, Harry smiled. It was a tiny, Mona Lisa smile, almost imagined but definitely there. "Lewis wrote that 'All that are in Hell, choose it. Without that self-choice there could be *no* Hell. No soul that seriously and constantly desires joy will ever miss it. Those who seek find.'"

After a long pause, I said, "I'm exhausted."

Harry smiled a bit more, "Talking about choice and Hell tends to have that effect."

"Thanks," I said, smiling a tiny bit, too. "That C.S. Lewis quote 'Those who seek find'—does that mean that I can avoid going to Hell?"

He nodded. "If you seek."

I sighed, staring at the ocean's dark horizon against the less-dark night sky.

Finally, I said, "Okay, what does this righting wrongs job involve?"

Harry stepped next to me. "You have an excellent skill set for what the Chairman has in mind," he said. "You are a combat veteran and a former U.S. Marshal. Your experience will be put to use in helping people—victims—that the law enforcement community isn't able to assist."

"How the hell am I going to accomplish what the NYPD or the FBI or any other agency can't? I'm not Superman."

"You will receive direction from me, something the police and federal agents don't get. The Chairman will make sure you have the resources you need to solve cases and help people."

"Why doesn't the Chairman help these folks directly? Couldn't He do it quick and easy?"

"He could, but then *you* wouldn't have the opportunity to help them."

I said, "The opportunity to help them—that's just the 'Mankind is our business' crap. Are you telling me we're all supposed to take care of each other?"

His large, dark eyes met mine. "Yes."

I didn't like to think about what he saw when he looked at me. I watched the waves roll in and gazed at the night horizon. "How 'bout if I right the wrong of Maggie's death?"

"No. You have been selfish and self-centered for the last five years. You chose to waste your life. If you choose to work for the Chairman, you'll do it for the benefit of others."

"Mankind is our business," I muttered.

"Yes."

After a long pause, Harry said, "Are you ready?"

"I guess so." I took a very long breath. "I should

probably come clean with you," I said. "I've actually read *A Christmas Carol*."

"You've read it thirteen times to be precise. Each year at Christmas. That's one of the things that made the Chairman think you were seeking."

I faced him. "Maybe I'll find."

"Maybe." He smiled. "Good luck."

In a microscopic burst of time, I found myself standing on the sidewalk outside the Dwayne, Horner & Metaxis headquarters on the sunny afternoon after Edmond Garner's shooting. I don't know how I knew it was the afternoon after the assassination, but I did. Ooooh creepy, I thought, smiling.

I was dressed in a navy-blue polo shirt, faded blue jeans, and white cross-trainers. A far cry from the beachwear and bare feet of a moment earlier. Ooooh, *very* creepy, I thought, smiling even more widely. Harry walked across the sidewalk, pointed at the spot directly in front of the main entrance, and asked, "Do you know anything about this?"

"Only what I saw on TV. Probably a helluva lot less than you. And, I guarantee that I know nothing compared to the police. I hope I'm not supposed to solve this."

"You're not in the crime business, you're in the—"

"Mankind business," I finished for him. "What does my first case have to do with . . . ," I gestured toward the place where I thought Garner had fallen, ". . . this?"

"You're going to be introduced to someone who

needs your help."

I scanned the area where Garner had fallen and then the buildings near this bit of lethal real estate. There were a few skyscrapers with non-opening windows and some shorter buildings without the correct sight lines. An older building a few blocks north of us, maybe five hundred feet away, had windows that opened and a clear line of sight to this sidewalk. The distance was not difficult for a good marksman with an appropriate weapon. I was out of practice, but I could probably have made the shot myself. And the building was far enough away that you could easily exit it unnoticed in the commotion that would have started when Garner flopped dead onto the sidewalk.

I pointed, "Is that the building the shooter used?"

He arched an eyebrow in reply.

"You already know if it is or isn't, don't you? Holy shit, can you give me a straight answer? "

"No. You're supposed to figure things out. And we don't usually use terminology like 'holy shit'."

"Sorry," I shrugged. "Was it the use of the profanity or the coupling of the profanity with a word like 'holy'?"

Harry shook his head and said nothing.

"Okay, yes," I said, "I think that could be the building. The windows open, not like climate-controlled skyscrapers. Far enough away that the shooter could exit the area without attracting attention. Close enough that it's a makable shot for someone with the right training and right weapon. Probably from five or six floors up. High enough for a good angle; close enough to the street for a quick exit. Probably took the stairs down."

Harry nodded slightly.

"Did I get it right?" I asked.

He ignored me and said, "Are you ready to meet the person who needs your help?"

"Sure. But could you take me—" I pointed to the older building "—to the office the shooter used?"

Harry stared at me.

"It will help me understand what I'm dealing with," I said.

I could have sworn that his chin tilted up a millimeter and that his eyes looked skyward for a fraction of a second as if seeking guidance from a higher authority. Then he was looking at me again so quickly that maybe I imagined the entire thing.

"All right," he said.

With no sense of motion or time passing, I found myself with Harry, in an empty office with windows that opened. Windows that overlooked the sidewalk where Edmond Garner had died. The office was old and kind of dingy, but it was clean as a whistle, not a dust bunny in sight. But there were smudges of fingerprint powder on the doorknob, the window sills, the window, and the table that was under one of the windows.

"Looks like the NYPD crime scene folks were here,"

I said.

Harry didn't bother to agree with the obvious.

I leaned close to the table, examining the fingerprint powder closely. There were no whorls anywhere on the table surface. "He wiped the surfaces clean, but I bet he was wearing gloves."

"How do you know that?"

"Doesn't that question confirm my hypothesis? Did you slip up there?"

"Are you trying to catch me in a mistake—or do you want to help? I repeat: How do you know that?"

"Everything about this murder is methodical and precise *and* careful. The killer was taking no chances. I bet the NYPD found no shell casings; the killer cleaned up and took everything with him."

"But the police can match the bullets in Garner to the the weapon."

"Yes, they can, if they ever find the weapon. As of right now, they can't even prove that this was the room the killer used. This guy knows his stuff."

"How do you know it's a man?"

"Playing the percentages. This kind of assassin is almost always a man." I stepped closer to the table and examined the surface again. There were two tiny smudges opposite the center of the window. I could picture a bipod with rubber-tipped legs being set-up and the rifle aimed at the sidewalk. I said to Harry, "Could I please see the lobby?"

"Why?"

"No one walks into a building carrying a rifle. I want to see their security, see how the killer snuck the weapon inside."

Without any sensation whatsoever, I was standing in the lobby, barely inside the doors, looking at the security desk and a walk-through metal detector. I pointed at the guards and asked, "Can they see us?"

"Of course they can see us."

"Are they wondering how we suddenly appeared?"

"They have no such awareness. As far as they know, we're simply . . . here."

"Wow, you really have great power."

"It's not my power."

"Oh . . . ?" I paused, then said, "Oh." I infused the single syllable with great weight, implying gigantic significance. "The Chairman, right?"

"What do you think?"

"I think I'm tired of your Socratic-dialogue methodology." I walked out of the building to the street with Harry directly behind me. "There's no way the killer could have walked in here with the rifle. It was probably in pieces, hidden by something that screened it from the metal detector. Probably a laptop. The guards made him turn it on, it worked, and they passed him through. With the rifle, disassembled, directly underneath the laptop in a briefcase of some kind."

Harry's face was still an emotional blank, but I was sure he nodded. "You are the right man for this mission. Are you ready to meet the woman who needs your help?"

"A *mission*? With a *woman*? This *is* getting interesting. Let's go."

My only reward for this sharp riposte was a microscopic grimace from Harry, and then—we relocated to the Upper East Side at the corner of 88th Street and Third Avenue. We were in front of a modern building with a floor-to-ceiling glass-wall at the entrance and a doorman behind a polished-granite service desk in the center of the lobby.

"Wow," I said, "You're better than the subway."

"Excuse me?" He seemed genuinely baffled.

"You're better . . . smoother, quicker, than the . . . " Absolutely no flicker of comprehension in his eyes. "Never mind," I finished.

Harry's eyes locked on me for a long moment then he walked into the lobby. It appeared that I was to follow him. "I'm Harry Mitchum," he said to the doorman." This is Jack Tyrrell. We're here to see Donna Kruger in 8J."

The doorman repeated our names to make sure he had them correctly, spoke into a phone, and said, "You can go up."

As we stepped toward the elevator, I asked, "Are we going to *whoosh* up, or are we taking the elevator?"

Harry shook his head in frustration. Well, I interpreted it as frustration. Maybe it was pure scorn. When the elevator doors opened on the eighth floor, he exited to the right. A beautiful, but haggard, blonde was standing in an open apartment door. She was wearing a black blouse and black slacks that showed off her figure and contrasted very nicely with the color of her hair.

"Hello, Harry," she said and faced me as we approached the door. "Is this the man who's going to help us?"

"Yes," Harry said firmly. I would have liked a chance to ask a question or two before agreeing to this case, but I realized that wasn't the way things worked with Harry and the Chairman. "This is Jack Tyrrell."

"Why don't you come in?"

We followed her into a large, airy living room. Lots of windows that overlooked 88th Street, white walls with framed posters for Monet exhibitions. There was a very long, dark-brown leather couch along one wall, and Donna waved at it, indicating we should sit down.

"Would you like anything to drink?" she asked. "Coffee, tea, water?" She smiled weakly, "Something with a bit more oomph to it?"

"No, thank you," Harry replied.

Donna sat in a white leather chair opposite us. She had large blue eyes and a wide mouth, but the eyes were bloodshot from exhaustion, and the mouth was tight.

Until the moment I saw Donna Kruger, I had thought this whole Mankind is Our Business thing a pain in the ass. Maybe a necessary one, but a pain nonetheless. Suddenly, it wasn't painful inconvenience—if I could make things right for, I wanted to do that.

"How can I help you?" I asked.

"It's my brother . . . " she began to cry very quietly. She paused to give herself a moment. "My brother killed Edmond Garner."

Donna dabbed at her tears with a tissue. I stared at Harry, whose face had no expression whatsoever. No expression that I could read. I gave up analyzing Harry and focused on the woman.

"Ms. Kruger?" I said softly. She didn't react to her name. "Donna, if you really believe your brother committed murder, you should be talking to the police, not me."

"My brother needs help. He doesn't need to be caught and punished. Ever since he came back from Afghanistan, he's struggled." She eyes were on mine. "My brother needs help."

"I'm no expert, but I think PTSD would be a factor in his defense—"

"He needs help!" She shouted, jumping to her feet, her eyes blazing. Then her shoulders dropped, her eyes went dull, and she whispered, "I need help."

I stood, stepped to her, and took her right hand. "Donna, I'm not sure what I can do for him. Or you."

Her face turned up to mine, "I don't know what's wrong with him. But my brother *needs* help. He killed

Garner."

"I know," I replied softly. I didn't really know, but I wanted her to feel as if someone was listening. Someone cared.

"And . . . he's not done, yet. He's . . . going to kill again . . . "

"I think you're in shock. You don't really mean that—"

"My brother is on a crusade. He is going to kill every Wall Street CEO he can."

2

Harry didn't say a thing. Neither did I. What was there to say? I wondered if Donna was the crazy one, or her brother, or both of them. Then again, maybe I was the crazy one—after all I thought I was in a relationship with my wife's ghost and believed that I was cavorting around Manhattan with Harry who was . . . who was . . . whatever the hell, I mean whatever the heck he was.

Donna was crying more freely now. I was still holding her right hand and tugging gently on it, guiding her to sit down on her long couch. I sat next to her.

"What's your brother's name?"

"Richard," she said between sniffs. "And that's Richard—not Dick or Rick." She forced a smile through her tears.

"When was he in Afghanistan?"

"2009 into 2010. He was with the Marine Regimental Combat Team 7 in Afghanistan."

"They saw a lot of action," I said softly.

"Richard certainly did. He has two Purple Hearts."

"He came home wounded, didn't he? With PTSD?"

She nodded, dabbing at her tears.

"And he never really settled in when he came home, did he?"

"No," she shook her head. "I think he originally hoped to make a career in the Marines, but when he came home, he couldn't take it. He was discharged in early 2011—"

"Honorable discharge, right?"

"Yes. But being out of the service was no better than being in it. He wasn't comfortable anywhere. He isolated himself, avoided visits with family or old friends. At night he'd argue out loud with the news reports on television."

"Since you think he might have killed Garner, I'm guessing that his arguments were with reports about the Wall Street types and the financial crisis, right?"

"Exactly. He couldn't find a job and he believed it was the fault of people like Edmond Garner. He tried to join the Occupy Wall Street movement, but he was too angry to stay with it. The Occupy people didn't make him feel welcome, but how could they? Richard was my brother, but when he talked about how he was going to kill the Wall Streeters, it terrified me," she stopped, swallowed, and took a deep breath. "If I was afraid of him, how could strangers accept him?"

I gave her hand a squeeze, "It's not your fault. It's not Richard's either."

We sat quietly for a moment. Harry's face was a blank. I couldn't begin to figure out what, if anything, was going on in his head. There was no sign of impatience, which made me think he was waiting for me to discover the reason Donna believed her brother's rants.

"Donna, where does Richard live?"

"His mail comes here—and that includes his VA benefits checks. He has keys to the apartment and comes and goes. He usually stops by for a hot meal and a shower once or twice a week. I guess he lives on the streets most of the time. I've invited him to use the couch, but he only does that in really cold weather."

"Does he carry identification? If anything happened to him, would anyone know to contact you?"

"Yes. I made him promise me that. He has his VA ID card and a New York driver's license. And an 'In Case of Emergency' card with all my info on it. As disturbed as he is, he *does* love me. I'm pretty sure he honors his promise to carry the cards with him at all times."

"I'm sorry to ask, but ... what makes you think that Richard would actually kill Garner?"

"Because he said he would. Over and over and over. Garner's been in the news a lot lately, testifying before

Congress about regulating the financial services industry, and every time Richard's been here in the last month, we saw Garner on the news, and Richard would scream 'I'm going to kill you first, *Edmond*. Then you'll be the gatekeeper welcoming your Wall Street brethren to hell.'"

No reaction from Harry.

"I can see why you're concerned," I said to her.

"He didn't just say it to the television. The day after Garner testified to Congress, Richard took one of my lipsticks and circled Garner's photo in *The New York Times*. Next to the circle, he wrote, 'Time to die!'"

"Do you still have that?"

She nodded, stood up, and walked down a small hallway into what I guessed was her bedroom. I shifted my attention to Harry. "What's going on? How am I going to help her?"

"You'll find a way."

Donna walked back into the living room, holding a folded newspaper and a photo album. She handed me the *Times* and put the album on the coffee table. Richard had circled Edmond Garner's photo with thick, garish lipstick lines. In the center of the circle, right over Garner's heart, was a smaller, solid circle, like the center of a target. Next to the photo, Richard had scrawled "Time to die!"

"Now do you believe he did it?" Donna asked.

"I'm sorry. I didn't mean to act as if I don't believe you—"

"But you didn't, did you?"

"No, I didn't. I'm sorry; I don't want to hurt you. But this isn't proof that he did it."

"What more proof do you need?"

I paused and considered her question: "Well, I'd like to talk to Richard himself, see if I can understand him more completely. And I'd like to see if he has the training and the weapon necessary to have killed Garner."

"He has the training. He was a sharpshooter or marksman or whatever it's called in the military."

I thought that over: anyone with any kind of marksman qualification could probably have made the shot on Garner. Anyone with the right weapon and scope. "What about a weapon? Do you know if he has one?"

"I don't. Maybe he could have gotten a gun through his friends on the street?"

"Maybe, but how would he have paid for it?"—

"He has money from his VA benefits. And I manage a small trust for him—money our parents left us. Given that he has no living expenses, he could probably afford a gun."

"Okay . . . he has the know-how, and he probably could get his hands on the weapon. That's still a long way from proof that he did it."

"Oh my God, what is the matter with you?" she was sharp in her frustration. She turned to Harry, "I thought you said he was going to help me."

"He is." Harry's tone was utterly lacking in

conviction. It would have made someone with a winning lottery ticket anxious.

"He's certainly not talking that way."

"He will help you."

"Donna," I interrupted, "I do want to help. But I need to get answers to these questions and a lot more if I'm going to do anything for your brother."

She stared at me with a hard look that would have done my second grade teacher, Sister Mary Torquemada, proud. (Okay, it wasn't Torquemada, it was Teresa, but the way that little old nun used those meaty hands of hers. . . .) I managed to return Donna's gaze without withering under her glare, but it was close.

Harry said, "He can't help you without information. He's an expert. Trust him."

"What makes him an expert?" She continued the hard look.

"Jack was in Army Special Forces—a Green Beret. He's a decorated veteran of combat in Afghanistan, like your brother. And he spent years in the U.S. Marshals Service. I wouldn't have brought him here if I didn't believe he could help you."

Donna's hostility subsided from a boil to a simmer, and I nodded my thanks to Harry.

I said to Donna. "I had a pretty difficult time settling in when I returned to the States." I hesitated and considered what I had admitted. "Look, to be honest, I was a mess when

I got back. A real mess. I've been where your brother is. If I can help him, I will."

She stood up, walked over to the window, and gazed out on 88th Street. I doubted she registered what she was looking at, but she couldn't sit still because her feelings were threatening to overwhelm her. She was silhouetted by the daylight coming through the window, and I noticed that she had one heck of a silhouette. And wonderful eyes and a wide mouth. Maybe a trifle too wide, and her cheekbones were probably a little too prominent, but still—what the hell is it with you, Tyrrell? You've seen plenty of attractive women in the years since Maggie's death, but you pick this strained, angry moment with Donna for the first time you respond emotionally—physically?— to a woman?

I hoped my feelings were as much a desire to help as plain and simple desire. And I hoped that from now on, whenever I met an attractive woman I didn't immediately classify her as a goddess. I exhaled a very long breath and checked Harry's reaction: his face was a calm, stony mask.

After a moment staring out the window, Donna asked, "What do you want to know?"

"When was the last time he was here? Do you think he'll be back soon? Could I meet him?"

"He was here the night before Garner was killed. He'll probably be back sometime in the next few days. I don't know about meeting him . . . "

"I'll give you my cell phone number—text me the

minute he shows up and I'll rush over. If you can introduce me as a friend, great. If not, we'll figure something else out. Okay?" I couldn't begin to tell you what the "something else" would be, but I had to meet Richard if possible.

"I . . . I guess so. I don't want him to feel I've betrayed him."

"We'll act as if I dropped by spontaneously—just a coincidence that he's already here."

"All right."

"Do you have some recent photos?"

"Why do you think I brought this out?" She opened the album and showed me a number of pictures of a young man in his mid to late twenties. He had a lean build, sandy hair that was darker than Donna's, and a fine jaw. His darker hair made me cast a furtive glance at Donna. If she colored her hair it was a good coloring job, very nice—snap out of it, Tyrrell! I refocused on the photos. One of them was Richard in uniform, looking every inch the Marine. Another showed Richard with shaggy hair, long enough to cover his ears and collar, and a beard that was more than stubble but a long way short of Santa Claus.

I pointed to the shaggy photo, "Is this recent?"
"Yes."

"May I have it?"

She pulled out the picture and handed it to me. I slipped it into a jacket pocket. "It's hard to tell from these photos—how tall is Richard?"

"He's six feet tall. 'Exactly,' as he always likes to say."

I stood up. "I have some contacts at the NYPD from my Marshal days. I'll ask around and see if anyone has had any contact with Richard. We might get lucky and find him that way."

"I don't want him in trouble with the law." Anger hardened her voice.

"I get it. I won't make trouble for him. Just put the word out I'm trying to find a homeless vet for the family. That's all."

Her withering glare had returned, and I manfully stood up to it again. Even though her eyes were angry as hell, I couldn't help but notice what beautiful blue eyes they were. Stay focused, I told myself. Focused.

After a moment, Donna decided she wasn't going to destroy me with a look, and her face slowly softened in resignation. "What's this going to cost me?"

"What?"

"What do you charge for this kind of thing? You're a detective, aren't you?"

"No, no, I'm not. I'm a guy trying to help someone out. "

"What's *your help* going to cost?"

"Nothing."

"Your help is free?"

"Yes," I said. Harry nodded almost imperceptibly.

There was another long pause as Donna considered me. Considered the situation, too, probably. "All right," she said. She picked up a business card lying next to the photo album on the coffee table and handed it to me. "My contact information." Then she extended her hand, "Thank you."

We shook hands as I replied, "You're welcome."

*   *   *

As we walked out of Donna's building onto the East 88th Street sidewalk, I jerked to a stop. "How the hell does a homeless guy get his hands on a rifle with a telescopic sight? And a laptop, and a specially outfitted briefcase to carry the weapon and the laptop?"

"His sister said Richard had money."

"That *might* explain how he paid for the stuff—but how did he find a seller? You don't walk into a surplus store and buy that kind of gear. Someone led him to it. Or maybe provided him with it."

"But he had money. Why would someone give it to him?"

"A homeless guy buying that kind of stuff is going to raise suspicions. But if you're using the homeless guy to do your killings for you, it's easier for everyone if you give him the tools to do it."

Harry said nothing but continued to look directly at me. This guy's propensity for eye-contact was unnerving. It was like being eye-balled by a hungry leopard.

I looked up at Donna's building as if that would

provide me with a clear understanding of what was happening. I said resignedly, "I need to find Richard, find out if he killed Garner, and find out if someone persuaded him to do it. Piece of cake."

"What will you do next?" Harry asked.

"Couldn't you put this whole thing on the express track? Tell me if Richard killed Garner and where he is now."

Harry didn't say a thing. His eyes were lifeless. There wasn't the tiniest hint of a smile or frown. This guy could have won a stare-down with the Great Sphinx.

"You know *if* Richard did it, and you know *where* he is, but I have to find out whether he's guilty then find him— is that it? Part of the whole redeeming myself thing?"

"What do you think?"

"I think it's a waste of time when you answer my questions with more questions."

"You have to do the work."

I sighed, "Okay."

"That doesn't include becoming emotionally involved with Donna Kruger."

"What?"

"It doesn't include—"

"I heard you," I interrupted. "But what difference does it make if I become emotionally involved with her? If it helps her feel better, isn't that helping her?"

"Yes, but you need to be selfless. You've been

pathetically selfish for a long time."

I looked up and down 88th Street, barely noticing the parked cars, the entrances to the laundry and the deli, and the front doors of apartments. "I've . . . I've been empty for . . . I've missed Maggie . . . and now—"

"No."

I faced him, "What the hell? She's very attractive—"

"And you want to rescue her."

"Yeah, so? Look, this is a ridiculous conversation. I'm a guy trying to help her with her brother. A guy she doesn't trust. Nothing's going to happen between us."

"But you wish that something would."

After a long moment, I said, "Maybe."

"When this is over, she won't remember you."

"What? How the hell is that possible?"

"Hell has nothing to do with it. Regardless of how Richard and Donna's story turns out, the Chairman will have Donna remember it without you."

"You're telling me that no matter what—"

"She won't remember you."

We were standing near the corner of 88th and Third Avenue, and I watched the traffic going uptown on Third. Taxis, delivery trucks of all shapes and sizes, a couple of SUVs probably going home to Westchester County.

"This selfless helping people sucks," I said.

"In the short term."

I didn't bother to check out his Sphinx-like face.

"I'm going to head down to the 19th Precinct and see what I can find about Richard." I took a few steps toward Third Avenue, realized I hadn't said goodbye and neither had Harry, and twisted around to look for him. He was gone.

Or was he gone? Had he ever been there in the first place? Was Harry real? I shook my head, wondering if I was a nut job of the first order. Maybe I had denied my PTSD and self-medicated with alcohol to the point of hallucinations.

Maybe belief in Maggie the Ghost, Harry the Supervisor, the Chairman, and Donna the Desperate was an elaborate, delusional denial of my real problems. Then again . . . maybe I really really could help Donna. Regardless, it was nicer to think I was of use than I was crazy.

"Okay," I said under my breath and began walking again.

*　　　*　　　*

"Jack Tyrrell." It was a statement, not a greeting. "What the hell do you want?" Paul Vidal, a tall, rangy Mexican-American stood up from behind his battered, gray desk. Vidal extended his hand, and we shook over the scarred desktop blotter. His office was barely big enough for both of us, the desk, a couple of filing cabinets, and a couple of chairs. All the furniture had the gray-steel look of government-issued furniture. The walls were painted a pale green that probably was supposed to be soothing but struck me as nauseating. Still, it was an office, with a door for privacy. One of the perks of being the lieutenant supervising the 19th Precinct's detective squad.

"Mind if I close this?" I asked, indicating the door.

"No. What's up?"

I closed the door and dropped into a seat on the guest side of the desk. "I could use some help finding someone."

"Jack, you know better than that."

"It's a guy named Richard Kruger. He's homeless but every once in a while checks with his sister who lives on East 88th Street to pick up his veterans' benefits checks. His sister's worried about him, hasn't seen him in a bit, but didn't want to report him as missing to the police. I told her I'd talk to you on the Q-T."

"You're putting me in a bind—"

"Paul, the guy's a vet like you and me. He needs help, and I promised his sister that I'd do what I could. Please?"

Vidal sighed and put a hand on his computer keyboard. "Give me his info."

I told him all the details that Donna had provided for me. He typed away, hit return, and read the results. "Your guy's a former Marine? Two Purple Hearts in Afghanistan?"

"That's him. You got anything else?"

"Yeah, his address is East 88th Street."

"Give me a break—has he had any arrests? Was he picked up and transported to a shelter when the temperatures dropped? Anything?"

"Nothing." He considered the computer, "Are you thinking this guy is going to get into trouble?"

"I really don't know. His sister is worried that he might. Said he's been making threats against people. She's worried he'll try to get a gun and shoot someone. How the hell would a homeless guy get a gun?"

Vidal had big hands with long slender fingers. He cupped his chin with his right hand, the thumb rubbing his right cheek, the fingers rubbing the left. It was an automatic behavior, done while he was thinking. "If he's got money, he spreads the word that he needs a weapon, and somebody knows somebody else who knows another somebody else . . . you know how it works, eventually, you get a guy who'll sell you a weapon. What kind of weapon?"

I shook my head, "Can't tell you." I couldn't tell him about my suspicions regarding the laptop and the briefcase either.

"There's a lot you're not telling me, isn't there?"

"Sorry. Kruger's sister, my client, doesn't want me saying anything. I've probably gone too far already."

"Hey, Jack, my help isn't free you know. Do you think he might be involved in an open case? Has he killed someone with this weapon you're talking about?"

"I'm not sure . . . ," I inhaled hard then said, "No. Probably not. But, to be completely honest, the sister thinks he might. I figure I'll check him out, hopefully find him, and be able to show that her brother's not involved in anything other than being a homeless vet."

He nodded, his eyes narrow. "If you get something, I want it."

"If I find out *anything* that tells me this guy is dangerous, I'll let you know."

"You'll let me know fast?"

"Sure." I felt guilty as I responded; I knew that Vidal's and my definitions of "fast" were likely to be very different. "And if Richard is arrested or whatever, let me know?

He gave me a tight smile, "Sure."

We both stood up, shook hands again, and I said, "Thanks."

Vidal didn't release my hand and maintained eye contact, "Nice to see you back in the game. 'Bout time you did something for the good guys."

I hesitated, thought of a hundred snappy comebacks, but settled for a simple reply, "You're right."

*   *   *

MANHATTAN, WALL STREET AREA: IN THE FORTY-EIGHT HOURS SINCE EDMOND GARNER HAD BEEN KILLED, BERNARD ABEL OF DUMORTIER INVESTMENTS HAD UNDERGONE A PERSONAL SECURITY TRANSFORMATION. He had hired a private security firm that specialized in protecting global executives who dealt extensively with the parts of the business world where law and order were foreign concepts. On the morning forty-eight hours after Garner's assassination, Abel's newly hired bodyguards drove him to work in an armored Lincoln Navigator. In the garage below Dumortier's offices, Abel exited the vehicle surrounded by a coterie of large men wearing body armor and was whisked into an elevator to go to his 34th floor office. The body guards allowed no one else to enter or exit the elevator. Once on Abel's floor, the body guards, still surrounding him, walked him to his office.

The office itself had been redone, almost overnight. Bullet-proof, tinted glass had been installed in all windows. His desk, which had been near the windows to give him a stunning view of downtown Manhattan, had been shifted to the far side of the office. Armored panels had been added to the desk. An assassin would need the very best in optics to find his target and an extremely powerful weapon to penetrate the glass and desk.

Bernard Abel was not alone in having a security transformation. Most Wall Street CEOs had revamped their personal security. Almost every building in the Wall Street area had beefed up security: more guards, more cameras, more metal-detectors, and in some cases X-ray machines and specially trained dogs. It would be almost impossible for anyone to carry a rifle into any building tall enough to fire into Abel's office and equally difficult to get to a window or roof that provided a shooting platform.

The young man who had assassinated Edmond Garner had chosen Abel as Victim No. 2 weeks before he pulled the trigger on Garner. So the young man was completely aware of Abel's routines, and he had watched all the security changes implemented in Abel's building and, more importantly, the security changes at the Hamilton Tower that he would use as his shooting platform. The assassin suppressed any guilt or anxiety he felt and was as methodical in planning Abel's killing as he had been in putting two bullets into Garner. He had the weaponry he needed and a cover story to gain access to the roof.

On the morning forty-eight hours after Garner died, the young man stood across the street, opposite the Hamilton Tower loading dock. He'd visited a hardware store and bought thick-framed safety glasses and navy-blue work coveralls that, at a quick glance, resembled the uniforms of the Hamilton Tower maintenance team. He was wearing the glasses and a faded old trench coat that had once been tan, over the coveralls. He also wore clear-latex gloves. He had the weapon in a duffle bag, resting on the sidewalk. He watched the loading dock and waited as a truck backed into the dock. The truck was long enough that the cab blocked the sidewalk. It also, the young man noted, obscured the view of one of the dock's security cameras and the security guards in a small glassed in booth on the far side of the dock. The two men in the truck cab hopped down and went inside the loading bay. After a few minutes, probably having finished their delivery paperwork with the building staff, the men began unloading their truck.

This was the young assassin's cue. He took off the old trench coat, dropped it in a trash can, and crossed the street. He pulled the duffle up and onto his shoulder and walked up the steps to the loading dock itself. One of the security guards began to move toward him, leaving the other at a desk inside the booth. The young man stopped and waited for the guard. No one was paying any attention to the young man or the guard approaching him—this kind of moment happened dozens of times a day.

The guard pointed at the duffle, "What's this?"

The young man swiveled and slammed the end of the duffle bag against the guard's head, knocking him down. Everyone's attention focused on the sprawling guard, and the young man calmly walked to the freight elevator at the rear of the dock near the security booth. He pressed the call button and waited, while the others helped the barely conscious guard to his feet. The elevator arrived, the young man stepped inside, pressed the button for the top floor, and watched the elevator door slide shut.

A minute later he was climbing the stairs to the roof. He pushed the door open, reached into his duffle, and pulled out a short block of wood that he used to wedge open the door. Then he walked to the side of the Hamilton Tower that faced Bernard Abel's office building. He pulled the M82A1A special application scoped rifle from the bag. Loaded with the armor-piercing, incendiary shells, the weapon was an absolute beast and would tear through every obstacle between the assassin and Bernard Abel. The young man placed the rifle on the low wall that ran around the edge of the roof. He attached the telescopic sight, knelt down, and looked through the sight. He counted the floors and then counted windows until he found Abel's. Due to the distance between the Hamilton Tower and Abel's office, the downward angle of his shooting would not be too steep. Thanks to the ultra-dark tinting on the glass, the shooter couldn't see into the office. But the tinted glass also confirmed that it was Abel's office—all of the other windows were much lighter.

The shooter calmly targeted the far left window of Abel's office, about three-and-a-half feet above the floor. He took a deep breath, exhaled, pulled the trigger, and waited for the recoil to subside. He aimed fractionally to the right of his first shot and pulled the trigger again. The rifle recoiled again, and in the same instant, the window of Abel's office shattered. The young killer aimed again, moved fractionally to his right, and pulled the trigger in the same second that his second shell crashed into the office. His third was on the way as he lined up a fourth shot. His third shell struck deep in the office, flame billowed out, and debris and broken glass exploded out of the office due to the force of the heat and fire.

The killer fired a fifth time as the fourth shell smashed into the office. From far below, he could hear faint screams as broken glass and shards of office debris rained onto the sidewalk.

He carefully scanned the entire office through the telescopic sight, carefully scanned the entire office. As he watched, a man in flames toppled to the floor next to the wreckage of what had probably been a desk.

The assassin calmly took the weapon apart, pulled a back pack out of the duffle, rolled the duffle flat, and tucked the duffle and weapon inside the pack. Then he unzipped the coveralls and pulled them off. He was wearing a blue, button-down Oxford shirt and khaki pants with no cuffs and no pleats. He brushed his hair back with his right hand and tucked the safety glasses in his pants pocket. At a quick glance, this young man bore almost no resemblance to the one who had bashed his way in through the loading dock.

He grabbed the block of wood from the door and headed downstairs, going several floors before emerging into a hallway and ringing for the elevator. Alone in the elevator, he pulled off the latex gloves and tucked them into the same pocket as his glasses. In the lobby, he walked past the security desk without a worry in the world—security guards screened people entering buildings not exiting them.

Out on the sidewalk, he did what everyone else was doing: he looked up at the flames coming from the jagged hole in the glass-walled tower and then at the scurrying panic of people on the sidewalk. After a long moment, he headed for the Fulton Street subway station.

3

The Thursday morning after meeting with Donna Kruger and my police buddy Paul Vidal, I woke up feeling clear-headed and energized. I got up from my bed and realized I hadn't felt like that since . . . before Maggie died. Before I sold out to the bad guys. It felt good. Maggie might have been a ghost or maybe an alcohol-driven hallucination. Harry might be from the Chairman. Then again, he could be a bit of insanity. I didn't care. Life was better since Maggie came back and Harry appeared.

I smiled, stretched, walked into my little kitchen, and set my coffee dripping. Into the bathroom for a hot shower and a shave. Threw on a T-shirt and blue jeans, ate a banana, drank my coffee, and enjoyed the view out my window of the sun shining on the trees on 76th Street. I finished the banana and noticed that the time was 9:22 AM—on the late side for me to wake up without a hangover. I grabbed the TV remote and turned on the set.

There was a picture of a skyscraper with a gaping hole in its side. At the bottom of the screen the crawl read, "BREAKING NEWS: 2nd Wall Street Assassination?" A woman's voice played over the picture, I guessed she was reporting from the building, "Unfortunately we have very little information right now. The NYPD has confirmed that shots were fired into the offices of Dumortier Investments and that there has been at least one fatality. The identity of the victim is unknown at this time."

A man's voice, probably the news anchor, addressed the unseen woman reporter, "Isn't Dumortier one of several Wall Street firms that beefed up security in the wake of Edmond Garner's assassination, which happened about forty-eight hours ago?"

"Yes, Dan, it is. We don't have a lot of detail on what was done, but we do know that Dumortier did harden their offices against attack, and a police detective on the scene told us that whatever was fired into the office was very heavy caliber, probably armor-piercing and incendiary, which explains the fire."

The anchor spoke again, still an unseen presence talking over the picture of the smoking building, "But the building's sprinkler system worked and did extinguish the fire, is that correct?"

"Yes it is, Dan. The fire seems to have been put out before it spread too far."

I hit the MUTE button on my remote and continued to look at the wounded tower. If Richard Kruger had done this, his sister had serious reason for worry. There was no way a double murder would end well for either of them.

Absolutely no way in hell. "Harry?" I spoke upwards to my ceiling. "Harry? I don't know how this works, but I need to talk to you . . . Harry?"

No Harry.

With the television still muted, I switched channels. All of the local and a couple of the cable news channels, including the business news channel CNBC, were showing video of the smoking tower, and then shots of the debris scattered all over the sidewalk.

"Harry?"

He appeared next to the TV set, wearing the same crisp white shirt, blue tie and light-gray suit as the first time I saw him. He didn't snap suddenly into view; he didn't slowly fade in. One moment he was there, while a moment before, he hadn't been. "Yes?"

"Who was killed at the Dumortier offices? Was their CEO one of the victims?"

He hesitated, clearly uncomfortable.

"For crying out loud, Harry, it'll be on the evening news. I'm just asking for a bit of advance knowledge. I don't want to waste time on this killing if isn't related to Richard Kruger's rage against the titans of Wall Street. Was it another CEO?"

"Yes. Bernard Abel, CEO of Dumortier Investments."

"One of the news reports said the killer might have used armor-piercing, incendiary shells because Abel had the office hardened against attack. Is that what happened?"

"Yes."

"Where the hell does a homeless guy get weaponry like that? I told you before that if Richard is the killer, he probably had help, someone to provide weapons and resources. Now I'm sure of it. He may be the trigger man, but someone else hired him to kill off Wall Street biggies. Someone—Mr. X—with money and the necessary connections. But why would Mr. X want to kill these CEOs? I can't imagine a rich guy with a homicidal beef against other rich guys."

Harry didn't say anything.

"You're not going to help me here? Not going to point me in the right direction?"

"No."

"Don't you want me to stop the killings before there are more victims? Or are you going to let more people die?"

"I don't know what will happen. Neither do you. But my instructions from the Chairman do not include my giving you all the answers."

"Are you telling me the Chairman is letting Richard Kruger and the guy behind him kill more people?"

"The Chairman doesn't let anyone do anything. People have free will; they make choices to do what they do."

"Are you kidding me with this free will shit?"

"Would you prefer that the Chairman treat you like

marionettes? Pull your strings?"

"Nice image. Tell me who's the guy behind the killings."

He didn't respond.

"Okay. Don't tell me. But are you willing to help me?"

"Yes. That's what the Chairman sent me to do."

"Great," I didn't sound very sincere. "Take me to see the security video from the buildings the shooter used. First for the Garner killing, then Abel. I'm pretty damn sure you know which building the killer used to shoot Abel, right?"

The only response was a silent stare. I grabbed my wallet and keys from the large decorative bowl on a shelf in the living room bookshelves and my tan windbreaker from the tiny closet near my front door.

"Let's go," I said. "I want to see those videos."

Harry broke off his stare as his chin barely tilted upward and his eyes pointed up—it was a small movement, and it happened fast. I wasn't sure I'd seen it, and then his eyes locked on my face.

"All right."

And I was standing in the lobby of the building I'd visited with Harry earlier that week—I was there instantly with absolutely no awareness of traveling. I whispered to Harry, "You've got to show me how you do that."

He frowned and pointed at the monitors of the

security desk. "What do you want to see?"

Instead of answering him, I said, "Can the guards see us?"

"Do you think we could watch the video you want to watch if they could see us?" He was impatient.

"Okay, just asking. Could you please play back from an hour before Edmond Garner was shot? You can run it through fast."

He nodded at the video, and the tape began. The security guard at the monitor sat frozen. The other guard and the people strolling through the lobby were motionless, stopped in their tracks. My mouth dropped open in amazement.

"What an amazing opportunity for pranks. I could really mess with some heads here."

Harry said quietly, "I thought you wanted to see the video."

"Sorry. I'm still getting accustomed to your magic act."

He shook his head and pointed at the monitor.

About twenty-three minutes of video scrolled by in a couple of minutes. We saw a man carrying a briefcase enter the lobby. He stopped and opened it, powered up the laptop inside the case.

"Stop the video, please."

Harry nodded at the monitor and the video froze. The picture quality wasn't great, but the young man was wearing a dark suit. It could have been Richard Kruger, but then again it could have been a lot of other thirtyish men.

"Okay," I said. "Can we go take a look at the security video from the building the shooter used to fire into Dumortier's offices?"

The transition was smooth and fast. The security set up in the new building was a lot different than the first building. We were in a small room adjoining the glass-enclosed booth off the loading dock. There were a dozen monitors on the wall with a pair of security guards, one man and one woman, scanning them.

"Could we please review the video from an hour before the Abel shooting?"

"Which video feed do you want?" Harry asked.

I checked at the monitors' current feeds and said, "Let's start with the loading dock. That's how I would have come in."

Harry nodded at one of the monitors, and the two security guards froze in their chairs. Every monitor stopped, too, except the one nearest us. On that screen, the video scanned fast forward through thirty-nine minutes before a man carrying some kind of duffle on his shoulder came into view. The duffle blocked his face, but when he clipped one of the guards with the duffle and knocked the guard out. After knocking down the guard, the man walked to what I assumed was the freight elevator, exposing only his back to the camera. It could have been the same man as the briefcase-toting assassin. But the tape was far from conclusive.

"Is there a camera in the elevators?" I asked.

"Not the freight elevator."

"What about the roof?"

"No."

I stared at the monitor where the duffle-bearing man had disappeared. "Thanks, I guess that's it."

We were back in my apartment in the blink of an eye, but more gently and swiftly than a blink.

"Are the police putting together some kind of task force on these killings?"

"Yes, but it's only coming together now. The first briefing isn't for an hour."

"Could you take me inside the briefing?"

Again Harry looked skyward quickly and minimally. I must be imagining it. "Yes," he said.

"Is Donna free right now? Could we go talk with her?"

"No. She's at work."

"Could I see her for dinner?"

"I am not a dating service. You are not allowed to pursue her socially."

"Cut me a break, will you? I'm not looking for a date—" not that I would admit that to Harry, anyway "—but . . . she might find it easier to talk over a meal. I might get some useful background on her, on Richard, on their family.

You never know what will lead you to a solution."

Harry's laser-like vision was targeting me, but I gave him my best, impervious return stare. And my impervious stare is pretty damn good—after all, once upon a time I was a U.S. Deputy Marshal and before that in the Army Special Forces.

"All right," he said. "Dinner."

I pulled out my cell phone and called Donna's office number. A young-sounding woman answered, "Donna Kruger's office."

"Hello, this is Jack Tyrrell. Could I speak with Donna, please."

"What is this in reference to?"

"Uh, I'm a . . . friend. Please give her my name."

"Hold please," and sent me into a light-jazz limbo. After a couple of minutes, Donna picked up, "Hello, Mr. Tyrrell."

"Please, call me 'Jack.'"

"Is that why you called me?"

"No, sorry," I found myself scrambling mentally and verbally—her tone was cold and hard. I hadn't expected a warm welcome, but I also didn't expect to be treated like a slimy substance you find on the bottom of your shoe. "I was hoping we could have dinner this evening?"

"Are *you* kidding me?" Her voice was positively arctic.

"I thought if we talked in a relaxed atmosphere you

might be able to give me more background on your brother, on your family—"

"—On me?" Her question cut me off completely and abruptly.

"Uh . . . yes. You never know what kind of incidental detail might help me connect the pieces and find Richard."

"*Really*?" Sarcasm made her voice razor sharp.

I sighed (I hoped it was to myself and she couldn't hear it) and said, "Never mind. Sorry to have bothered you." I hung up before she could say anything else that I'd regret.

Harry said, "That went well."

"You're a real pal."

He shrugged. Harry may have been interested in helping me right wrongs and saving me in the process, but he clearly could not have cared less about my feelings. Strange guy—assuming "guy" was the right term.

As I was about to put my cell phone back in my pocket, it rang. Caller ID showed it was Donna. My eyebrows climbed my forehead with doubt; I took a deep breath and said, "Hello."

"Mr. Tyrrell, I want to apologize," her voice wasn't arctic. More like a cold day in March. I realized she was trying, but this was hard for her. "I'm sorry I spoke to you the way I did."

"It's okay. I realize you're under a lot of stress. I honestly didn't mean to bother you."

"You didn't. I guess I'm in a bothered state these days." Her tone was getting warmer and warmer. She was a mild day in April now.

"You're in a tough place. I understand. Well, thanks for calling back, I appreciate it."

"Do you still want to have dinner?"

"Yes . . . uh, that would be great."

We set a time for me to meet her at her apartment and hung up. By the time we finished, the call had become a completely normal conversation. I shook my head in pleasant bewilderment at what had happened and slid my phone into my pocket. I checked Harry to see what his reaction was.

He said nothing. His face was expressionless.

I said, "Any further comment?"

"Is any required?"

"No. None at all." I smiled. I was sure that blank-face Harry was chagrined over what had happened. And I was enjoying that. I asked, "You want to grab some coffee while we wait for the task-force meeting?"

"Excuse me?"

"We could grab some coffee and talk. Get to know each other. Like partners."

"We are not partners."

"Of course not," I said, "but I thought . . . never mind. Bad idea, forget it. You probably can't eat or drink."

"Yes, I can." He was almost indignant.

"Well then?"

"Fine," he sighed.

"Great, there's a cafe on Broadway—" I held up my hand in a STOP gesture "—we'll walk. No *whooshing*."

"No *what*?"

"Whooshing. That thing you do when you take me someplace instantaneously."

Harry was searching for the appropriate response but couldn't find it. "Fine," he said again.

In the cafe, Beatles songs were playing over the PA system—Beatles songs from the "Can't Buy Me Love" and "A Hard Day's Night" era, not the "Sgt. Pepper's Lonely Hearts Club Band" era. We ordered and collected drinks from a barista and settled side by side on a faux-leather couch. We put our drinks on a small, coffee table with old issues of *Forbes*, *The New Yorker*, and *Sports Illustrated* scattered across its top. I had a cappuccino, while Harry had a green tea. Don't know what I would have guessed he'd drink, but I'm pretty sure I wouldn't have gone for green tea. Seemed kind of zen. And Harry struck me as very western, very Judeo-Christian. But why I thought that I couldn't have told you. It was just an impression.

"I hope you don't mind my asking," I said, "but how old are you?"

"Humans don't comprehend time the way we do. You perceive time as accumulating. For you as the day progresses, it seems to be 'later.' As your life progresses, you are older. But time doesn't accumulate for us. My age would not make sense to you."

"Okay . . . , but . . . for the sake of discussion, if your age could be counted in human terms, something approximating years, how old would you be?"

"You have a need to define things, to understand things, don't you?"

"I wouldn't be much of an investigator if I didn't define and understand. But don't change the subject: How old in human years? One hundred? Two hundred?"

He said nothing.

"Wow," I muttered softly, "were you around when the pyramids were built?"

His cup of green tea halted in its arc from the tabletop to his mouth, suspended at the end of his arm. After a moment's pause, it resumed its course, and he sipped from it.

"All right," I said, "age is a bad topic 'cause of the paucity of my comprehension. Could I ask you something else?"

"More defining?"

"Absolutely. What about the Bible? Is it true?"

"What do you think?"

"What difference does it make what I think—I don't know anything. You, on the other hand, have inside information."

"And you want to know what really goes on without

making any effort at personal discernment?"

"*What*?"

"Discernment is working to see, to understand, to know. If I give you the answers, you won't do any of the work of discernment. Discernment is similar to your investigations: part of what makes you a good investigator is you like the pursuit of knowledge, you like doing the work of finding the truth. The same thing is true in the process of discernment."

"You're telling me I have to do the work."

"Yes. You have to do the work. Now, what do you think: is the Bible true?"

I wasn't crazy about this turn in the conversation. The last thing I wanted to do was say the wrong thing to Harry. After all, if the Chairman was who I thought He might be, well . . . He was absolutely the last Being you ever wanted to tick off. Then again, if He was as merciful as the religious types said, maybe ticking Him off wasn't such a big deal.

"Is it true?" Harry asked.

"Well . . . I guess so . . . I don't mean that I think it's literally true. That doesn't make any sense. For instance, the Bible doesn't say anything about evolution, but I think that's how we got here. But . . . I think the Bible is spiritual truth. It's an attempt by ancient men—who had nothing approaching modern science—to explain God and how He works with us. It seems nuts to me to think the Bible is literally true."

"Hmm."

"Does 'hmm' mean I'm right?"

He shrugged, "It means you have done a tiny bit of thinking about these issues and that you are trying to discern. There may be hope for you."

"Didn't Maggie's interceding for me already prove there's hope?"

He reverted to his normal state and said nothing.

"Okaaaaaay," I said, stretching out the long-A vowel sound. I sipped my cappuccino then asked, "What about God—is He really there?"

"Shouldn't that have been your first question? Why waste time asking about my age and the truth of the Bible if you don't know about God?"

"I was sneaking up on the big question. Is He really there? Is the Chairman . . . God?"

"If you don't already believe that He's there, why are you even talking to me?"

"Because . . . " I hesitated, completely unsure what I was feeling. "I . . . I need to . . . hope. I want you to be . . . real. I'm not sure that you and Maggie aren't delusions."

"Maybe your need for hope is a yearning for God."

It was my turn to stop my cup in its arc from the table to my mouth. His words impacted deep inside me. I said very softly, "Holy moly . . ."

Harry smiled and said, "Exactly."

There was nothing else to say. At least on that subject. I drank more cappuccino, paid close attention to the lyrics of "Ticket to Ride," and said, "Where does Richard Kruger sleep?"

"That was quite the conversational shift."

"Standard interrogation tactic: Ask questions from different directions. Sometimes the truth pops out. Where does he sleep?"

Harry shook his head, "It's time for the task-force briefing. Are you ready?"

I took one last sip and answered, "Yes," and—whoosh!, we were in a bland, functional conference room inside One Police Plaza in downtown Manhattan. I knew we were in the headquarters of the NYPD because the conference room windows overlooked Park Row and the east side of the graceful, Beaux-Arts designed Manhattan Municipal Building. Maggie and I had gotten our marriage license in that building. I sighed at the memory and focused on the task-force meeting.

There was a podium at one end of the room. A long, rounded-at-the-corners rectangular conference table stood lengthwise, and the seats around the table were filled with men and women wearing business suits or NYPD uniforms with three stars or more on their shoulder boards. If I remembered the police ranks correctly, these folks were chiefs or higher. I guessed that the suits were people from various federal law-enforcement agencies, probably the FBI, the U.S. Marshals, and the ATF. Probably Homeland Security.

Another ring of chairs was set against the walls and windows of the room. There was a lot of official heat in that room. A tall, slender African-American wearing a chief's uniform stepped to the podium. "If we could please come to order?"

The room went silent.

"Thank you," the chief continued. "I'm Chief of Detectives Albert Hall. This task force is being headed up by my office, and we're coordinating with the Federal Bureau of Investigations"—he gestured toward several men and women in suits—"the U.S. Marshals Service, and the Bureau of Alcohol, Tobacco, Firearms and Explosives, as well as Homeland Security." More gestures indicating each group as he spoke. "We're also receiving intel from the CIA, military intelligence, and the NSA as to possible assassins."

"In other words, a tremendous amount of resources are being devoted to this. Captain Beirne, please update us on the current status of this case."

A beefy, red-haired Irishman took Hall's place at the podium. He must have been almost a half-foot shorter than the chief, and he had to adjust the microphone down.

"Okay, our first victim was Edmond Garner, shot three times with .308 caliber shells. Given the caliber and the distance, we think the weapon was probably a Remington M24, fitted with a multi-shot magazine. By using laser-sighting from the point of impact, we were able to find the empty office that the shooter used. There was some gunpowder residue around the window frame but no other evidence.

"Second victim, Bernard Abel, was killed in his office that had been fortified with dark-tinted, bullet-proof glass windows and armored panels on his desk. The shooter used something a hell of a lot heavier than what hit Garner. What little we found points to .50-cal, armor-piercing incendiaries. Probably fired from something like an M82, but we don't know what the weapon was. Abel's office was destroyed with four or five shots, and there was a lot of fire damage even though the sprinklers went on fast.

"We believe the same shooter is behind both homicides—I'll tell you why in a minute—and if we're right, that means the shooter isn't attached to a particular weapon but uses whatever he needs to get the job done. And the Abel shooting indicates a level of knowledge about the security around the victim. So either the shooter has a stock of weapons handy all the time, or he was able to get what he needed because he knew that Abel was going to be a lot harder to kill than Garner.

"Any questions?"

One of the women at the table said, "Mancini, FBI." She was a *very* nice-looking FBI agent. Long, dark hair pulled back in a ponytail, light-gray suit, and horn-rimmed glasses gave her a sexy librarian appeal. Her nose was a tiny bit too long, her face a tad narrow, but she was quite attractive. For crying out loud, Tyrrell, first Donna Kruger now the FBI agent. Five years with a complete lack of interest and now every woman was an object of desire. Are Mancini's hair and figure more important than the details of two homicides? Can't you pay attention to the discussion for five minutes? Focus on what Mancini is saying and not her looks. She asked, "Why do you think it's the same shooter?"

"Because fifteen minutes ago, we got a note, copied to local and national news media. It'll be on the air and online pretty damn quick." Beirne glanced up from his notes and nodded at a young, uniformed officer at the door, who began passing around paper sheets to everyone. Beirne resumed, "Let me read the note to you, while it's being handed out:

"To Law Enforcement,

"You have failed to punish the Wall Street thugs who pillaged the economy for their own gain and who have been a plague on the common man. You have had years to do what is right and instead, done nothing.

"Now I will make things right. I will punish the Wall Street criminals. Edmond Garner and Bernard Abel are the first victims. They will not be the last."

"In justice, the Real Lawman"

I leaned over to Harry and said "The Real Lawman

89

has a nice style, using words like 'pillage' and 'plague' and 'punish'. Very *punchy*."

Harry's answer was to point at Beirne, indicating I should pay attention.

"Does anyone know we're here?" I asked.

Harry gently shook his head and pointed again. I paid attention as he directed.

Beirne was saying, " . . . we suspect that we're not dealing with a crazed loner. The quality of the shootings, the different weapons, the thorough prep that went into each shooting, all argue for a professional hitter. But if our guy is a pro, someone's got to be paying him. Professionals don't kill for free."

Mancini leaned over the table and asked, "Does it have to be a pro? Maybe the unknown gunman is ex-military, someone back from Iran or Afghanistan." She quickly checked the file in front of her, "From the forensic analysis, neither assassination demanded the best marksmanship. Any moderately skilled shooter could have done both. There are probably quite a few vets with the skills to pull them off. And with enough trauma-driven anger as motivation."

Beirne nodded as she finished, "Thanks Agent Mancini, that's a good point. We're checking that possibility through our connections with the military intelligence community. They're looking up veterans with the necessary marksmanship quals, discharged in the last 10 years, suffering from PTSD, with a last-known address in this area."

"And you'll ask them to expand the search from the New York area if we don't get much on this first pass?" she followed up.

Beirne nodded.

A lean man in a dark-brown suit raised his hand and began asking his question before Beirne recognized him, "What's doing with all the Wall Street types? What's happening with their security?"

"Probably moving to Antarctica," someone muttered. There was grim laughter around the room.

Beirne shook his head. "As I said, Abel's office had been fortified, and the shooter was still successful. We're recommending that the other possible targets avoid their offices, their primary residences, their summer homes— anywhere they're likely to be tracked down. The best defense is a good hiding place. The U.S. Marshals Service Witness Security Program is advising them on the specifics."

I leaned toward Harry and said softly, "I'm very familiar with Witness Security—those guys are good."

The suit who had asked the question about security piped up again, "Assuming every single potential victim goes into hiding, what's going to stop the killer from disappearing? And if the killer disappears, won't the victims come out of hiding after a while? And won't the killings start all over again?"

Beirne shrugged, "I don't know. We have to catch the shooter. Catch him fast. The best way to do that is work the angle that he's a hired pro. We need to find who hired him. The FBI and SEC are looking into the financial markets to see if they can spot anything that might give someone a motive to go after Wall Street CEOs. NYPD's got forensic accountants going over the records of Garner and Abel's firms, to see if any clients got burned and might want revenge.

"You all were given sheets with a breakdown of the activities of every agency in here. Please, if you have any ideas, let me know, and we'll make it happen."

There was a long silence. Beirne stepped away from the podium, and Chief Hall returned to it, raised the microphone, and said, "If there are no further questions, let's get to work. Our next briefing will be tonight at 2000 hours."

As the men and women of the task force filed out of the room, I said to Harry, "They think there's a Mr. X behind it all."

"You already suspected that."

"It's nice to have my professional opinion validated." I walked over to the window, pointed to the Manhattan Municipal Building, and said, "Maggie and I got our marriage license there."

"I know."

"Do you know everything about me?"

He didn't bother to answer.

"Okay," I exhaled slowly, "I don't suppose you'd care to reveal Mr. X to me."

"No."

"That might save lives."

"We've discussed this before."

"Oh, bullshit. Free will . . . I have to do the work to redeem myself . . . people die in the meantime."

Harry responded with his patented, silent stone-face.

"Fine," I said. "How 'bout showing me where Richard Kruger is?"

"No."

"Look, we both know he's the trigger man. If he weren't, Donna wouldn't need my help."

He raised his eyebrows a fraction of an inch. I wasn't sure if that was an acknowledgment or not.

"Richard's being used. The faster I get to him, the faster I can help him and Donna."

"You're seeing her tonight. Maybe you can find a way to find him."

Before I could reply, Harry had whooshed me to my apartment. Alone. "That's not fair," I said out loud.

There was no response. Exactly the same as if Harry had been standing in front of me. If this guy was a product of my own fevered brain, I'd managed to create a thoroughly aggravating being. Why would I impose that on myself?

"Harry," I said to the air, "you make my head hurt. And you are a major pain in the ass."

No surprise: that comment didn't elicit a response.

*   *   *

"Mr. Tyrrell isn't it?" the doorman at Donna Kruger's building asked me. Boy, this guy was good.

"Yes."

"Ms. Kruger asked me to send you up. That's 8J."

"Thank you." As I walked toward the elevator, I heard him speak softly into the house phone, "Mr. Tyrrell is on his way."

Donna was standing in her doorway as I stepped off the elevator. She was wearing a light blue, wrap dress that ended slightly above her knees. The dress showed off her figure and her legs. I hoped my khakis, blue-on-blue-plaid button-down shirt, and Docksiders made an equally favorable impression on her. I saw my thoughts as if they were in comic strip balloons. For crying out loud, Tyrrell, cool it.

I smiled at Donna, "Hello."

She smiled weakly in return, gently waving me into her apartment. "Would you care to come in?" As I stepped inside, she asked if I wanted something to drink.

"Water would be great, thanks."

"From the tap? Or maybe you'd like some Perrier?"

"Perrier would be nice." I sat on her couch as she disappeared into her kitchen.

She was back quickly with a pair of glasses filled with sparkling water and ice cubes. She handed me one and sat down on the couch. I noticed that she sat as far from me as she could. "Have you seen the news?"

"You mean the open letter from the killer? Yes, I saw it."

Her eyes glazed over; she appeared to look right through her drink. "He's going to keep killing."

"The letter doesn't prove anything about your brother."

"Why not?"

"Remember the issue of *The New York Times* you showed me?"

"Of course," she snapped impatiently.

I ignored her tone and continued, "It was brief and raw. A simple, ugly statement: 'Time to Die'. Whoever wrote the letter to the NYPD and media took the time to be much more eloquent. Your brother's note was a burst of anger. The letter was a warning and a threat."

She sipped her water, clearly puzzling over what I had said, then asked, "What does it mean if someone else wrote the open letter?"

"It could mean that someone is trying to claim credit for killing without actually killing anyone. But I think the letter is from whoever is behind the killings. It's not from the shooter."

"You think someone has hired Richard?"

"Well . . . if Richard is the killer, it makes sense that he has a sponsor, let's call him Mr. X. The two shootings were done with very different, very good weapons. That argues for a lot of resources that a homeless man wouldn't have. For what it's worth: that's the theory the NYPD and its task force are working on."

"You know what the NYPD is doing? How?"

"Our friend Harry Mitchum has a lot of connections."

She nodded, "That makes sense. He found you."

I replied gently, "I didn't think you approved."

She smiled at me. "You're not too bad." Her smile wiped away the exhaustion on her face and made her eyes sparkle. She was a seriously pretty woman.

Pull yourself together, Tyrrell. I returned her smile, "Should we make some dinner plans? We can keep talking about your brother over food. Assuming I don't make you mad and you end up throwing the meal at me."

"I think I can contain myself. Do you like Chinese? We could order some from a place down the block and have it delivered here. That way if I pelt you with food, it won't be in public." There was hope for her, yet. Get . . . A . . . Grip, I told myself.

"Sounds great. I love Chinese food. After all, can a billion people be wrong three times a day?"

"That is a large statistical sample . . ."

Donna produced a menu, we made some choices, and she called the restaurant. Hanging up, she said, "About twenty minutes. Do you want a drink?"

"No thanks. Perrier's fine."

"Would it offend you if I have a glass of Merlot with our Chinese food?"

"No worries, my wife used to drink Merlot with Chinese food."

She smiled and went into the kitchen. I heard the soft chug-chug of wine being poured, and a second later Donna emerged with a glass of red wine in her hand. "What do you mean your wife 'used to drink' Merlot—did her tastes change? And would she be upset if she knew you were having dinner with me?"

I smiled uncomfortably, "No, she would not be upset. Maggie is the understanding type; I'm sure she's pleased that I'm trying to help someone. She's . . . uh . . . she passed away five years ago."

"Oh, I'm sorry."

"Me, too."

Donna drank her wine then said softly, "You still talk about her in the present tense."

You'd talk about her in the present tense if you had seen her ghost a couple of nights ago, too, I thought. I said, "Well, I haven't done a particularly good job of adjusting to her death. Haven't figured out the whole grieving thing."

"In my experience, no one ever figures that out. Not really. People adjust over time, learn to manage their loss."

There was something very familiar to me about her tone; her quietly supportive voice suggested understanding and caring. "Are you . . . are you a shrink, by chance?" I asked.

She chuckled, "Yes, I am. Is it obvious?"

"I don't know if it's obvious to everyone, but it is to me. Maggie was a shrink, a PhD in psychology."

"Oh."

I was an emotional basket case, struggling to breathe normally. The echoes of Maggie, my beautiful, blue-eyed, Merlot-drinking, psychologist wife, were reverberating every time Donna spoke or moved. "May I use your bathroom?" I asked.

Donna pointed me down a little hallway. I threw cold water in my face. Over and over. I stared at my dripping reflection in the mirror and resisted the temptation to talk to myself. I dried my face, took a deep breath, and went back to the living room and Donna.

"Are you all right?" she asked.

"Oh, me? Yeah, fine, thanks."

"Really?" Her voice was firm yet gentle. She wanted an answer to her question not an evasion, and her tone was warm enough to indicate support and an open mind. I knew from my experience with Maggie that indicating all that in a simple, one-word question made for a very effective therapist.

"I think . . . " I hesitated—yeah, go ahead, tell her what you think—"I think I'm supposed to help you. Not the other way around."

"Maybe we can help each other."

I nodded, "Let's focus on you for right now. But I appreciate your offer, and I won't forget it. Promise."

"I probably shouldn't be offering to help you. Here I am a therapist, and I've been no help at all to my brother."

"Maggie always said you can't have your boyfriend as a patient. Later, she changed boyfriend to husband, but you get the idea."

She agreed, "No matter how well trained you are, no matter how good your experience is, you can't help the people who are really close to you."

"Well, you can help them as a family member or a friend but not as a therapist."

She gave me a tired, world-weary smile.

The phone on the wall near her front door rang. She walked to it and answered, "Yes . . . oh, great . . . yes, please send him up." She hung up the phone and said, "The food is here."

I stood up and pulled out my wallet.

"What are you doing?" she asked.

"Well, I . . . uh, I was going to pay for dinner . . ."

"Since I'm not paying you for your help with my brother, I think I'll buy dinner."

When the delivery man arrived at her door, she handed him thirty bucks and took the dinner from him. I followed her into the kitchen, and we served ourselves delicious steamed dumplings (pork), shrimp in lobster sauce, and mixed vegetables in garlic sauce. I almost made a joke about not getting intimate after consuming the garlic but stopped before I said anything truly stupid. Sometimes it's a very good idea to shut up.

We returned to the living room couch and used Donna's coffee table as our dinner table. We both took few bites before conversation resumed.

"Unless you prefer to eat in silence, would you mind if I ask a few questions?" I said.

"No, not at all," she managed to be delicate even as she spoke with a mouthful.

"Do you have any idea if Richard tends to live in a particular place? I've seen homeless folks clustered in front of the doors of St. Jean de Baptiste for instance, or in some of the parks. Has Richard ever mentioned anyplace to you?"

"I don't mean to be negative, but shouldn't you have asked me this before?"

"Yes. I'm sorry that I didn't. I guess it was too hard for me to believe your brother was a killer—I didn't ask some of the questions I should have."

"But now you think he is the killer?"

"I hate to say it, but I think he probably is."

"Oh my God," she gasped softly. "It makes it real to hear you say that."

"I'm sorry. I don't mean to hurt you."

"You're not. But I'm worried for my brother. What's going to happen to him?"

"Well, first we need to find him, and that's why I need to know if you know any places that are regular hang outs for him."

She thought it over for a moment, "Richard often mentions the Met. Maybe he's in the woods near the museum."

"Hmm, not too far from here, and there's a bridge under the Park's East Drive with a pedestrian walkway, where he could shelter from the rain and snow." I continued to think about it and began forming a plan to reconnoiter the area after dinner.

"What happens after you find Richard?" Donna asked.

"We'll get him help. I don't want to see him in prison anymore than you do."

"Won't he have to stand trial, be evaluated?"

I hesitated, not sure what I could do for her brother, then realized: "Harry has some amazing connections. I bet there's some way we could get Richard help and avoid prison."

"That would be wonderful. Can Harry really do that?"

"I hope so. He can be a real miracle worker." I took a sip of my water. "Look, there's another problem. While Richard may be the shooter, he's not the driving force for the killings. There's no way a homeless man could have scoped out the locations, no way he could have gotten the disguises or the weapons. Someone, Mr. X, is sponsoring him, giving him the tools, and manipulating Richard's anger. I need to find Mr. X or Richard will never be safe."

Donna had stopped eating and was staring at me, "Because Mr. X will clean up the loose ends by killing Richard?"

"Probably."

"Oh my God." She looked at her plate but appeared to be staring right through the plate and the table. "Can you keep him safe?"

I really didn't know the answer to that. I swallowed hard, "I'll do my best."

*   *   *

When I said goodbye to Donna, there was a moment as we lingered in the doorway when it seemed the right time to kiss her. I certainly wanted to kiss her goodnight, but Harry's warning about my not getting involved and her forgetting me when this was all over reverberated in my head.

"Thank you," I said.

"You're welcome."

"I'll be in touch the minute I have anything to tell you."

"Hopefully soon," she said.

"Hopefully." I walked to the elevator, pushed the call button, glanced back, and said, "Goodnight."

"Goodnight."

The elevator doors rolled open, and there was absolutely no good reason on earth for me to hang around a microsecond longer. I stepped inside and made my exit. As I walked out of the elevator into the lobby, I nodded to the doorman and glanced through the glass door of the building. I stopped in mid-step because I saw a dark figure duck behind one of the parked cars across the street. Someone was watching the building. Maybe that someone was waiting for me.

I walked out the front door and turned left and then left again going downtown on Third Avenue. If more than one person had staked out Donna's building, and anyone followed me in a car, he wouldn't be able to pursue me because of the one-way direction of the streets. I hustled along Third Avenue toward East 87th Street, to head toward the East River and against the west-bound traffic. As I turned left onto 87th Street, I checked back up Third Avenue. A man in a dark-gray trench coat was walking quickly in my direction. I broke into a quick jog on the 87th Street sidwald, rushing toward Carl Schurz Park.

Fortunately for me, the light was in my favor when I got to Second Avenue. I ran across Second, half-turned and checked behind me. Mr. Trench Coat was in pursuit, pounding along about one hundred feet away. But he had to wait for traffic at Second, and I ran much faster. Even though I had every necessary license and permit to carry a weapon in New York City, I wasn't carrying anything at the moment. On the other hand, I was pretty damn sure that Mr. Trench Coat was packing, and it would make me very unhappy if he used it on me. I needed to reach Carl Schurz Park—and the added safety factor of the heavy police presence around Gracie Mansion, the New York City mayor's official residence, at the park's northern end.

I was badly winded as I ran across East End Avenue into the park's 87th Street entrance. Carl Schurz Park stretched for about a quarter mile from East 90th Street on the north end to East 84th Street on the south end. The park was a block wide, about two hundred feet, and there were trees and shrubs, a playground, and a dog run. The eastern edge ran along the East River and rose to an elevated walkway that had been constructed over the FDR Drive, Manhattan's east-side highway and parallel to the river. The elevated walkway was reached by stairs set along the side of a long stone wall that rose from the park.

As I ran into the park, the obvious move would have been to hop behind the nearest bushes and wait for my pursuer, but I wasn't going to make the obvious move. That's the kind of thing that gets people killed. My lungs burned, but I ran as fast as I could toward the elevated walkway over the FDR and along the East River. I ran up the steps to the walkway and headed south.

There was no place to hide on the walkway. There were benches on the walkway where a park visitor could sit and enjoy the view of the river rushing below and the lighthouse at the northern tip of Roosevelt Island, which is in the middle of the river between Manhattan and Queens. But the benches wouldn't hide a starved cat. I kept running south on the walkway, ran away from the police at Gracie Mansion, ran where there was no cover. I stopped halfway between two walkway lamps where the shadows were darker. I heard the racing footsteps of my pursuer but couldn't see him. I walked quietly over to the railing on the park side, climbed over, and hung at arms length from the railing. My body was hanging in the shadow of the stone wall that supported the walkway. Only my hands were visible at the bottom of the railing, and I hoped that I had chosen a dark enough spot that Mr. Trench Coat wouldn't see them. My toes found a tiny purchase in a seam between the wall's stones, so that I was able to stand high enough to see over the walkway.

The sound of the footsteps changed as Mr. Trench Coat came up the walkway steps. I could see him as he reached the top, stopped, scanned north then south, and wondered where I was. He decided to come south, probably to avoid the police surrounding the mayor's home.

As he came closer, I could see he had a gun in his right hand—an automatic, probably a 9mm, but lethal regardless of the caliber. He threw a glance behind the first few benches he approached and saw there was no way I could hide behind one. Instead, he looked over the railing, scanning the park below. He didn't look down the wall

105

itself—after all, anyone hanging on the railing would have been trapped, and he must have known I wasn't that stupid, right?

I lowered myself until only my hands were still visible and listened as the soft pad of his shoes came very close and then slowly began to fade away. I pulled myself up until I could see over the walkway again. He was moving farther south; the pistol dangling in his hand.

My arm muscles were burning more fiercely than my lungs had been a few moments earlier when I was racing along the streets. But if Mr. Trench Coat checked behind him, he'd spot me and I would be dead. If I was going over the rail, there was no time to hesitate. I pulled myself up, changed my grip to the top of the rail, and slowly and silently climbed over the railing. I slipped off my Docksiders, left them next to the railing, and rushed after him on my bare feet. I was only about ten feet away on the walkway when Trench Coat must have seen me out of the corner of his eye—there was a grunt of dismay, and he raised his gun toward me.

I lunged for him, left shoulder forward, crashing into his right arm. He staggered back, still upright, still holding the gun. I slammed my fist into his Adam's apple. He gasped as he fell backward and dropped the gun. I rushed forward and kicked it out of reach. I should have grabbed the gun—Trench Coat was completely disoriented and groaning in pain. But he was very tough; he wasn't close to quitting. He put his hands on the ground and pushed himself upright. He was big, too. He had me by an inch and twenty or thirty pounds. As if being bigger wasn't enough, he was pissed off. Truly and completely pissed off. I took a step toward the pistol as he staggered to his feet and dove at my legs.

We went down, and he was throwing short, hard jabs to my gut. He was pounding the air out of me. I grabbed both sides of his head and gouged at his eyes with my thumbs. That stopped the jabbing. He shouted in pain and rolled away from me. I gathered my feet beneath me to stand, but he was too quick and caught me on the side of the head with his fist. I rolled with the punch and kept rolling— to the gun. I grabbed it and pushed off the ground into a firing crouch. He was rushing toward me but stopped when he saw his own pistol aimed at his heart. He froze and raised his hands.

"Turn around," I said.

"Go fu— " he began. I quickly jumped forward and whacked him in the side of the head with the gun. He dropped like a rock. I prodded him with my foot. No reaction. I gave him a swift, short kick to the ribs. Nothing. He was out. Thank God.

I took a close look at the gun. A Glock and a very good weapon. I considered pocketing it for about ten seconds but realized that there was no way in hell I could afford to be stopped by the police with a weapon that wasn't registered to me. Well, Officer, I was in a fight. . . . I ejected the shell in the pistol's chamber and popped the magazine out. I wiped the pistol, shell, and magazine off on Mr. Trench Coat's trench coat and holding them carefully, so as to leave no useable prints, I dropped them into the East River. I was going to walk off and leave my pursuer where he was, but thought the better of it. A man sprawled on the walkway would attract a lot more attention than some guy sitting on a park bench in the middle of the night. The guy on the bench looks like he consumed a little too much booze. Whereas the guy sprawled on the walkway looks dead. I put my hands under his arms and dragged him to the nearest bench, then heaved and huffed and puffed until I had him in a semi-sitting, semi-collapsed position. The guy was very big; it took a hell of a lot of work to get him onto the bench. I sat down on the other end from my former pursuer. I was exhausted and needed to rest for a minute. I hoped that if this guy were part of a team that was following me, the other team members were still outside the park. I couldn't have fought off a Girl Scout selling cookies at that moment.

After a short rest, my breathing returned to normal and my muscles stopped burning. I considered my unconscious friend on the far end of the bench. It occurred to me that it could be very useful if I went through this clown's pockets. So I did. There was a wad of dollar bills, which I stuffed back into his pocket, some keys, and a flip phone. No smart phone for this character. No wallet or identification, either. I sighed. Some kind of ID would have made things too easy for me. I checked the recent calls on his phone and noticed that two numbers occurred over and over: 917-555-4348 and 917-555-5962. I typed them into the contacts on my phone, labeling them as "Bad1" and "Bad2." I shoved the keys and phone back into the pockets where I had found them.

I patted Mr. Trench Coat on the knee and said softly, "Nice having this chat. Thanks." He didn't reply, which I didn't take personally. I collected my shoes, put them on, and walked back the way I had come, toward the park's 87th Street entrance. Near the entrance, I took to the cover of the shrubs and slowly made my way toward the street. If Mr. Trench Coat had a back-up team, I wanted to spot them before they spotted me.

It took me a few minutes to reach the entrance, where I saw two men sitting in a silver Audi A6. Not the most recent model, but not very old, either. They were parked on the far side of East End Avenue and had a view of almost the entire side of Carl Schurz Park. Occasionally, the red glow of a cigarette was visible through the windshield. Okay, I thought, not going to leave the park this way. I made my way back to the raised walkway and hustled south toward the park's 84th Street end. I passed Mr. Trench Coat, still unconscious, still alone, and unnoticed on his bench. As I walked, I thought: Who the hell are these guys?

They probably worked for whomever was using Richard Kruger to kill Wall Streeters. Mr. X, as I fondly called him. But how the hell did Mr. X know to come after me? He didn't. No one but Harry and Donna knew I was working on these killings or that I had a theory about a Mr. X being behind the murders. Which meant that Mr. X had his goons watching Donna Kruger's place. In case she was worried about her brother. In case she had reached out for help. The last thing Mr. X wanted was for anyone to help Richard. The whole point was setting up Richard as the killer, as the Real Lawman, who wrote the letter to the police. Richard would take the fall for the murders when the time came.

Mr. X could have hired a professional to kill the intended targets and then disappear without a trace. But that's not what Mr. X wanted. He wanted a shooter gift wrapped for the police. Probably after Richard apparently committed suicide. Didn't all looney killers end up killing themselves? The murders would appear to be over, the case solved. The police wouldn't look for a motive beyond Richard's insanity. Mr. X would remain hidden, out of sight.

That meant that Mr. X had a motive that went beyond the punishment called for in the Real Lawman's note to the NYPD and the media. The angry, crazy calls for justice through death were a smoke screen.

And—if I waas right that Richard was the fall guy for Mr. X, he was in more trouble than Donna knew or suspected. He was trapped between a law-enforcement task force and Mr. X. His options had narrowed to a life in prison or death.

I left the park at 84th Street and turned right, walking west until I came to Second Avenue and was able to hail a cab. I had to find Richard and find him fast. But first, I was going home to get my gun.

That's when the chilling thought hit me: If Mr. X's guys had been watching Donna's place, was she safe there? Once the guys in the car outside Carl Schurz Park realized that Mr. Trench Coat was a long time emerging from the park, they'd go in and look for him. After they found him unconscious, how long would it be before they made a move on Donna? I really didn't know if she was in any more danger than she had been, but I felt that I had to get her out of there. Fast.

No time for my gun.

4

I climbed into the cab, telling him to go to Third Avenue and 87th Street. He grumbled at the short fare, but I shut him up by handing him a $20 and telling him to keep it. Two minutes later, I was getting out of the cab and walking uptown to East 88th Street and Donna's building. I continued past her building on Third, scanning down 88th Street as I crossed it, heading uptown. At first glance, there didn't seem to be anybody loitering on either sidewalk or sitting in any of the parked cars. I walked up Third and ducked into a newstand, where I bought a copy of the *New York Post* and a cheap Navy-blue baseball cap with "**I ♥ NY**" on it. I pulled on the cap and headed back to 88th Street. At the corner of 88th and Third, I opened up the *Post* and held it in front of me as if I were reading it. As disguises go, it was less effective than the masks the folks in *Mission: Impossible* wore, but if anyone was watching Donna's place, they wouldn't recognize me immediately. I turned left onto 88th, on the uptown side, opposite the lobby to Donna's building, moving slowly as if I didn't want to trip over my own feet while reading the paper. I walked about a hundred feet when

I saw a black Audi A6 with two men sitting in it parked across the street. From what I could see, they were both big, unkempt types from the same mold as my friend Mr. Trench Coat. There was a white guy with a mustache and shaggy hair, and a black guy with a shaved head. First the silver Audi sedan at Carl Schurz Park with two guys in it, now a second Audi sedan with two more guys in it, here near Donna's building. This made me me wonder if Mr. X had hired all his thugs from a Rent-a-Thug franchise and had bought the cars in bulk to receive a volume discount.

The urgent problem for me was the car's position. Using the side view and rear view mirrors, they could easily track my movements. They could cover their front simply by looking out the windshield.

"Oh, crap,"I said softly. I walked farther down the sidewalk, until I was a few yards behind their car. I dropped my hands slightly, craning my neck to create the impression of a man searching for the street number of the building nearest me. Then I glanced in their direction. Neither man was looking at me. I dropped the paper, rushed through the space between two parked cars and across the street. I planted both hands on the Audi trunk and vaulted up, then dove onto the roof in a semi-fetal position, keeping my hands and feet out of sight. My landing made a dull, loud boom.

There was startled cursing and both doors rocked open. The white man on the passenger side of the car emerged first by a split second. My right foot caught him flush in the mustache. He spun away from the car and flopped onto the sidewalk, his pistol hitting the ground in a sharp clattering noise. The driver was straightening out of the car as I encircled his neck with my left arm and pulled him against the top of the door frame, smashing his shaved head against the metal. He grunted and tried to struggle, but I slammed his head into the frame again then dropped his limp body to the street. His pistol fell from his hand and made the same clattering noise.

I slid off the car, and hauled the driver back into the car. Huffing and puffing, I ran around to the far side and repeated the hauling process with the other man. I looked up and down 88th Street, but no one was paying any attention to us. More than one hundred feet away, pedestrians were moving in both directions at the Third Avenue intersection. It was amazing what you could get away with in New York City. I grabbed the two Glocks— both pistols like Mr. Trench Coat's—and climbed into the back seat of the Audi. (Mr. X, whoever he was, did all right by his thugs: Audis and Glocks. Bad guys with good equipment.)

Leaning over my unconscious companions in the front seats, I patted them down and went through the content of their pockets. Like Mr. Trench Coat, they had cash and phones but no wallets or ID. I quickly noted recent calls on both phones—the Bad1 and Bad2 numbers I had seen on Mr. Trench Coat's phone appeared many times. I stuffed the cash and phones back in their pockets, and on a whim, pulled the key from the ignition. No point in making life easy for these guys.

There was a small box of tissues on the console between the bucket seats. I yanked a bunch out, emptied both pistols, ejected the magazines, wiped everything down with tissues and got out of the car. I walked eastward, away from Donna's. There were some smaller buildings along this part of 88th Street with trash cans in front of them. I dumped the Glocks in one and then much farther down the street dumped the ammo.

I headed back toward Donna's, keeping an eye on the boys in the Audi. Figured I'd give myself a running start in case they woke up. Not that I expected either man to regain consciousness any time soon. I made it inside Donna's building without a sign of life from either.

The doorman said, "Hello, Mr. Tyrrell. Here to see Ms. Kruger?"

"Yes, please." I heartily wished there was a way to get to Donna's without being announced. If her apartment was bugged—and given the thugs, Audis, and Glocks that were in abundance, I was pretty sure that Mr. X had bugged her place—once the doorman called her on the house phone, the bad guys would know where I was. My only hope was that the team I had incapacitated were the only bad guys close at hand.

"Go on up," the doorman said.

"Do you have a pad of paper and a pen that I could borrow?"

"Uh, . . . sure." He dug into the service desk and handed me both items. I scribbled a couple of quick notes, one per page, tore my notes off the pad, and handed it and the pen back to him.

"Thanks."

As I rode up in the elevator, it occurred to me that, until tonight, I hadn't seen any action of any kind since Maggie and I were shot. But in the last hour, I had taken out three guys. I smiled in grim satisfaction. It was nice to know that I still knew the steps to this particularly violent waltz.

The elevator doors rolled open. Donna was standing in the doorway. She said, "Hello, did you forget—"

I held my finger to my lips, and she stopped speaking and looked very puzzled. I held up my first note:

"Your apartment is watched & could be bugged."

Her eyes went wide, and she faced me and mouthed the word, "Really?"

I nodded and held up my second note:

"You need to leave. Pack a small bag & come with me. Fast."

Her head snapped up when she finished this note. Her eyes were wide with fear now.

I mouthed, "It's okay. Pack."

She nodded and walked toward her bedroom. I gently closed her front door most of the way, careful to stay out of sight if anyone was watching her apartment with a telescope. I hadn't shut the door all the way, so if anyone were listening they wouldn't hear it click.

Donna didn't mess around. She was back in five minutes. I had expected some kind of small suitcase, the kind you carry onto an airplane. Instead, she had a black, ballistic-nylon backpack, just big enough for a few toiletries and a couple of changes of clothes. It was nowhere near as obvious as a suitcase would have been. The backpack certainly didn't give away the fact that she was leaving the apartment for the night. I smiled; Donna was quick and smart. She locked her door, and I grabbed her hand and led her to the stairwell.

Once in the stairwell, I said quietly, "Is there another way out of this building? Beside the front door?"

"There's a service door to the side, but it opens onto the sidewalk about twenty-five feet from the front door."

"Well, that's not a lot of help, but we have to use what we can. Lead the way."

She led me down several flights, through a couple of short corridors and finally to a steel door with a horizontal push bar instead of a doorknob. I pushed on the bar and opened the door about an inch to the outside. There was no sign of anyone, gun in hand, waiting for us. No sign of anyone watching the building. That didn't reassure me, my field of vision through the one-inch opening was too narrow to comfort me with the lack of an obvious enemy. The only thing that was comforting was the black Audi with its two unconscious passengers. Without thinking, I patted my pocket with the Audi key. We had a getaway vehicle.

I closed the door slowly, "There's a black Audi parked about fifty feet from here. We're going to use it to get out of here."

"You're very lucky to have found parking this close to my building."

"You have no idea." I started for the door, had a second thought, and said, "Listen, uh, there are two guys in the car. Two bad guys who were watching your apartment. We're going to take the car from them."

Donna was stunned, "Are you crazy? Do you think they'll just let you borrow their car?"

"Well, it's not really about 'letting' me—I kinda knocked them out and took the keys."

"Oh, my God."

Her mentioning God made me wonder what Harry Mitchum had been up to while I was tackling all the thugs on the Upper East Side. Maybe Harry wasn't allowed to give that kind of assistance. For that matter, maybe I wasn't supposed to be assaulting people by way of helping Donna. I shook my head—worrying about how I could or couldn't help Donna would drive me crazy. I dismissed all these unproductive thoughts and looked at her. She was staring at me as if I were a baboon wearing a sun dress and walking in the Easter Parade on Fifth Avenue.

"If I didn't knock them out, they would have done the same to me. Or worse. And then who knows what would have happened to you."

"I . . . I guess . . . I guess you had to . . ."

"You'll have plenty of time to consider my behavior and decide on the morality of it later. Right now, we have to get to the Audi, dump the bad guys out of it, and get the hell out of here before their reinforcements arrive."

"Are you sure there will be reinforcements?"

"Uh . . . yeah, these aren't the first bad guys I had to knock out this evening."

"Oh, my God."

"Sorry . . ."

I slowly pushed the door open, leaned through, and scouted as much of the street and sidewalk as I could see. We seemed to be enjoying a Bad-Guy-Free environment.

"Come on," I said and ran like hell toward the black Audi. I reached the car, opened the passenger door, and tugged the bad guy. He toppled out, landing on the sidewalk with a soft thud. I dragged him over to the nearest group of garbage cans and propped him against the wall of the building. Donna was stopped in the middle of the sidewalk with an astonished expression on her face.

"Are you going to leave him there?"

"Yes, but he won't be alone." I hustled to the driver's side, checked up and down the street to make sure I could get away with this little operation unobserved, opened the door, and pulled the driver out, my arms circling his chest. This guy was no bantamweight, but a sense of urgency helped me get him next to his companion. I lined up a couple of garbage cans to screen the Mustache and Shaved Head. They weren't invisible, but casual passersby might not notice them, either.

Donna was still stuck to her spot in the middle of the sidewalk.

"Get in," I said, rushing around the back of the car and climbing behind the wheel. Donna was next to me in the passenger seat. As I pulled out, I heard a roaring engine. There was a flash of silver racing toward us in the rearview mirror. I stomped on the accelerator but not in time—the silver blur slammed into our rear bumper. We could hear glass smashing, either our taillights or his headlights or both, and metal crunching.

I kept the accelerator mashed to the floor, and our car shot forward. The silver Audi I'd seen at Carl Schurz Park was right behind us—the two cars screaming across East 88th Street at 60 mph.

"Who the hell is that?" Donna shouted over the roar of the car's acceleration.

"More bad guys."

"I thought you knocked them out."

"Not all of them!"

The light at Second Avenue was turning yellow. We screeched through the intersection at 80 mph with the silver

Audi so close I could practically smell the driver's cheap after shave. He was going even faster than I was and slammed into the rear of our car again. There was more metallic grinding and breaking glass. I manhandled the steering wheel, fighting for control of the vehicle. He hit me again, and the impact shot us free of him as we crossed the 88th Street and First Avenue intersection. I made it cleanly, but his Audi bounced off the side of a large, brown UPS truck. The Audi didn't stop, but the collision gave us a buffer of a couple of car lengths.

"You're crazy," Donna shouted. She twisted around, looking back through the rear windshield. "You haven't lost him."

"I'm aware of that." I was close to 100 mph, and driving down a narrow, New York City street at that speed was making me sweat with fear. We were closing in on York Avenue and running out of road—88th Street ended about a tenth of a mile away at East End Avenue and Carl Schurz Park, where I had begun my evening's fun. We were almost in the center of the intersection of York and 88th when I slammed on the brakes and shoved the automatic stick shift into second gear. The tachometer redlined, the engine roared, our tires screeched as the rubber bit into the road, and we lurched left on York.

We didn't make the turn cleanly, skidding sideways and slamming broadside into parked cars. I fought the wheel, maintained control, and accelerated away.

The silver Audi's driver attempted to follow me but overshot the intersection and crashed headlong into a car at the northeastern corner of York and 88th.

I sped up York while glancing into the rear view mirror. The silver Audi backed onto York Avenue, straightened out and shot up York in pursuit. One of his headlights was out. I drove through successive red lights at 89th and 90th and again at 91st; honking horns clamoring at me at each intersection.

"You're a maniac," Donna shouted. "You're going to get us killed."

"Hope not," I shouted back.

At York and 92nd I ran one more red light and pulled a sharp right turn onto the 92nd Street entrance to the FDR Drive. Within seconds I was hurtling south on the drive. We flashed past Asphalt Green and under Carl Schurz Park. There was no sign of the one-headlight Audi in my rear view mirror. I drove as fast as I possibly could, keeping the speedometer at 60 to 65 mph, which can be extreme on the FDR. Roosevelt Island's northern tip with its lighthouse was visible to our left. I kept driving south as quickly as I could manage and exited on 63rd Street, heading west.

I hadn't seen the pursuing Audi since we had gotten on the FDR. With a reduced sense of urgency, I slowed to a normal pace for Manhattan traffic. I made a right turn on Third Avenue, heading back uptown but only for a few blocks before going left on 67th Street. Then left almost immediately on Lexington Avenue, heading downtown to 63rd Street, where I turned right to resume my westward direction.

"What the hell is going on with you?" Donna asked. Now that we weren't racing around town, she spoke in a normal tone of voice.

"Just making sure we're not being followed."

"Are we?"

"Nope." I stopped at the red light at Park Avenue, took a deep breath, exhaled, and relaxed my shoulders, which had been clenched up to my ears. The light changed, and we crossed Park. "Do you have a place you can stay? A friend?"

Donna thought for a second. "Sure. Brenda Mills, my college roommate, lives in Chelsea. I'll call her." She pulled out her cell and was about to place the call, when I reached over and took the phone.

"Sorry. The bad guys may have cloned your phone. Can't take the chance."

"You expect me to show up unannounced and beg for a place to stay?"

I mulled that problem over for a second. "Tell her a pipe burst in the apartment above yours, your apartment is flooding, you were scrambling to get out, your phone got wet, and you're sorry, but could you please stay with her for a few days, blah, blah, blah."

"Are you kidding me?"

"I'm sorry, but the people chasing us are deadly serious. And I mean *deadly*. They're assassinating high-powered Wall Street types with sophisticated weapons. And a bunch of them have been chasing us around tonight in nice cars with very good pistols. Cloning your phone is not out of the realm of possibility. And given their behavior tonight, you can't take any chances. So, yeah, I want you to show up on Brenda's doorstep, tell her my cock-and-bull story. Okay?"

Her face was turned to the window as 63rd Street ended at Central Park, and I went left, heading downtown on Fifth Avenue. "Okay," she said softly.

I stopped for the red light at 62nd Street and Fifth Avenue, "I'm going to hang onto your cell. It might come in handy."

"How do you plan for us to stay in touch?"

I accelerated as the light changed to green, "Give me your friend's number, I'll call you."

"Maybe your cell has been cloned."

"Ugh," I admitted. Then, on second thought, "They've only known I'm working for you for about twenty-four hours, and I've had my phone at all times. It's not very likely."

"Can we afford to take that chance?"

I was about to answer when headlights came hurtling toward us from 60th Street. The silver Audi slammed into my side and bulled us sideways right off of Fifth Avenue and pushed ours onto the short drive that loops around a small plaza for the statue of William Tecumseh Sherman atop his steed. I stomped on the gas pedal, pulled hard on the steering wheel, and was able to separate from the silver car. He slammed into my tail as I continued hauling on the steering wheel and got my car onto Central Park's East Drive. We jerked away from our pursuer and raced up the drive. He was so close behind me that I couldn't see his one good headlight in my rear view mirror.

"Oh my God—where the hell did he come from?" Donna shouted.

"Damn, this car has GPS. They knew where we were all the time."

"Now what are we going to do?"

"Lose 'im somehow."

We rocketed past the Wollman Rink below us to the left and the Central Park Zoo to our right. A few seconds later, we went over the 65th Street Transverse, still rushing north. As we approached Terrace Drive at 72nd Street, I didn't signal or slow down until the very last second then wheeled hard to the left. It was the sharpest, highest speed turn of my life—I think the Audi lifted off its left wheels. Donna was shouting something, but I was concentrating too hard on controlling the car to listen to what she was saying.

Behind us, the silver Audi careened through the turn, but he skidded sideways and slammed over the curb. We gained hundreds of feet of breathing room before he was roaring after us. I raced across the bridge above Bethesda Fountain; Terrace Drive curved to the left then right again. I pressed the brakes hard, slowed down, shut off my lights, and bumped softly over the curb and off the road.

"But he's got GPS on this car," Donna said.

"Yeah, but our relative positions are changing too fast, the GPS won't reset quickly enough for him."

The silver Audi shot past us. I floored the gas pedal, banged down over the curb, and took off in pursuit. About a hundred feet ahead of us the silver Audi's brake lights came on, and we could hear the tires screeching.

"Hang on!" I shouted.

We crashed into the silver Audi's rear bumper at about 50 mph and rocketed the other car right off the road. It disappeared into the dark, launched toward the statue of Daniel Webster. Well, poor Daniel was on his own. I jerked our car to the left, and seconds later we were out of the park at West 72nd Street, the Dakota looming to our right as we drove south on Central Park West.

Driving as fast as the traffic would allow, I dug into my pocket and handed her my cell. "Put Brenda's number in there."

We were past 63rd Street when she handed it back to me. I checked the rear view mirror —no sign of our single-headlight pursuer. "I'm going to drop you at Columbus Circle. Take the subway to your friend's. Wait for my call."

"Okay."

I pulled to the curb, "Don't go anywhere until you hear from me."

"I won't" she said, climbing out of the car. She slung her backpack over her left shoulder and leaned back into the car, "Thank you. Be careful." She shut the door without waiting for an answer, ran across the tiny plaza and down the stairs into the subway station.

I checked my mirror again, reassured to see no one following. I drove through Columbus Circle and downtown on Broadway to 56th Street. Made a left, drove east until just the other side of Park Avenue, and parked at the first open space I came to, which was a fire hydrant, of course. Let Mr. X pay the ticket. I ran a block over to Lexington Avenue and then up a couple of blocks to the subway station beneath Bloomingdale's at 59th Street. Took a No. 6 subway to 86th Street, exited the train, and ran upstairs to the street. Throughout all these changes, I kept checking my back trail—anyone who was following me must have been the Invisible Man because no one was in sight. I walked to the nearest bus stop and waited for few minutes for the cross-town bus, which took me through Central Park for the second time that evening. I got off at Columbus Avenue then walked downtown toward 76th Street.

I needed to go home. I needed to get my gun.

*   *   *

When I reached the corner of Columbus and West 76th Street, I turned onto the uptown sidewalk of 76th, scanning the parked cars on both sides of the streets. Every time I neared the front stoop of a brownstone, I scouted the stoop for a possible attacker. This was a time-consuming method, but after everything that had happened that evening, I was going the safety-first route. I doubted Mr. X's team had had a chance of messing with my cell phone—but staking out my home seemed highly likely. As if to prove the point: there was an Audi A6 in what seemed, under the glare of the street lights, like a light-blue metallic color. The car was pointed away from me, parked next to the uptown sidewalk, but I could see two broad-shouldered guys in the front seat. From the angle of their heads, they appeared to be watching the front door of my brownstone. Looking at the front steps where Maggie had died.

I hid behind the balustrade of the nearest brownstone stoop and sighed with fatigue. It had already been a very busy night. The idea of taking out two more bad guys was exhausting. And to be honest, I wasn't sure I could do it. But I had to get them out of my way so I could go into my apartment and get my gun. Once I had my gun, I could forgo the roughhousing and just shove my pistol up their noses. Until then, I needed some non-gun methodology to get past them.

Using my cellphone—God, I hoped this wasn't cloned—I dialed 9-1-1.

"9-1-1 emergency, how can I help you?"

I pitched my voice higher and breathier than it was

normally, "There are these men outside my window, and I . . . uh, I think they're shooting up."

"Excuse me, but what do you mean shooting up?"

"Well, one of the men, well, he looks like he has a needle in his arm. Like in the movies, you know what I mean?"

"Where are these men? What is your location?"

"I'm on—" I glanced at the front door above me, "—45 West 76th Street."

"Where are the men?"

"Oh, the men? They're in a car parked outside my building."

"Do you know the make and model of the car?"

"It's one of those European cars, a sedan. It could be an Audi."

"Do you know the color?"

"It's a light metallic color. Gray, maybe. Blue? I'm not really sure."

"Okay, thank you. I'm dispatching a unit to your address now. Please stay on the line."

"Yes, yes, I will."

I waited until a police cruiser pivoted off Central Park West onto 76th Street. No siren, and the flashing lights went off as soon as the car turned onto 76th. I hung up on the 9-1-1 operator and began walking down the street toward Broadway. The cruiser pulled close to the Audi, and the officers stepped out of it. I didn't linger; I walked away from this little police drama. After I put several car lengths between me and the action, I crossed the street and walked back to my brownstone. I cast a glance at the Audi, and the driver noticed me going by. He had red head with a military buzz cut that made his head look like a cement block with red fuzz on top. All I could see of the other man was dark curly hair. Neither of them looked happy to see me. I gave them a brief wave, trotted up the stairs, and let myself in.

Once in my apartment, I wasted no time.

I went to the bedroom closet and pulled a small metal case from the shelf. I unlocked it, took out the shoulder holster and put my arms through the straps, then grabbed the Ruger SR9 with a 17-round magazine (and one in the chamber, although, because of living with Maggie, I never stored it that way). The SR9 fired 9mm rounds, like the Glocks I'd removed from the bad guys. I shoved the Ruger into the holster and grabbed a couple of extra magazines from the case.

After I put the case back on its shelf, I pulled a dull-gray backpack from the closet, threw some fresh clothing in the pack, and tucked in a small toilet kit and my cell phone charger. Then I grabbed my windbreaker from the closet and put it on to cover the holster and gun.

I shut off all the lights, walked through the darkened living room, and looked out the bay window onto 76th Street. The police officers were climbing back into their cruiser, as the two gentlemen in the Audi looked up at my window. I hustled out of the apartment and the building and down the stoop. The police cruiser was driving away, already nearing the corner at West End Avenue. I didn't hesitate.

I rushed across the street to the Audi, the Ruger already in my hand. I could see the bad guys' faces contort in disbelief, and then they were scrambling under their own jackets going for their guns. I swung the gun at the driver's window, smashing the glass. I stepped back, out of the driver's reach, and pointed my gun at Buzz Cut's head before either man had his pistol out.

"There's no way I miss at this range. Got it?"

They nodded.

"I want you two gentlemen, to pull out your guns *very slowly*, by the butt end of the grip."

They were chagrined that I'd gotten the drop on them and muttered unflattering things about my appearance and parentage. But they did as they were told and held the guns out in front of them.

"Good. Now, *very slowly*, reach behind and drop them on the floor behind your seats."

Again, they both complied.

"Now, give me the keys."

As he reached toward me with the keys in his hand, I extended my left hand. My right held my pistol rock steady, pointed at his head. To incentivize him to behave. He handed me the keys without any kind of trick. His language wasn't tricky, either, merely a string of harshly growled obscenities.

"Yeah, right," I said, "my maiden aunt curses better than you." I stepped back but kept the Ruger pointed at him. "Empty your pockets onto the front seats. And spare me the commentary while you're at it."

"Huh, what?" Buzz Cut asked.

"Empty your pockets and shut up."

They dumped cash and cell phones but no wallets.

"Get out, both of you."

More obscenities directed at me, but they continued to do as they were told.

I quickly patted down Buzz Cut and found nothing. "Come around," I said to Curly. He quietly submitted to being patted down. Once again, nothing.

I stepped to the trunk and opened the trunk lid. "Come on, get in."

"You gotta be fu —" Buzz Cut started.

I interrupted him by stepping closer and pointing my gun at his nose.

"Get in."

They moved to the open trunk, but Buzz Cut wasn't done protesting. "No way. Fuck you."

I waved the pistol to distract him and kicked him in the balls. He bent double and staggered, and his buddy Curly had to grab him to keep him for falling.

"Shut up and get in the trunk," I said.

Curly helped Buzz Cut into the trunk and then

climbed in himself. It was very crowded for two large, grown men. You could even say it was *extremely* crowded. I couldn't have cared less. I sat in the driver's seat and checked out both cell phones. There were many calls to Bad1 and Bad2. The other numbers in the recent call list appeared once or twice. I scooped up all the cash and dumped it, the phones, and the car keys onto the floor behind the front seat. Then I got out of the car, taking the two guns, both Glocks, with me. For what I hoped was the last time that night, I wiped guns and magazines and dumped them in different garbage cans in front of various brownstones. This disarming dangerous thugs was getting old.

I walked quickly to Broadway, crossed that boulevard, and hailed a cab going uptown. I told the driver to go uptown and take the 79th Street Transverse and stop at Fifth Avenue when we reached the other side of Central Park. That would put me east of the area in the park where, according to Donna, Richard Kruger probably lived. *Maybe* lived. *Occasionally* lived?

I had nothing better to go on. Going into Central Park at night wasn't a safe activity even for a highly trained, gun-toting man like me. But the park was as good a clue as I had. Hopefully Mr. X's thugs didn't have a way to track Richard. Hopefully they wouldn't get to him first.

5

The taxi stopped at the southeastern corner of Fifth Avenue and East 79th Street, and I stepped out of it. The ornately grand, spotlighted Metropolitan Museum of Art stretched north for four blocks on the far side of Fifth Avenue. Water played in the fountains in the two broad plazas near the museum's main entrance. Central Park wrapped around three sides of the museum. I wished I could just sit and watch the fountains at play in front of the Metropolitan, but I needed to find Richard. Find him fast.

I crossed 79th then Fifth and walked into the park. As soon as I was under the trees, I took my gun out of the holster. To my right, the huge glass slope of the museum's south side glowed from the light inside. To my left, I could hear the soft rush of traffic from the 79th Street Transverse. Ahead of me, the path curved around the backside of the museum and toward a pedestrian tunnel under the park's East Drive. Light from the street lamps filtered through the trees, creating bright spots and dark shadows. The homeless were probably gathered in the shadows, under the protective branches of the trees. It was also possible that some of Mr.

X's employees were also in the shadows. With Glocks at the ready. I paused and took a deep breath. This was not my idea of a good time.

A bit of night sky was visible through the trees. I looked up and said quietly, "Harry?" I waited. "Harry, a little help, please?"

"What kind of help?" he said, standing to my left. The suddenness of his appearances and disappearances was hugely unsettling.

"What kind of help?" I repeated with an incredulous tone. "How 'bout showing me where Richard is."

"You're doing fine without any guidance."

"Is that your way of saying he's here?"

Harry shrugged.

"Okay, play the Mystery Man of Faith. Do you think you could help me with any bad guys who might be lurking? I mean, I am supposed to be on a mission from the Chairman, right? Is a little help too much to ask for?"

"You don't seem to have needed any help so far."

"Couldn't you have provided a bit of assistance with all the, uh . . . gentlemen I had to take out tonight?"

"You didn't need help. Whatever you need, you'll be given."

"Oh, that means I won't get any help with anything that falls within my experience or training?"

"You already did."

"What?"

"You were given the necessary experience and training."

I thought that comment over for a minute. "Are you telling me that the Chairman *gave* me what I needed in advance of my needing it?"

"What do you think?"

"I think it's a coincidence."

"Coincidence is the Chairman's way of remaining anonymous. No proof that something happened due to his agency."

"Yeah . . . right. Look, my wife convinced the Chairman to pick me for this mission, in part because of all my experience and training. But if it hadn't been me, the Chairman would have found someone else."

"But it was you."

"Like I said: coincidence. I happened to be available when you needed someone."

"Or the Chairman acted anonymously."

I glanced up at the cars driving uptown on the East Drive and took in the shadows around that part of the park. "Fine. Whatever you say. Are you going to help me now or not?"

"If you need it." With those words, Harry was gone.

"Shit . . . !" I did a 360, as if that would help me find my disappearing companion. Was he whooshing out of sight because he had imparted the necessary information for tonight's lesson? Or was I too angry with him to sustain the delusion of his existence?

Frustrated with Harry, regardless of his real or imagined state, I lifted the Ruger and spoke directly to it, "All right, let's go find Richard. And, you, . . . keep me safe from . . ."

I walked down the path to the pedestrian tunnel under the East Drive toward Belvedere Castle and the Great Lawn.A few low-wattage light bulbs hung from the ceiling of the tunnel, and in the dim light, ragged forms huddled under blankets and coats. It was a mild June night—my windbreaker was more than I needed—but the homeless were hunkered down as if they were saving the heat for the winter that was six months away. Most of them seemed to be asleep, but one black man was sitting up, reading a week-old copy of the *Daily News*, watching me as I walked through the tunnel.

"What can I do for you, my man?" he asked. His voice was raspy; he sounded parched. But the tone was friendly.

"I'm looking for a guy named Richard. Richard Kruger. White guy, six feet tall, lean, sandy hair. Do you know if he's around here?"

"Yeah, sure. Richard likes to sleep up near the road. Likes the sound of the cars going by. It's a . . . what do you call it?"

"White noise?"

"White noise. Exactly."

"So if he's here, he'd be up that way?" I asked, pointing toward Belvedere Castle and the Great Lawn.

"Yeah, that's where he'll be. I saw him earlier, he should be there."

"Great, thanks." I started to step past him, stopped, and asked, "Could I buy you a hot meal?"

"Sure. That'd be nice."

"Okay if I give you the money for it?"

"That's nice. Thank you."

I handed him a $20. "You take care."

"I will. You, too."

"Thanks," I said and walked west, hoping he would actually buy a meal with the money.

On the far side of the tunnel, the path rose slowly. To my right, uptown, was the gigantic grassy space of the Great Lawn, where people played softball and attended open-air concerts. About a quarter-mile away, almost directly in front of me, Belvedere Castle was perched on top of a huge rock outcropping. Very picturesque. Not that I could see it in the dark. Up the short slope toward the East Drive, I could see people lying and sitting near the bases of a couple of trees. Figuring I might as well start close at hand, I walked up the small hill to the nearest tree. Two men were sitting under the tree, one a short white guy with dirty red hair and the other a short Hispanic guy.

"Hi, I'm looking for Richard Kruger, do you know if he's here?"

"Sure," the red-head said, twisting to his right and shouting, "Hey, Richard, you got a visitor!"

To my left, a man scrambled to his feet and took off running toward the Great Lawn. He was twenty-five or thirty feet ahead of me and was moving fast. The only lights on the Great Lawn are set along the perimeter walkway—Richard was sprinting west through the dark center of the lawn. I wouldn't have been able see him at all except that he was wearing neon-lime green running shoes that seemed to glow in the dark. I ran after those flying shoes, but he had a good start and wasn't wearing a backpack or carrying a two-pound gun. I raced after him, shouting, "Richard! I'm a friend of Donna's—I'm from Donna!"

He didn't hear or heard and didn't care. His lead on me was expanding, and in a few seconds he would reach the trees on the western side of the Great Lawn and be lost, even with those neon-lime shoes shining in the dark. He could hide under a bush or behind a tree, go north or south in the park, or exit the park into the Upper West Side.

"Richard, I want to help! Stop, please!" Shouting was costing me breath; I was losing more ground to him —

And he was gone, disappearing into the deep darkness under the trees. I staggered to a stop, bending over, hands on my knees, whooping for breath.

I stared at the spot where he had disappeared, wondering how I was going to explain to Donna that I had found her brother but lost him. I had taken out five men with guns and cars tonight, but I couldn't grab one homeless guy in a pair of sneakers.

"Shit," I gasped.

*   *   *

I left the park at Columbus Circle and found one of the last, remaining public phones in New York City. I called my cousin, Tom Corcoran, and asked if I could stay with him. Given the difference in our surnames, I figured it would be safe—no easy way for Mr. X to find me. I was probably being paranoid, but I was afraid that if I used my credit card to check into a hotel, Mr. X might be able to track my charges. Instead I was checking in with my cousin, who lived in a loft on West 13th Street in the Meatpacking District. Tom had lived there since before the area was hit by gentrification, which was lucky since he wouldn't have been able to afford his large apartment afterward.

Tom's wife, Judy, gave me a peck on the cheek as I walked in their front door. She was short and cute with bobbed, reddish-brown hair. "How are you?" she said with a wide smile. "It's good to see you. It's been too long. Way too long."

"I know. It *has* been too long. My fault."

"Oh, sweetheart, no one's looking to blame anyone."

"No, but it is my fault."

"That's for sure," Tom's voice cut in. He walked into their front foyer from the living room. He was stocky, prematurely bald, but with a puckish grin that made him look younger than he was or his bald pate suggested. Like Judy, he was happy to see me. He gave me a big hug. "Where the hell have you been?"

"I guess I've been in hiding ever since Maggie died . . . I'm sorry."

"And now you've come out to play?" he asked.

"You could say that . . ."

"Good," Judy said, stroking my arm.

They were incredibly warm people, always had been. I was a jerk of cosmic proportions for avoiding them for such a long time. "I'm trying to avoid some very unpleasant people. I don't know how long I'll need to stay."

"Stay as long as you like," Tom said. "We have the space."

"Are you working on something?" Judy asked.

"I will happily tell you all about it, well, as much as I can. But could I drop my bag in the guest room first?"

She laughed, her brown eyes sparkling, and pointed down the hallway that ran along the living room. "It's still in the same place. Help yourself."

"Thanks." I walked down the hallway, which was painted sheet rock with metal doors in it. The living room was to my left, with an uninsulated double-wall of sheet rock separating it from the hall. I knew the bedrooms had insulated walls and were sound proof. Kinda. Since I wasn't expecting to entertain any overnight guests in a noisy, energetic fashion, the quality of the soundproofing wasn't going to be an issue. I knew these walls and this loft very well 'cause Tom and I had put up the walls about twenty years ago.

The guest room wasn't big, with narrow windows running high along the back wall, a double bed against the right-hand wall, and a closet and bathroom opening off the left. I dumped my pack on the floor, dropped my windbreaker and holster onto the bed. I'd unpack later, especially since it would take all of thirty seconds.

Tom and Judy were waiting for me at the high, granite-topped island in their kitchen, which was outfitted with bare wooden floors, brushed-steel cabinets, and appliances. A dining table and chairs occupied the end of the living room nearest the kitchen, but they ate almost all their meals sitting on stools at the island.

"You hungry?" Judy asked. "I have leftovers: barbecued chicken or pasta."

"The chicken sounds great."

"Salad? Oil and vinegar?"

"Perfect."

She went to work warming the chicken and tossing a salad. Tom sat down opposite me and pushed a water bottle at me. "Do you want anything else?"

"No, thanks" I picked up the water, "this is fine."

Tom asked, "What's happening? Who are you hiding from?"

"Don't know."

"Do you really need to hide?"

"Oh yeah. I mixed it up with five different armed men tonight. They followed me out of my client's. Once I took care of them, I had to hide her."

Judy paused in the midst of making the salad, "Should I be worried by the phrase 'took care of them'? You didn't kill anyone, did you?"

"Not a single person. Not that they probably don't all deserve it. But I didn't kill anyone. Just knocked them out and disarmed them. Well, three of them. The last two, I disarmed and then locked in the trunk of their car."

"Jack!" Judy was shocked but chuckling, "Isn't that going a bit far?"

"I guess I could have killed them. But I probably would have dumped the bodies into the trunk anyway."

"Who's your client?" Tom asked.

"A woman."

His eyebrows arched, "Oh? A woman? Old, young, rich, poor, beautiful, or not really?"

I took a long moment considering how best to answer. "She's a beautiful blonde in her mid-thirties. Not rich, but not worried about money."

"And just what are you doing for her? Protecting her from some danger?"

"Yes, I'm protecting her, although that's not the reason I'm working for her."

"Are you falling for her?"

"No, I'm not falling for her."

"Really?" Judy asked. "Your face doesn't match your words."

"Give me a break, you two."

"Would it be the worst thing in the world if you did?" Judy asked. "Hasn't it been long enough?"

I sighed, "Yeah, I guess it's been long enough. But it's . . . it's not going to happen with her." It hurt to admit that despite my feelings for Donna, nothing would happen between her and me. Tom and Judy were probably the only people in the world I could have admitted it to.

"Okay, you're not falling for her," Tom said, "and you're protecting her, but that's not your main job. What are you doing then?"

"Trying to find her brother. Afghanistan vet, now homeless. I suspect that he is being used by some very bad people."

"Suspect?"

"I'm pretty damn sure, but I can't prove a thing. I don't even know who the very bad people are."

"But you're sure they're out there?"

"Hmmm, pretty sure. After all, I did have to disarm five of them this evening."

"Is that why you're here?"

"It is. Speaking of hiding out, would it be all right if I bring my client and her brother here at some point?"

"Sure, but when you do, you'll have to sleep on the

living-room couch."

"Yeah, right, like I could fit on that miniature piece of furniture." There was nothing miniature about their couch, but my six foot two wouldn't fit comfortably on it. "Some pillows and a blanket on the floor will do fine."

"When should we expect these extra guests?" Judy asked.

"Not sure. I almost had the brother tonight, but he got away from me."

Tom grinned, "You slowing down in your old age?"

"It's been a really long day. *Really* long. And he had a head start."

"And a bunch of old ladies using walkers got in the way," Tom replied, "not to mention the blind man and his seeing-eye dog directly in your path."

"I'd forgotten what a sympathetic soul you are."

Judy saved me, for the moment, by putting a plate of food in front of me.I dug in; it is amazing what an appetite you build when you're fighting armed men all evening. Tom and Judy sat with me and made familial small talk, but they steered clear of the subjects of Maggie or what the hell I had been doing for the last five years.

When I had finished eating, I offered to clean up, but Judy wouldn't hear of it. She washed my plates, as we all talked a bit more.

Finally, a few minutes before midnight, I said, "I gotta hit the hay. Thanks again for putting me up."

"Don't ever be a stranger again," Judy said.

I kissed her cheek, and Tom walked me to the guest room door. "I'm glad you're getting it in gear."

"Me, too."

He smiled and walked back to his wife. I went into the guest room, picked up my cell phone, and called Donna. When her friend Brenda answered, I introduced myself, apologized for the late call, and Brenda handed the phone to Donna.

"Are you all right? Are you safe?" She was *very* worried.

"Yes, I'm fine. What about you? Did you make it to Brenda's without any trouble? No one followed you?"

"No trouble. And I don't think anyone followed me."

"They would have snatched you off of the subway if they could have. You're safe as long as you don't leave Brenda's apartment."

"I do have a job you know. My patients need me."

"Don't go to work tomorrow. Call in sick."

"I don't work a 9-to-5 job—I have appointments with patients. I can't call in sick."

"If you *were* sick, would you call into your clinic or service or whatever?"

"Of course."

"Well, tomorrow you're sick. 'Cause if you show up to work and our friends from tonight are waiting for you,

you might never go to work again. Then what would your patients do?"

"You play rough," she replied.

"I'm a nice guy by comparison to the folks we met tonight."

"Okay. I'll call in sick. How long am I going to be doing that?"

"I'm not sure. Sorry."

"You're just taking care of me."

I was making my best effort, anyway. I decided not to tell her about the lovely gentlemen who had been waiting outside my apartment. But I had to tell her about finding and losing Richard. "Listen, I found Richard in Central Park, right where you thought he'd be—"

"Oh my God, that's wonderful! Is he there, can I speak with him?"

"I lost him."

"What?" she sounded horrified, not bewildered. "How?"

"He ran away from me. He was too fast. I'm sorry."

There was a long pause. It was very uncomfortable, waiting for her response to that piece of bad news. "What do you do next?" she asked.

"I find him again. Does he have any other favorite places?"

"I think he's only talked about sleeping in Central Park."

"My guess is that he won't go back. Anywhere else in the city that he's always been fond of?"

"He likes places by the water. Riverside Park on the Upper West Side. Battery Park downtown. Those tiny little parks on the East River in the 50s, beyond Sutton Place near the Queensboro Bridge."

"You mean the Ed Koch Queensboro Bridge."

"Sorry, didn't mean to disrespect Hizzoner."

I grinned at her reply, "That's enough parks for starters. Let's hope I get lucky in one of them."

There was quiet on her end, then I realized she was laughing very softly. "Oh?" she asked. "You're hoping to get lucky?"

"Please . . . you know what I meant." I was laughing a bit, too.

"I'm sorry," she said. "I'm tired, I'm getting punchy."

"We both are. Get some sleep."

"Goodnight."

"Goodnight," I said.

I washed up, brushed my teeth, then changed into clean underwear to sleep in. I lay on the bed, with the lights out, and stared at the ceiling. Apparently, I was going to spend tomorrow touring some of Manhattan's parks. There were worse ways to spend the day. But as a search methodology, it was lousy. The odds that I'd find Richard were very poor.

It occurred to me that if finding a homeless man was a challenge, communicating with him might be pretty darn tough, too. How the hell did Mr. X tell Richard who to kill? How did Mr. X get weapons and clothing to Richard? If Richard had a cell phone it would be easy, and I knew that some of the homeless did have phones, but Richard struck me as the phone-free type. He was too paranoid to be easily reachable.

Well, if there was no cell phone, how did they communicate?

Maybe Richard stood at the ready at one of the few pay phones remaining in the city—at the appointed hour every day or so, he'd wait for a call. Or maybe there was a drop spot. Messages left at a predetermined place that Richard checked regularly. I hoped I got lucky with the parks tomorrow. If I didn't, I was going to have to stake out pay phones near the Metropolitan Museum of Art. And try to find every possible drop spot in the area and stake it out. All this on the theory that if you were Mr. X and trying to get in touch with a homeless man, you'd do it somewhere near where he usually slept.

I rolled on my side. My brain refused to disengage. I couldn't go to sleep. If it was difficult to communicate with Richard, how much harder would it have been for Mr. X to find him in the first place? How on earth did you go about recruiting a homeless man with the necessary talents to work as a hit man? Maybe you wandered the parks, talking to homeless men until you found a veteran or two. You kept searching and talking until you met a vet so severely traumatized that he was ready, willing, and able to do the unthinkable. How long did it take, I wondered. How long did Mr. X have to look before he found a Richard? Traumatized, disillusioned, and angry enough that he was manipulated into killing.

My eyes burned with exhaustion. But I couldn't stop my thoughts from bouncing around inside my skull. And bouncing erratically and illogically from one thing to another: I segued from wondering about how Mr. X found Richard to how Donna found me. Had she been praying and then Harry appeared as the answer to her prayers? Did she have an awareness that Harry was a response to prayer?

And what could she possibly think of me? Did she think I was dangerous due to PTSD like her brother? Or was I the one worried about that? Maybe she was happy to have help. Maybe anyone who seemed capable and competent was good enough as far as she was concerned. Maybe . . . maybe when this was over . . . the hell with Harry . . . maybe I could ask her out . . . what would Maggie think?

I fell asleep thinking of Donna. And Maggie.

*   *   *

My cell phone's alarm went off at 7:30. I shut it off, stretched, and went into the bathroom for a shower. The previous evening's activities had left me with a sore spot or two, but I felt wide awake and full of energy. It's amazing what a night of playing with bad guys does for your psyche. It was distinctly possible that I was still on an adrenalin high. And/or that I was on a gratitude high, thanks to Maggie's intercession turning my life around. I felt better than I had for years. Since before Maggie died. Before I accepted the bribe.

Tom and Judy were both awake and getting ready to leave for work. Tom was an engineer with a construction firm; Judy was a public-school teacher. I smiled as I lifted my first cup of fresh coffee to my lips: I was going to work, too—for the first time in five years. Maggie had resurrected me when she put me on the path of making things right for others.

"You look happy this morning," Tom said. "You figure out how to find your homeless guy?"

"Not sure."

"Are you going to ask out your client?" Judy asked.

"Not sure."

"Will you be back for dinner tonight?"

"Not sure."

"Can you say anything besides 'not sure'?" Tom asked.

"Not sure . . . "

"I set you up for that."

I shrugged. Judy gave me a peck on the cheek; Tom patted my shoulder as they left. I had a second cup of coffee and two pieces of toast with raspberry jam. I rinsed my cup and my plate, went into my room, slipped into my holster, pulled the gun, checked it, and put it back in the holster. Pulled on my windbreaker to conceal my lethal hardware and left the Corcorans' loft.

Out on West 13th Street, I debated where to go first. The Meatpacking District is about as out of the way as it gets in Manhattan. It wasn't near any subway lines, and I didn't have a clue about the bus routes in this part of town. But the district was a lot closer to Battery Park than to the Queensboro Bridge or Riverside park. I decided to go to the Battery first. I walked downtown on Bleeker Street through the western part of Greenwich Village to the subway stop at Sheridan Square. The Village oozes charm with its short, well-maintained brownstones and quiet streets. I took a deep breath of the air before descending into the subway and hopping on the downtown 1 Train. I rode the subway to South Ferry, climbed to street level, and walked across the street into Battery Park.

Immediately to the north of the park was the Wall Street area. To the east, behind me as I walked west toward the Hudson River, was the Ferry Terminal. To my right, a few blocks uptown on West Street, stood the new tower at 1 World Trade Center. In front of me, in the park itself were trees, broad walkways, and almost at the river, Castle Clinton. The word "castle" is a bit grand for a solid, squat, single-story fort or battery built to defend New York Harbor in the early 1800s. As the park grew around the battery, it took the fort's name. I could see the ferries for Liberty Island and Ellis Island directly across the walk from the castle, and I enjoyed the view of Ellis Island's magnificent, multi-domed buildings and, a little to the south, the Statue of Liberty, standing nobly alone in the harbor.

At that moment, soaking in the beautiful vista, I thought of Maggie and the day we spent at Ellis Island, visiting the museum and marveling at the quiet heroism of the immigrants who had come to America with almost nothing beside the clothes on their backs and hope. I sighed and thought that I'd give everything I had to have five more minutes with Maggie. To hold her hand one more time. I wished I could shake myself like a dog does when it's wet. Shake off these thoughts and memories. Well, buddy, you're here to hunt, not wallow in nostalgia. I walked onto a pathway that led away from the Hudson and under the trees of the park and scanned every direction for those neon-lime running shoes.

Unfortunately, Richard saw me before I saw him. In fact, all I saw was the blur of a dark trench-coated figure and those ridiculously fast, neon-lime running shoes. He was heading north, toward Wall Street. I was after him as fast as I could, pounding hard with the wind from my running making my eyes tear. Richard knocked over a young man in a suit, leapt over a bench, and ran off the walkway under the trees. Richard had been slowed by knocking down the man in the suit, and I went over the bench more cleanly than he had, gaining a few steps on him. But he was fast. He zigzagged behind a tree, trying to lose me. I didn't waste time following his move and gained a bit more, but we were getting very close to the northern edge of the park at Broadway. He cut too close to a tree and stumbled over its roots. He took a couple of long, staggered steps, trying to maintain his balance.

And that's when I took him down with a full-body tackle.

He was a whirling dervish trying to escape, but I was bigger and my law-enforcement training had taught me a trick or two about restraining people who didn't want to be restrained. I pinned his arms behind his back and knelt on his pelvis.

"Richard, please, I don't want to hurt you."

"I'm not Richard!"

"Come on now, stop it, I need to talk to you. I'll buy you a meal."

"I got nothing to talk with you about. I'm not Richard."

"Right, sure," I said and forced him to roll over.

It wasn't Richard. He had the same shaggy, sandy hair and stubbly beard. The same lean build on a six-foot frame. But he had brown eyes. His nose was more pronounced and his jawline weaker than Richard's.

"Who the hell are you?"

"Joe," he grunted.

"Why did you run away last night when I was looking for Richard?"

He frowned but said nothing, squirming uneasily.

"Did he pay you to decoy me? I mean to decoy anyone who came looking for him?"

"I don't know what you mean."

"Did he give you money to get up and run if anyone came to the park and asked for him?"

His frown was now a snarl.

"Please, I need to find him. I think other people are looking for him; they want to kill him."

"That's bullshit. They give him money."

"They *gave* him money *before*. But now he's a problem for them, and they're going to fix the problem by killing him."

"Straight up?"

"Yes. Straight up."

"And you want to keep him safe?"

"I do. His sister sent me. I'm an Afghan vet like Richard."

His eyes went wide with confusion and hope. "Hey, I'm a vet, too. Iraq. My National Guard unit got mobilized, and off I went."

"Come on then, help me find Richard. Let me help him."

He was chewing that one over. I kept my mouth shut but stood up and helped him to his feet.

"Okay," he said, "I guess I'll help you. That offer for a meal still good?"

"It is. Want to find a coffee shop?"

"No, there's a cart back near the boats for the Statue of Liberty. Let's go there."

"Sure." We walked back toward Castle Clinton and the Hudson River. "Joe, have you tried the VA, tried to get some help? Maybe the readjustment counseling?"

"Man, I tried everything."

"Maybe you should try again. You might be ready for their help now."

"I don't think so . . . but maybe."

We walked in silence to the cart. Joe wanted a sausage and peppers hero and a Coke. Not what I would have had for breakfast, but I said nothing and paid for the food. We sat on a bench with a view of the harbor, the Statue of Liberty, and Ellis Island. I sat patiently enjoying the view and waited for Joe to make serious inroads on his hero.

"When did Richard ask you to fake out anyone looking for him?"

"I don't know . . . two, three nights ago."

"Did he tell you why?"

Joe shook his head and chewed a huge bite of sausage. After a minute, he was able to shove the food to one cheek with his tongue and said, "No. He said someone might come looking for him and gave me ten bucks if I'd run away when someone did. Said we kinda look alike, thought it would fool someone until they caught up with me."

"Did he tell you where to run to?"

Another head shake. "No, just keep going out of Central Park and not to come back for a day or two."

I mulled that over. Richard hadn't wanted to leave Central Park. My theory about his using a nearby pay phone or drop spot seemed stronger than before. But what made Richard think to set up a decoy? If he was worried about the bad guys, he'd also leave Central Park. If he was worried about someone like me, he wouldn't leave because he would want to maintain contact with Mr. X through the phone or drop. I gazed at Ellis Island without really seeing it and thought, looks like I'm going back to Central Park. And this time, I wasn't going to chase the first pair of neon-lime shoes that flashed at me.

I stood up and handed Joe a $20. "Get yourself another meal with that."

"Thanks."

I took a few steps, stopped, and returned to the bench. "Joe, please get help. When I came back from Afghanistan, I was a mess. I was suffering from PTSD. I was depressed. I didn't get any help, I just bulled my way through. I even managed to get married and get a job as a U.S. Marshal. But all the crap from the war came back, and I lost everything."

"You seem okay now."

"I'm working on it. I finally got some help." I dug out one of my cards—the same ones I handed out to my less-than-reputable clients. "That's my phone number. Call me if you want help. Please?"

"Maybe," he nodded as he chewed. "Maybe I will."

*   *   *

I got on an uptown 4 Train at Bowling Green, which is barely north of Battery Park (and not very far from my former place of employment, the U.S. Marshals Service offices). I really wanted to ride all the way to the Bronx, get off at Yankee Stadium, and watch the Bombers play an afternoon game with the Baltimore Orioles. There were a couple of problems with that scenario: even though the Orioles were in town, they were playing the Yankees that night, and I had finding Richard was too urgent a priority to delay for baseball.

At East 86th Street, I left the subway station and walked west toward the Metropolitan. It was an absolutely gorgeous day. Sunny, mild temperatures, a soft breeze making the Manhattan air feel fresh. It was my fervent wish that Richard wouldn't spoil it by rabbiting on me. If he did run, I hoped he wasn't as fast as Joe of the neon-lime running shoes. Another high-speed foot chase was more than I could handle.

I entered Central Park at the museum's north end at 84th Street, walking past the huge, glass-walled wing that housed the Temple of Dendur. It was a small temple as

Egyptian temples go, about the size of a small summer cottage on the Jersey shore. I walked on the path that ran parallel and in between the back end of the museum and the East Drive. I came from the north instead of the east to the area where Joe had run from me last night. A few homeless people were lying on the grass that sloped up to the East Drive; they seemed to be sunbathing but with all their clothes on.

The path descended toward the same tunnel I had gone through the night before. This morning, there were only pedestrians. The homeless were outside on this warm day. I walked through, stopped at the other end, and did a visual check of the slope from north to south. There was a man with sandy hair sitting under a tree with his back to me. He wore a faded, olive-green fatigue jacket and was talking with another homeless man. It might well have been the tree Joe was sitting under last night. I took a deep breath in preparation and began climbing the short slope. The one homeless man noticed me and pointed me out to the sandy-haired man, who twisted around. It was Richard.

I stopped in my tracks and spread my empty hands outward. "I want to talk with you, Richard," I said. "Your sister sent me."

He didn't run. But I wouldn't have bet that he would stay where he was.

"Donna's worried about you. That's why she sent me."

"Yeah? Why you?" His voice was raspy, raw from too much sleeping outside.

"I'm a vet from Afghanistan like you. She wants me to talk to you, see if there's anything we can do to help you."

He considered that for a moment but didn't reply. He also wasn't running. I thought that the longer he listened the less likely he was to run.

"Can I buy you a cup of coffee? We could talk," I said.

"I don't need you to buy me a cup of coffee—I have money."

Of course you do, I thought. Mr. X's money. Payment for services rendered. "Okay," I smiled, "you buy me a cup of coffee."

Richard smiled, shaking his head, "No . . . you offered first. You buy."

"Sure."

He was relaxed and loose-limbed as he stood up slowly. He grabbed a black, plastic garbage bag (which I figured was his luggage) and stepped down the slope toward me, "I know a place on Madison we can go. They won't give me a hard time."

I nodded, falling into step with him, taking his measure as we walked along. He was a little dirty, a little shaggy, but I'd seen construction workers who were less presentable. And virtually every homeless man I'd seen in the last couple of days was worse. Richard was what a homeless guy looked like (and smelled like) when he got to wash his clothes and himself once or twice a week. Richard wasn't a spit-and-polish Marine anymore, but he didn't provoke any nose-wrinkling. Or attitude-wrinkling either.

As we came close to the park's exit at East 79th Street, I noticed a silver Audi A6 pulling to the curb on Fifth Avenue. Both back doors opened and out climbed Buzz Cut and Curly, the pair I'd locked in an Audi trunk last night. If I were a nice guy, I would have been relieved that they were all right. Instead I cursed the luck that brought them here. I grabbed Richard by the arm and dragged him into a heavy thicket of bushes between the path and the 79th Street Transverse.

"Do you communicate with someone by a drop?" I whispered savagely.

His eyes were wide and startled, "How the fu—"

"Never mind. Do you?"

He nodded, frightened. He pointed back the way we came. "Over there."

"Okay. We're going to stay here and keep quiet."

Buzz Cut and Curly walked past us, talking. When they were about a hundred feet beyond us, they stopped, checked around to be sure they were unobserved, and shoved a small manilla envelope into the knothole of an oak tree near the path. They checked around one more time, sauntered back out to Fifth Avenue, and climbed into the waiting Audi. As soon as it was pulling away, I was moving toward the oak, pulling Richard along.

"Hey, what's in there is mine—"

"Don't worry, you can keep the money." It chilled me to think what he had done to earn it.

I dipped my hand into the knothole and pulled out the envelope. There was a thick wad of bills, which I handed to Richard, who smiled and twisted away from me, counting the bills out of my sight. Guilty conscience? I read the note enclosed with the money:

Meet me tonight. 8:00 PM. Usual place. Vadim

"There's a note. It says that Vadim wants to meet you tonight. Usual place. Who's Vadim?"

"He's . . . well . . . I, uh . . . I work for him sometimes."

"Doing what?"

"Oh . . . this and that."

I was sure I had never heard assassinations being described as "this and that," but I understood Richard's reluctance to confess to someone he had met five minutes earlier. After all, I hadn't even bought his cup of coffee, yet.

"Where is the usual place?"

"Oh . . . " he shook his head. "No . . . I think I'll keep that to myself."

"Okay." I would push him later for the information—if I had to. "Still want that cup of coffee?"

He smiled wolfishly, flashing his wad of cash at me. "You still buying?"

"I am."

*   *   *

We arrived at the coffee shop on Madison Avenue at the perfect time, after breakfast and before lunch. We settled into an empty, chrome-trimmed booth with a Formica table top and cushioned banquette in a pinkish rose hue. Both of us ordered coffee.

"You want anything to eat?" I asked.

"No, thanks."

I thought it over for a second and asked the waitress for, "Two eggs, over easy, whole wheat toast, and really well-done bacon. So well-cooked that anyone else would send it back, okay?"

"Home fries with that?"

"Yes, please."

The waitress called my eggs order into the cook through a service window and came back in a second with two white mugs and a coffee pot. She poured fresh cups for each of us and put a small steel pot of milk on the table.

Richard put milk in his coffee, turning it light brown. Then a couple of teaspoons of sugar. I drank mine black. I waited until we each had a few sips before saying anything.

"Would you be willing to come meet with your sister?"

"Why? Why does she want to see me?"

I sipped more coffee and carefully considered what I

should say next. "She's worried. She thinks you may have killed Edmond Garner and Bernard Abel."

He pushed the cup away, as if the coffee contained truth serum. His face was white with tension. "What do you think?"

"Me? I don't think you killed them."

He stared at me, eyes wide with fear. His hands gripped the table his knuckles were white with tension.

I said, "I *know* you killed them."

He sat frozen for a long moment. Then he bolted, sliding out of the booth at lightning speed.

He wasn't my first fugitive—I knew he was going to turn rabbit, and I clamped down on his arm, pinning him to the tabletop. He fell sideways back onto the banquette.

"Richard, I was a U.S. Marshal. You're not going anywhere. Relax, drink your coffee."

He resettled in his seat, and I let go of his arm.

"You were a Marshal?"

"Yes."

"And you think I killed someone but you're not taking me in?"

"I *know* you killed someone. Two someones. And, *no*, I am not taking you in. I work for Donna, not law enforcement. She wants me to help you. Here I am."

My eggs arrived with the almost burnt bacon and the home fried potatoes. I removed a slice of toast off the little side dish, forked some egg, potato, and bacon onto the dish and shoved it toward Richard. "Hope you don't mind, but I figured you're probably hungrier than you want to admit."

He considered the food for a long moment then picked up his fork and dug in. We ate in silence. If it's possible for silence to have a temperature, ours became warmer and more comfortable as we ate.

"I don't get it. Why do you want to help me?"

"'Cause your sister asked me to. And I'm a vet like you, I needed help when I came back."

"Yeah? Who helped you?"

I smiled, "My wife."

"Lucky you. A lot of women wouldn't stay."

Lucky me. It had never occurred to me that I was a lucky man. But right then and there, sharing a late breakfast with a homicidal homeless man and remembering my dead wife, I realized that I *was* a very lucky man.

"Yeah, I'm very lucky to . . . have her in my life."

Richard poked at his egg with his fork, breaking the yoke and mixing the yellow with his home fries. "You, uh . . . you know how I got this money . . . and . . . and you still want to help me?"

"Yes."

"Have you told Donna? I mean . . . you said you *know* I did it—does she know?"

"She suspects. She loves you anyway. She wants to help you no matter what."

He was making more of a mess on the plate. "She

165

can't . . . she can't . . ."

I reached over and put my hand on his arm. He stopped swirling his fork through the egg and potato mixture he had created. "She can. She does."

He put his left hand over mine and asked desperately, "Are you sure?"

"Yes."

After breakfast, I splurged and bought us a cab ride downtown. Richard declined the cabbie's offer to put his trash-bag luggage in the trunk. I called Brenda's apartment from the taxi.

"Is everything okay?" Donna asked when she came on the phone.

"It's fine. Richard and I are in a cab headed downtown—"

"—you found him! That's wonderful. Is he all right?"

"He's fine. I need you to listen to me: Throw your stuff together. We're picking you up in about five minutes."

"But I'm safe here . . ."

"Please do as I ask. We'll see you in a few minutes."

There was silence on her end of the call, then "All right." She hung up.

I hoped I hadn't scared her, but I had my reasons for picking her up, reasons that I didn't feel particularly comfortable discussing with Richard listening.

The taxi pulled to a stop on West 17th Street west of

Eighth Avenue. A school, a paved playground, and basketball courts stretched the entire block to West 18th Street. Brenda lived in the same brownstone where my sister had had an apartment years ago. I remembered many nights sitting up late with my sister and Maggie, talking about movies or music or the latest man in my sister's life.

Before I climbed out of the taxi, I said to Richard, "Can I trust you to wait here?"

"Yeah, of course."

"Good." I opened the door, stepped out of the car, and stopped.

Donna was rushing down the brownstone's front stoop, across the sidewalk, and all but dove into the back seat of the cab. She threw her arms around Richard's neck and kissed his beard-stubbled cheek. "I'm so glad you're all right." She was in tears.

Richard was crying, too. "I'm sorry, I never wanted to hurt you . . . I'm sorry . . ."

I got back into the taxi, trying not to disturb their reunion, and gave the cabbie Tom and Judy's address.

Donna threw her arms around my neck and kissed my cheek. "Thank you," she whispered.

"You're welcome," I said, smiling.

Despite my smile, I had the uncomfortable feeling that finding Richard was the easy part of making things right for Donna. Keeping him out of jail was going to be much harder. Keeping him alive might be extremely difficult.

Keeping anyone else from dying was impossible.

6

"Lunch, in the form of pizza, will be here in about fifteen minutes," I said, hanging up the wall-mounted phone in Tom and Judy's kitchen. Richard and Donna were seated on stools at the island. Donna had moved into the guest room, what had been my room last night. Richard, looking pretty darn good after a shower, would be sleeping on a couch in the loft's living room. I'd make a cozy bed out of one of the area rugs with a sheet, pillow, and a light blanket.

While we were settling in, Richard had borrowed a razor. He was a good-looking guy when he was cleaned up and fed. He had sharp blue eyes like Donna and even features. We'd tossed his clothes in the washing machine and found some of Tom's stuff that fit him. I hoped my cousin would forgive me for invading his closet.

We were all drinking water from tall glasses. Donna was seated next to her brother. I sat across the island from them.

"Richard," I said, "I need to ask you a few questions. They're probably going to make you very uncomfortable, but I need the truth. I can't help you unless I really know what's going on."

"Well . . . " he glanced sideways at his sister and shifted on his seat.

"Richard," I said, waiting for his attention to return to me. I spoke quietly, "Donna and I already know the worst. You killed those two men. But we're going to help you. First, you need to explain what happened to us."

He sat in silence, staring at the granite island, his right middle finger tracing an invisible pattern on the shiny stone surface.

"Okay?"

He slowly nodded.

"Okay. How did the men who hired you to do the killing find you ?"

He winced at the word "killing," and I realized that every time I mentioned the word, he winced. He had done what he did, and done it lethally well, but he was unhappy about it.

"How did they find you?"

"You know the red head? The guy we saw in the park today?"

"Buzz Cut? The guy with the badly chopped hair? "

Richard smiled in spite of himself, "Yeah, Buzz Cut. Well, he and a couple of other guys were circulating through the park for a couple of days, maybe longer . . . I'm not sure . . . anyway . . . they'd talk to us homeless and kept asking who were the veterans.

"They always talked to veterans. At least that was the rumor, that the red head—I mean Buzz Cut—was talking to veterans."

"What do you mean rumor? Is there a grapevine among the homeless?"

"Of course there is. How do you think we find out stuff?"

"Sorry. Anyway, Buzz Cut finally found you."

"Yeah." Richard seemed reluctant to go further.

"Did he talk to you about killing people?"

"Not at first. He asked me about my experience in the Marines, said he was one, too. Seemed like he really was in the shit in Afghanistan. We talked about that, then we talked about other stuff, and finally we talked about those freakin' guys on Wall Street, how they lost all that money, screwed up people's mortgages and savings, and they still got big bonuses. Shit, what a deal." His tone of voice was getting hotter and firmer as he talked. There was no hesitation anymore. "Bastards, they all belong in jail. But they're collecting bonuses. Shit. Then Buzz Cut said 'they should all be shot,' and I said I'd shoot 'em if I could."

Richard stopped for a long moment, as if considering his own words. His tone was much gentler when he resumed, "I guess I shouldn't have said that. 'Cause Buzz Cut said, 'if you really mean that, I can make it happen.' And he did, he made it happen."

His hand restlessly traced the veins in the island's

171

granite. "We . . . kept talking . . . and I got angry, really angry . . . I couldn't make anything work right . . . but these guys on Wall Street . . . and Buzz Cut telling me there was something I could do, and he'd help, I could put my anger to use for America . . . I was so angry . . . I was drinking . . . I . . ."

Richard fell silent and tears rolled down his cheeks.

"Thank you for telling us," I said.

"I betrayed everything I stood for."

I shook my head, "No, you didn't. You were manipulated. You needed help, but instead of help, you were taken advantage of and used."

He wiped the tears away with the back of his wrists. "I want to do what I can to make this right."

"I know. You can answer some more questions. Okay?"

"Okay," he said.

"How did they communicate with you? Was the drop I saw today the only way?"

"Yeah."

"Did they leave weapons for you there?"

"Near there. There's another tree that's kinda hollowed-out near the ground. They left stuff there, or behind some rocks. It was easy."

"How often did you check the drop?"

"Every day."

"How often did you see them?"

"Hardly ever."

"After your first conversation with the Buzz Cut?"

"Well, he and I talked a couple of times. But after that, no."

"Do you know any of them besides Buzz Cut?"

"No."

"Who's Vadim? He signed the note we found earlier."

"Yeah, that's the boss. I never met him, but he signed all the notes. He's Russian."

"How do you know that?"

"Sometimes Buzz Cut called him that instead of Vadim. You know, sometimes he called him 'the Russian.'"

Donna interrupted to ask, "Why sign the notes? Why allow your middle man to talk about you?"

"A control thing. He wanted Richard to know the money came from him and not Buzz Cut." I turned to Richard, "Does Buzz Cut have a name?"

"Uh . . ." he thought it over for a minute and smiled, "yeah, his name is Al."

"Do you know his last name?"

He shook his head.

"Does he speak with any kind of accent?"

"Brooklyn."

I held up the note we'd found at the drop. "Where's the usual place?"

"The Fifth Avenue sidewalk in front of the Central

Park Zoo."

"How often have you met someone there."

"I met Al there a couple of times. Before I said the thing about shooting them all."

"Just a couple more questions, Richard, and then we're done. I promise. Okay?"

"Okay."

"After the . . . shootings, what did you do? Did you police the area, did you get rid of the weapons? What did you do after?"

"Of course, I policed the area. I picked up all the shell casings. Wiped down any surfaces for gunshot residue and fingerprints, even though I wore gloves. I didn't leave a trace," he said proudly.

"No, you didn't," I said, as much for Donna's benefit as his. "What about the weapons?"

"Well, first I got rid of the shells and gloves in a sewer. The weapons were always in a case of some kind, so I brought them back to the park, wiped them down, and then sunk them, case and all, in the Lake, you know, the big pond kind of in the middle of the park in the 70s. I'd hide in the Ramble—do you know the Ramble?"

"I know it." It was a large, densely wooded area on the Lake's winding northern shore. The perfect place to hide.

"Yeah, I'd hide there until it was dark, get out of the clothes I wore for shooting, sink the weapons, cases, clothing, everything. Pretty good, huh?"

"Pretty good." Until the next time the Lake (a place name without any charm whatsoever) was dredged. But who knew when that would happen. And even if the police found the guns and connected them to the shooting, they probably couldn't connect the guns to Richard. He'd done a good job of hiding his tracks. Al and Vadim had recruited the right man for the job. I only hoped that Harry Mitchum had recruited as well as they had.

"Richard, you're not going to the meeting tonight."

"But I have to. Vadim expects me to."

"Well, I have a feeling that Mr. Vadim may not actually be there. Besides, you're retired as of now. I think you're probably safe from the police if you stop now. You did a good job with the physical evidence—I know that for a fact from the police. They're not hunting for a homeless man. They're hunting for a professional assassin." I didn't mention that they were also looking into the possibility of the killer being a vet. "You've stopped now. If you let Donna help you get off the streets, you'll be virtually impossible to find."

"Really?" Donna was surprised. "Is it that easy?"

"I didn't mean to make it sound easy. We have a mountain or two to climb before Richard's safe, but the most important thing is," I faced Richard, "you've stopped doing what Al and Vadim want. And you have to stop living in the parks and streets, 'cause that's where they'll look for you."

"I don't know if I can." He was worried, and he

175

looked from me to Donna.

She put her hand over his. "I'll help you. It will be all right."

*   *   *

The roof of Tom and Judy's building had been finished as a large patio with stunning views in all directions. The Empire State Building was visible to the northeast, more than two miles away, and to the south, the new tower at 1 World Trade Center rose into the sky. Much closer at hand, a few hundred feet to the west of my cousin's home, was the High Line, a park built on the remains of an historic freight rail line elevated over the streets of Manhattan from below West 13th Street, stretching north along the west side to the rail yards in the West 30s. Beyond the High Line was the Hudson River, and clearly visible across the Hudson, was Hoboken, the birthplace of Frank Sinatra.

The rooftop patio was empty. It was early afternoon, and everyone was eating lunch or at work. I strolled across the wood-plank platform built inches above the roof and enjoyed the vistas.

After a few minutes of sight-seeing, I said, "Harry, I need you."

Once again, he appeared. No sudden popping into view, no slow fade-in as he became visible. One second, he wasn't there, and a micro-second later, he was.

"You don't seem to need me at all," he said. "You

coped with the bad guys; you found Richard and reunited him with Donna. All on your own."

"Yeah, thanks for that assessment. As gratifying as it is, that's not what I want to talk to you about."

"What do you need?"

"Help for Richard. I think he is safe from jail, assuming I can resolve things with Mr. X."

"What do you mean 'resolve'? You're not going to kill Mr. X, are you?"

"Only if I have to. I'm not sure what 'resolve' is going to end up meaning. But I'm pretty sure Mr. X, whose name is probably Vadim by the way, wants to have Richard take the fall for these killings. Law enforcement will think the trail ends with Richard, and our homicidal buddy Vadim rides off untouched and unharmed."

"Unless you kill him."

"Was that a joke?" I waited for a response but only got the tiniest arching of Harry's right eyebrow. "Nice," I said and continued, " Anyway, I have to find Mr. X or Vadim and settle things so that Richard is safe. I need your help in two ways."

"Yes . . . ?"

"First, if the police Task Force meets again, I need to be there to see what the status of the case is."

"The next meeting is at 8:00 PM this evening and then 8:00 AM tomorrow. Unless something happens, in which case they will meet sooner."

"Oh, will something happen?"

"I'm not a prophet."

"Damn it, Spock, I'm an angel not a prophet!" I said, grinning. Harry's face was as blank as I'd ever seen it. If it was possible to be more blank than its previous blankness, it was more blank. "Come on, *Star Trek*? Haven't you ever seen it?"

Harry shook his head.

"Okay, sorry you don't do cultural references. Will you get me into the morning Task Force meeting? I'm not available this evening; I have a rendezvous with the bad guys."

"Yes."

"Good. Now, the other thing I need is to find Richard some kind of psychological help. But I need it to be someone we can absolutely trust 'cause there are all kinds of legal and moral issues I can't begin to untangle. I was hoping that you had someone working for you, someone like me, but a shrink who can help Richard."

"You want to know if I'm the case manager for a shrink who can help Richard?"

"Exactly. I mean, I'm not the only person who works for you, am I?"

"No, but you are the most inconvenient."

"Whoa, two jokes in one conversation. Wow. Do you have someone or not?"

"Yes, I do."

"And you'll set that up?"

"Yes."

"Same kind of introduction that you made for Donna and me?"

"Yes."

I took a deep breath, "Listen, about Donna, I know you said I can't become involved with the people I help because this has to be selfless, but . . . what if . . . well, what if becoming involved would help her?"

Harry's eyebrows pinched together. I couldn't tell if he was angry or suspicious. Or both.

"I'm not trying to say we're made for each other, but I really like this woman. I feel drawn to her, and I think it's mutual. Wouldn't it be a good thing . . . for her, I mean . . . if she found someone who cared for her? Someone who could make her happy for a while?"

Harry's eyebrows smoothed out. "Yes, it would. But that someone won't be you."

"I thought you weren't a prophet."

A Mona Lisa smile almost happened. "I'm not. But I know how these things work."

"Oh, shit," I groaned. "I have to work for others. Not allowed to reap any happiness for myself."

"Haven't you been happier since Maggie came back to you?"

That stopped me, literally, in my tracks. I had been walking toward the west-side of the patio, looking toward the High Line and the Hudson. I *had* been happier since her first appearance. Maggie had given me hope, which I'd been without for more than five years, from the moment I hit bottom and took a bribe. But now, even though I missed Maggie terribly and was incredibly frustrated by the inability to get close to Donna, I was happier than I'd been in a long time. Maggie's gift of hope was lifting my spirits. Or my soul. Or whatever. I looked back at Harry.

"Yes, I'm happier. And I don't mean to sound ungrateful, I really don't. But is this all there is? Am I going to be alone the rest of my life?"

"I don't know."

"That's the best you got?"

He nodded, "I'm sorry. I can tell you that if you are supposed to have someone in your life, you will."

"Thanks for that, I guess." I sighed. If Harry was a character created by my damaged psyche, he was an awfully inconvenient one. And where did he get these little sayings like "if you are supposed to have someone in your life, you will?" Were those springing from some internal font of wisdom? Or had he really been sent to me by Maggie and the Chairman to utter these gems? I shook my head and said, "Okay, you'll get me into the next Task Force meeting, right?"

"Yes."

"And you'll connect Richard with a shrink?"

"Yes."

"Care to give me a whoosh to my next stop?"

"Give you a what?"

"A whoosh—we talked about this before, that thing you do where you disappear and appear suddenly."

"No. I don't care to give you a . . . *whoosh*."

"Oh, come on . . ." my voice hung in the air as Harry whooshed out of sight. I spoke out loud, as if Harry could still hear me, "It's such a long walk to the subway from here . . ."

*   *   *

My friends Valerie and David Berk were both lifelong New Yorkers and retired Wall Streeters. But they weren't the driven, fanatical investment types. They didn't eat, drink, and breath the markets. They had made lots of money and retired. Now, they lived well, and they supported a preposterous number of charities. They also were inveterate arm-chair detectives, and they had always been more interested in my work than I was in theirs. Not that I couldn't have used some good investment advice . . .

I arrived at their Sutton Place apartment a little after 3:00 PM. A tall, slender redhead opened the door and gave me a big hug and kiss. "What a surprise to hear you on the phone—it's so good to know you're ALIVE!" Valerie said. That seemed a bit of hyperbole, but I wasn't going to argue with her. "David," she called into the depths of the apartment, "it's the long-lost Jack Tyrrell!"

David emerged from some far end of the apartment.

181

He was a inch taller than I was, broad-shouldered with dark-brown hair and a graying beard. He walked across the thick, wall-to-wall cream-colored carpet and shook my hand. "We wondered what the hell happened to you."

"Well, I . . . kind of dropped out of sight after Maggie died . . . sorry."

"It's nice to have you back in sight," Valerie said. "And you're working?"

"Yes, and I need your expertise."

They led me through their living room with its floor-to-ceiling windows overlooking the East River, Roosevelt Island, and the pagoda-shaped Queensboro Bridge a few blocks uptown. David showed me to the den, a smaller room with bookshelves, a dusky rose, upholstered couch and matching arm chairs. Even though they'd been retired for years, a muted TV was on CNBC, the market ticker rolling across the bottom of the screen.

"Would you like a drink?" Valerie asked.

"No, thanks."

"Well, then," she said, settling onto the couch next to me while David took an arm chair. "How can we help you?"

"I'm not free to go into detail—"

"—Of course!" David interjected.

"Oh shush," Valerie said, then to me, "go on."

"I've been thinking . . . well, . . . if the recent Wall Street killings weren't the act of some anti-Wall Street fanatic, I'm wondering if the killings were motivated by something happening in the markets."

"Like someone muscling in?" David asked. "Like the old-fashioned protection rackets?"

"Exactly."

Valerie and David smiled at each other. She said, "We were talking about that this morning. Once upon a time, gangsters would go into a small-time store and threaten the owner if he didn't buy protection from them, right?"

"Sure. You think that's what's happening here? On a larger scale?"

"On a much, *much* larger scale," David replied. "If you've got a huge, criminal enterprise, and you're making a ton of money, but you're hungry for more money, this would be a good play."

"Gives you a legit revenue stream," Valerie continued, "*and* a way to launder your less legitimate income."

"Makes sense to me," I said, "but who would want to do that?"

Valerie and David looked knowingly at each other. David said, "The Russian mafia."

Valerie added, "Vadim Kirilovich Bezukhov to be precise." She opened a laptop.

Ah, Vadim himself, I thought. Out loud, I asked, "Why him and not someone else?"

David shrugged, "There are a few Russian mafiosi

who could attempt to shove his way into the markets in this violent fashion, but he's the most likely. He was suspected to be behind the murder of the *Forbes* editor in Moscow a few years ago. And there are rumors he tried to buy a piece of a firm in the UK, and when that didn't pan out, he tried with one here in New York. But his reputation precedes him, and nobody legitimate wants anything to do with him or his money."

Valerie turned the laptop around to show me what she'd found: multiple headlines about killings in Russia, killings with Bezukhov as the prime suspect. There was also a picture of Vadim Kirilovch Bezukhov vacationing with Vladimir Putin at a Black Sea resort. Bezukhov was taller and sleeker than Putin—a poster boy for what used to be called Eurotrash.

As I scanned the picture and headlines about Bezukhov, Valerie said, "It's Bezukhov, if it's anyone. As you can see, he has quite a track record, impressive connections, and he's already doing business with a couple of American corporations with operations in Moscow."

"I'm confused: If he's already in business with Americans, why can't he get a piece of the action with a company here?"

"Everyone knows that if you do business in Russia, you're shaking hands with the devil. It's completely corrupt," David replied. "And once you get into the financial markets here, you'll have the Feds so far up your rear end you'll think they're using a proctoscope."

"David!" his wife said, but she was grinning appreciatively. "Crude though that terminology is, it's accurate. That's why we think Bezukhov is killing people— he's frightening his real target into cooperating with him."

"Do you have any ideas who the real target is? The one he wants to buy?"

"It's going to be someone with a heavy commodities presence."

"Why do you say that?"

"Bezukhov is involved in the Russian oil business," David said. "Attaching himself to a big player in the U.S. commodities market ties in very neatly with what he's doing in Russia."

"Were the two men who were killed, Garner and Abel, big commodities players?"

"Not particularly, but that's not surprising," Valerie replied. "If you're Bezukhov, you don't want to kill the biggest and best, you want to scare the biggest and best into allowing you to buy into their firm."

"Any ideas which firm he's targeting?"

David said. "Our guess is Woronov & Smith or Krassner McGill. Both firms have been very active in oil for years, and, well . . . " He hesitated.

His wife chimed in, "It's only our opinion, but neither of these firms has a sincere commitment to playing by the rules. They're the kind of people who'll do anything they think they can get away with if there's a profit in it. They'd be highly susceptible to Bezukhov's persuasive methods."

"Wouldn't most people be susceptible to the threat of homicide?" I asked.

David shook his head, "Some of these guys are beyond arrogant. It would never occur to them that they could be targeted much less killed. And as they were dying, they'd be thinking, 'what a fucking mistake this is! They killed the wrong guy!'"

I did a mental review of what Valerie and David had told me. "Why are you convinced it's the Russians? Why not some other organized crime trying to burrow into legit businesses?"

"Could be. But the original mafia, the Italians, bought into pizzerias, waste management, and construction. The joke was you couldn't buy a slice of pizza unless it was from a mob-owned joint. The drug cartels, the Colombians and Mexicans, seem to use savage violence and bribery to get what they want. Not a lot of interest in going legit. But the Russians, they want it all. Violence, bribery, expanding criminal enterprises, and legit revenue streams. And they think they're entitled to it—they believe they can do anything they want."

Valerie smiled, "My mother told me not to marry a Russian Jew . . . "

David grinned and continued, "Look at Putin and the

stunt he pulled in Crimea. Basically stole a huge chunk of real estate from the Ukraine. And the Soviets were no better. Khrushchev built a wall smack through Berlin and later shoved missiles into Cuba. Stalin signed a treaty with Hitler partitioning Poland, among other things, and then late in World War II, he made a promise to Churchill and FDR that he would allow free elections in Poland after the war. He had no intention of honoring the treaty with Hitler, and he never held free elections."

"Before the Soviets and KGB thugs like Putin," Valerie said, "you had the Tsars, and they could be every bit as bad as the guys who came after them. Russian leaders have a centuries-old tradition of doing whatever the hell they want."

"And getting away with it," David added.

"Ooooo-kay," I said. "Russians it is."

"Vadim Bezukhov in particular," Valerie said.

"In the law-enforcement community, we'd say you had a hard-on for this guy."

Valerie smirked, "You betcha."

"Are you going after this guy?" David asked. "Even with your background, Bezukhov is no one's idea of a good time on a Saturday night."

I paused as I thought that over. "I hope not, but I may not have a choice in this."

"You'll need help if you go up against Bezukhov."

"I have help."

"Whoever they are, they'd better be really good."

I thought about Harry Mitchum and the Chairman. "I have reason to believe they are the absolute best there is."

"Reason to believe . . .?" Valerie cocked a skeptical eyebrow at David. They were not reassured. "Have you seen your team in action? Can they handle Bezukhov?"

"I . . . believe they can. I'll find out."

"I don't mean to sound . . . patronizing," Valerie said, "I'm worried about you. You haven't operated at this level for a long time. Do you have to do this?"

"No, I don't *have to*. But someone needs my help, and I'm going to do this. I'm making a choice to do this. A choice of my own free will."

The Berks exchanged another glance then returned their focus to me. Valerie sighed then forced a smile, "Sure I can't offer you a drink?"

"No, thank you." I stood up. "I have miles to go before I sleep."

David winced at the quote from Robert Frost's poem, "I hope you mean 'sleep' in the literal sense of going to bed."

"Me, too. Right now I gotta eat before I'm off to meet my new buddy Vadim. Actually, it probably won't be Vadim himself, but whatever . . ." I shrugged nonchalantly.

"You're scaring me," Valerie said.

"I scare myself."

It took a while to say my goodbyes—Valerie made

me promise to be careful and take care of myself about a dozen times, hugging me in between several of my promises. The idea that I was messing with Vadim Bezukhov absolutely terrified both of them. To be honest, it didn't leave me feeling warm and fuzzy, either.

After leaving the Berks', I walked west to Third Avenue, found a coffee shop, and ate a tuna sandwich for dinner. Going all the way back downtown to Tom and Judy's place and then turning around to come back to meet Vadim (or whomever) at the Central Park Zoo would take too long. Since I was packing my trusty Ruger and a nasty attitude, I had no need to return to the Corcorans. Assuming Harry would channel the Chairman's help to me if I *needed* it, I was all set.

I had to admit, my faith in my pistol was a lot more substantial than my faith in the Chairman. And, I had an uneasy feeling that faith wasn't supposed to be like that.

After I finished my sandwich, I walked west and crossed Fifth Avenue, continuing uptown toward the zoo. I was on the sidewalk opposite Central Park, which provided a good location to check out whoever arrived to attend the meeting. It also provided a good place to make a run for it if the situation demanded a hasty retreat.

Because it was June, it was still daylight at 7:53 PM. I slowed as I neared the southern part of the zoo at 63rd Street. People strolled in both directions on both sides of Fifth Avenue. That was comforting. It meant that the bad guys were less likely to do anything rash. Anything that would be damaging to my health.

Speaking of bad guys, there they were. Ol' Buzz Cut and my first friend, Trench Coat, paced near one of the benches along the stone wall that separated the park from the sidewalk. I could see the upper part of the brick buildings of the zoo beyond the wall. The park was lower than Fifth Avenue, and the side of the wall along the sidewalk was considerably shorter than the side facing into the Central Park. I scanned the parked cars on my side of Fifth Avenue and didn't see anymore of Mr. X's—I mean Vadim's—team lurking, but I knew they could easily be there. I checked my watch; it was 7:57. What the hell, I'd be early.

I jaywalked across Fifth Avenue and walked directly up to Buzz Cut. His eyes went wide when he recognized me. Trench Coat also recognized me and reached inside his coat for his gun.

"Don't," I said.

He froze.

"I'll drop you where you stand if you don't take your hand out of your coat right now."

He was considering testing me—I could see it in his eyes. But he had no idea how fast I was and decided not to find out. I was relieved. I had no idea if I was fast enough to carry out my threat, but I doubted it.

"What are you doing here?" Buzz Cut growled at me.

"I'm here for Richard. Did you have instructions for him?"

"For him. Not you."

"I'd be happy to give him a message."

"Get lost."

"Well, if that's your attitude, I have a message from Richard. As of now, he doesn't work for Mr. Bezukhov. Would you please inform Mr. B of that fact?"

"How the hell did—?"

"Shut up," I interrupted. "You only need to tell Bezukhov that I know what he's doing. Tell him that Richard isn't helping him anymore. He needs to leave Richard alone. Got it?"

"Who the fuck do you think you are?"

"I'm the guy who took five of you out the other night. I'll do it permanently if I have to. You're the guy who's going to inform Bezukhov that Richard's not working for him. You also need to tell him that he's finished. No more killing."

"Or what?" Buzz Cut was clearly unimpressed with me.

"Or I'll stop him."

"You think you can stop my boss?" he snorted derisively. "You and what army?"

"You do not want to mess with my army." Please let that be true, Harry. Please. I said to Buzz Cut, "Believe me."

"Sure," he smirked, shrugged, and swung hard for

191

my gut with his right fist.

I parried his fist to my right and stomped on his left knee with my right foot. He grunted in pain as he went down, automatically grabbing his knee. I spun toward Trench Coat, who was pulling a gun from under his coat. I kicked out toward his arm with my left foot. I connected but without the time to plant my right foot, I was only able to stop his gun hand from emerging. The gun went off with a *phitp* sound, an almost silent burp, tearing a hole through his coat. The bullet hit the park's stone wall and ricocheted up into the overhanging trees.

My right hand clawed at his eyes, slamming into his cheekbones, forehead, and his left eye. He screamed in pain, and I kneed him in the balls. He fell to the sidewalk, and his gun, a Glock pistol, clattered on the ground.

Around us, people were shouting and scurrying back and forth. A few people had their smart phones up and were video-recording the fight. Just what I needed: video of me brawling with dangerous men on YouTube.

I kicked the Glock out of Trench Coat's reach then twisted toward Buzz Cut, who was running downtown. Well, he was hobbling actually. It seemed I'd done quite a number on his knee. I grabbed the Glock and took off after Buzz Cut.

He scrambled over the wall and dropped into the park near 62nd Street. I went over the wall about thirty feet uptown of him—I wasn't following right behind him as I had no desire to get shot. He ran to the nearest path and headed uptown. I cut through the bushes and trees, running hard, and lunged at from the bushes. I hit him around the shoulders and tackled him in the middle of the path.

I pulled his arms behind him, pinning them to him by kneeling on his back, grabbed his hair and bounced his face off the ground to make sure I had his attention.

"I don't ever want to see you or any of Bezukhov's guys again, got it?" I was breathing hard and the words came out in a savage almost-whisper. "Tell Bezukhov he's finished."

I bounced Buzz Cut's head off the path again, rolled him over, and pulled a Glock from under his jacket. Then I stood up and walked west as fast as I could. I stopped in the middle of the bridge at the northern end of the Pond (another charmless name of a Central Park feature), wiped the two Glocks down, and dropped them into the water below. At the rate I was going, I was personally driving a sales increase in Glock pistols. But I didn't linger on the bridge with that thought. I ran off, zigzagging through the southern part of Central Park as the evening twilight descended. I checked my back trail, saw no one following, and left the park at Columbus Circle. I hurried down into the subway station and caught a downtown A Train.

As the subway pulled out, I said, "Harry?"

Faster than I could blink, or think for that matter, he was there. Standing next to me, hanging off the same passenger grab bar.

"Harry, some bystanders took video of me brawling near the zoo, I need—"

He cut me off. "You won't be identifiable."

"Are you sure?"

His reply was a look that would have melted rock. "Why did you confront those men? Wouldn't it have been better to follow them to Bezukhov?"

"One guy—me—trying to follow two guys who don't want to be followed? Not much point in trying. I knew going into this meeting that the only thing I could accomplish was to stir Vadim's pot. So I stirred."

"Why?"

"You mess things up for someone, it forces them to take action they might not have wanted to take. Forces them into the open. Makes them vulnerable. At least, that's what I'm hoping for."

"But you didn't find what they wanted from Richard."

"They wanted him to kill someone else."

"And you don't know who that is."

"They were never going to tell me that. But now someone else will have to do the killing."

"Creating greater exposure for them."

"Exactly." I stared out the subway window and watched the darkness outside rush past. "I wish I could stop the next one."

"Maybe you will."

"Not unless I get very lucky. Or you help me."

"I'm not a prophet. I don't know who's next."

"Couldn't you ask the Chairman?"

"He wouldn't tell me."

"Why not?" But before he could answer, I said, "Free will, right? All the players involved in this make their own choices. Even if some people have to die."

"Free will is a double-edged tool. It allows for happiness and joy, and it causes sorrow and pain."

"That's not very comforting when someone is going to be killed."

"No, it's not."

7

EAST HAMPTON, ON THE ATLANTIC OCEAN: CHARLENE MERCIER SAT IN THE SATURDAY MORNING SUNLIGHT ON THE WOODEN DECK OF A HAMPTON BEACH HOME, watching the Atlantic Ocean waves roll onto the beach. There were sand dunes between all the houses along this beach and the beach itself, but the deck was high enough that she could see the waves rush in. She drank coffee and thought, if I have to go into hiding, this is a nice place to do it.

She'd moved into Derek Anthony's place within hours of Bernard Abel's being blown out of his office. Charlene and Derek had been romantically involved for about six months, ever since they'd met at a charity event at Lincoln Center, but they'd been keeping it quiet while his divorce was finalized. That was paying an unexpected dividend now in that almost no one knew she had any connection to Derek, and no one would look for her at his house in the Hamptons.

Charlene was a slender African-American with short, dark curls. She had large eyes and high cheekbones.

On more than one occasion, Derek had said that he would love to cast her in a movie. She had paid no attention to the flattery. Not that Derek couldn't have cast her. He'd produced a number of African-American romantic comedies and action movies that had easily paid for this house. He wasn't the household name that Spike Lee or Tyler Perry were, but Derek couldn't have cared less. Like Spike, Derek had a Masters from NYU's Tisch School of the Arts. Unlike Spike, he also had an MBA from NYU's Stern School of Business.

Charlene was no slouch either. She'd grown up in New Orleans and still had a soft, Southern accent to prove it. She'd earned her MBA at NYU, climbed the investment-bank career ladder, and now was the CEO of Trott-Fogarty LLC—one of the first African-American women ever to hold such a position.

But now, despite all her success, or maybe because of it, she was hiding from the assassin who'd murdered Edmond Garner and Bernard Abel. And while she seemed to be enjoying Derek's house in solitary splendor, in fact she was sharing it with a team of six men, all ex-military, hidden in positions surrounding the house, armed with high-powered rifles and sniper scopes. Keeping her safe.

Charlene squinted through her sunglasses to see against the morning sun beating on the Atlantic's surface. She thought she had spied a large powerboat, but couldn't be sure. After a long moment, she gave up the attempt.

Squinting into the sunlight was giving her a headache. She drank more coffee, leaned back on her chaise, and closed her eyes. Her body felt warm and relaxed in the sun.

Despite the sun glare, Charlene had spotted a large powerboat that bobbing just offshore. On the boat, a man went through the ritual of setting fishing lines out. He was short, only about five foot six, light brown hair, narrow blue eyes, a small scar on his left cheek bone. The man had never gone fishing in his life. He was the professional hired to finish the mission that Richard Kruger had begun—the new incarnation of the Real Lawman, the serial murderer of Wall Street CEOs. The Real Lawman watched Charlene Mercier through a pair of Zeiss binoculars. With the sun over his shoulder, he had no trouble seeing her. She appeared very comfortable as she settled back on her chaise.

He lifted a small black-plastic radio transmitter, about the size of a smart phone with an aerial extended about eighteen inches. Press the small, red button, and a signal was transmitted. His thumb hovered over the button.

He checked Charlene Mercier's position once more. She was still lying on the chaise. He smiled and pressed the button.

The entire deck disappeared in an explosive cloud of smoke, splintered wood, and sand. Windows shattered, and the beach-side of the house disintegrated. The smoke slowly cleared, curling into the air over the beach in a long, high plume. Charlene Mercier's bodyguards, who'd all been thrown from their hiding places by the blast, slowly picked themselves up and approached the explosion site.

The roof had collapsed into a hole in the sand where the deck had been. Burnt pieces of decking and deck furniture were spread all over the beach and dunes. One of the bodyguards stopped walking toward the house and called to the others. He pointed at the tall dune grass at his feet. They rushed to him and looked where he was pointing.

Charlene Mercier's charred, mangled remains were sprawled amidst debris on the sand. Smoke rose in wisps from her corpse.

Out on the ocean, the powerboat was making good speed away from the shore.

*   *   *

Harry whooshed me into the morning Task Force meeting at One Police Plaza. It was the same conference room as before, with the view of the graceful Manhattan Municipal Building. We arrived at 9:21 AM, but the meeting hadn't yet come to order. I admired the municipal building and thought of Maggie and the day we'd gotten our marriage license there. Would I ever feel that kind of hope again?

Looking away from my memories, I whispered to Harry, "Has something happened? Why is the meeting starting late?"

"You don't have to whisper. They can't see or hear you."

"Fine," I said in a normal, conversational tone, "has

199

something happened?"

Harry pointed to the other end of the room where Chief Hall was stepping up to the podium to address the meeting.

"I'm sorry about the delay this morning. As you probably know, we've had another murder—" he checked his watch, "almost ninety minutes ago."

Hall nodded at a young officer at the conference table. The image of a very pretty black woman was projected on the screen behind Hall's left shoulder. He gestured with his thumb over his shoulder, "This is Charlene Mercier. CEO of Trott Fogarty. She was killed this morning in an explosion at an East Hampton house owned by Derek Anthony." He nodded at the young officer, and a photo of the house, taken from a helicopter, was displayed.

There was a crater in the sand on the beach side of the house. It had probably been a beautiful home, but now one entire side was shattered, and the roof was partially caved in.

Chief Hall continued, "Natural gas has been ruled out—the explosion was centered under the wooden deck. The gas line that feeds the house is intact, no damage."

"Crime-scene investigators think it was probably C4, detonated by a small radio receiver with a powerful battery. What looks like a radio aerial was strung out on top of the sand, trailing toward the ocean."

Agent Mancini, the sexy FBI woman, asked, "Was

Ms. Mercier on the deck at the time of the explosion? Are you thinking that the bomb was triggered by a radio signal from a boat offshore?"

Chief Hall nodded, "Yes to both those questions."

"Why was she at the house?" Mancini asked. "And do we know Mr. Anthony's whereabouts at the time of the explosion?"

"I'm going to answer the second question first: Mr. Anthony and Ms. Mercier were involved. They were keeping quiet about it because he's in the middle of a rancorous divorce. After Edmond Garner and Bernard Abel were killed, Ms. Mercier went into hiding at Mr. Anthony's. She moved out there within hours of Abel's death. Mr. Anthony hadn't been out to visit—this morning at the time of the explosion, he was having breakfast at the Regency with three other film producers."

"If he were going to kill her, he'd have a trigger man do it," Mancini pointed out. "His solid alibi doesn't mean he wasn't behind it."

"No, but he doesn't have an obvious motive. We're checking him out, but right now it doesn't look as if he stood to gain a thing by her death."

"Whereas, if she's Wall Street Murder No. 3, the killer's motive seems to be established," Mancini said.

The beefy, red-haired Captain Beirne, seated near the podium, spoke up, "That's what we think, but the details of this killing are very different. Aside from the obvious of guns vs. explosive, the Mercier killing doesn't look like the work of a lone assassin. Although the earlier murders showed some pretty efficient advance work, whoever got to Mercier knew her routines and knew her life. The bomb and the radio detonator were planted at least a few days ago, because no way someone crawled under the deck and buried it while the lady was surrounded by all the private security she had on location. And if our boat theory is correct, the killer had to get a boat, scout out Anthony's house and make sure Mercier was on the deck and then signal the detonator. It all indicates an organization with resources."

Yup, I thought, sounds like my buddy Vadim. Exactly what I needed: To tangle with a homicidal Russian who had lots of money and resources.

Chief Hall added, "Not only an organization, but we might be dealing with two separate killers given how different the methods were."

Since I had tucked away the man who'd killed Garner and Abel, I could confirm that there were at least two different assassins. Which meant my mission to stop the killings was getting tougher all the time.

A man with dark hair and a sharp, solid jaw that you could have broken rocks on, asked the logical follow-up question: "Lopez, DEA, if we're talking an organization with lots of resources, does that mean organized crime? Is someone trying to intimidate his way onto the Street and then grab a legit revenue stream? Maybe do some money laundering at the same time?"

I leaned over to Harry, "This is why Bezukhov wanted to pin everything on Richard."

"Then why kill Charlene Mercier the way he did?"

"I removed Richard from the equation. If he was going to kill again, he needed another killer."

"But he planned this killing before you took Richard away."

"Yeah, he probably always had a Plan B."

Around the conference table, there was speculation about which group of organized criminals might have committed the third murder. The mostly drug-based Hispanic cartels were dismissed. The Italians were dismissed—they already had what they needed in waste management and construction. The Albanians were considered, but there was general agreement that while the Albanians were violent enough to murder their way into an industry, they probably weren't evolved enough to want to get into Wall Street. Not yet.

Finally, after more than ten minutes of analysis, the law-enforcement professionals arrived at the conclusion that my personal, arm-chair detectives had gone to directly: the Russians. Several Russian mafia chiefs were mentioned, including the Berks' prime suspect—Vadim Bezukhov. It was agreed the FBI, in the person of Special Agent Linda Mancini, would take the lead investigating the organized-crime aspect, with a special focus on the Russians.

Hall said, "Unless anyone has anything else, we'll be back here at 2000 hours tonight. Thank you, all."

The meeting broke up, but people remained grouped into small bunches, swapping ideas and asking questions. The killer had metamorphosed from a crazed but clever lone gunman into a shadowy sinister organization. That didn't feel like progress to anyone.

*   *   *

Harry magically set us down in front of One Police Plaza. He probably would have objected to the word "magically." But I don't know how else to describe it.

"What now?" he asked.

"As I told you, you need to connect Richard to a therapist of some kind, hopefully someone who could take him into a therapeutic community on an anonymous basis."

"That will be done by dinner time."

"Dinner time? Today?"

Harry gave me his patented, blank, cement-wall stare.

"Okay, that's great," I said. "I like your style. Not to mention speed."

"What are you going to do?" Harry asked.

"I've got to check some phone numbers with Paul Vidal, my friend at NYPD. And, I have to figure out a way to carry this fight to Bezukhov."

"Why?"

"I want to stop the killings. And I want to make sure

this guy doesn't come after either Richard or Donna. Since I haven't got a single item of evidence or even a coherent theory to offer the police, I need to push Bezukhov somehow. Get him annoyed, make him take chances to eliminate me."

"What if he succeeds in eliminating you?"

"Well . . . then you won't be helping me help others any more, will you?"

Harry folded his arms across his chest. I hadn't seen him do this before, and I have to admit, I was clueless as to whether he was annoyed, amused, or apathetic. Or all of the above.

"I'm open to suggestions," I said. "I really am. But based on our brief history to date, you don't make suggestions."

His reply was silence. I thought his arms might have tightened across his chest.

"Is silence consent? Meaning no suggestions?"

I waited but there was no verbal response.

"Absent any further discussion . . . " I said, pausing to give him one last chance to interject with a good idea, "I'll have to come up with some way to aggravate the hell out of Bezukhov."

"You should find it no trouble being aggravating."

My head snapped back and my eyes went wide. "Oh my," I said. "Well played."

Harry resumed his stony silence.

"Would you mind," I began, "taking me to the 19th Precinct—?"

He disappeared on the "p" of "precinct."

"Damn," I said under my breath and walked toward the subway station under the Manhattan Municipal Building. I took a 4 Train uptown and got off at 59th Street, right under Bloomingdale's. I walked the few blocks to the 19th Precinct.

Paul Vidal was at his desk in the detective squad. His office door was open, and he looked up when I knocked on the door frame. He seemed tired, and for a moment I had the impression that he hadn't left the squad since I'd seen him three days earlier.

"Are you coming for a new favor or to do me one?" he asked wearily.

"Both." I plopped down in one of his guest chairs without being asked. "Remember the homeless vet I was looking for?"

"Yeah, uh . . . " he pushed some papers around on his desk, and said, "yeah, Richard Kruger, right?"

"Yes. I found him. He'll be in a therapeutic community getting help by the end of day."

"That's great," he smiled. He was genuinely pleased. The natural reaction of one vet hearing that another was being taken care of. "Nice work. Where'd you find him?"

"Central Park. His sister knew that he liked to hang out near the Met, and I got lucky."

He nodded, still smiling, but then the smile faded; he

pushed some more papers around, scanned a report of some kind, and looked at me. "Were you in a fight with two armed men on the Fifth Avenue sidewalk near the zoo? Last night?"

"Heaven forbid."

He frowned and tapped the report, "A guy matching your description took out two armed men. Grabbed their guns and disappeared into the park. You don't know anything about that?"

"Nope."

"You're a little too cute for your own good."

I shrugged. I wasn't going to help him arrest me, and Paul knew there was nowhere near enough evidence to follow up.

"These guys that you didn't beat up, do they have anything to do with Richard Kruger?"

"Not that I know of. Do you have names for the guys? Maybe I know them."

"No, we don't have names. They both ran away. Staggered away, actually, from what witnesses said."

"It's amazing what happens on the streets of this town."

"Yeah, isn't it." He grinned tartly. "What kind of favor do you want?"

"I have a couple of phone numbers, I was hoping you could do a reverse look-up for me."

His eyes locked with mine. I heard his fingers

drumming on the desktop.

"Listen, if you'd rather not," I said in my best Jimmy Stewart "aw shucks" tone of voice, "you know, we could forget the past and—"

"I'm not forgetting the past. I owe you, and I'm grateful. What are the numbers?"

I checked my phone for the numbers of Bad1 and Bad2 and read them to Paul, "917-555-4348 and 917-555-5962." He typed them into a database as I spoke. We waited a few seconds, and he read the results with a cocked eyebrow. "Hmm, they both came back as ''unknown.' Probably burn phones, you know, prepaid cell phones?"

"I know." I hadn't really expected results that would lead me to Vadim Bezukhov.

"Where'd you get those numbers?" Paul asked with forced nonchalance.

"Some people I've been working with."

"*Some* people you've been working with?"

"Yeah, basically."

"And that would not include the two guys you did not beat up last night?"

"Absolutely not," I said. I hated lying to Paul, but I salved my conscience with the idea that my lies were serving the greater good.

"Is there anything else I can do for you?" Paul asked with a total lack of sincerity.

"Since you're asking . . . would you happen to have

an address for Vadim Bezukhov?"

Paul's mouth dropped open and stayed open for a long moment. He exhaled loudly, "Are you *fucking* kidding me?"

"I wanted to know if he has a Manhattan address."

"You're talking about the guy in the Russian mafia, right?"

"Well, *allegedly* in the Russian mafia."

"You are outta your mind . . . "

"I could really use that address if you have it."

He stared at me for a long time, shorter than an eternity but longer than a TV commercial, and began typing into his computer. "I hope you know what you're doing. This guy is supposed to be as bad as it gets. People die who just *think* about messing with him."

I dropped my facetious innocence and said, "I wouldn't contact him unless I *had* to."

"You sure?"

"Yes. Believe me."

Paul nodded slowly, scribbled something on a small pad of paper, ripped out the page, and handed it to me. "Please don't show up dead."

"I'll do my best."

Outside the precinct house, I lingered on the sidewalk, afraid to look at the piece of paper with Bezukhov's address. I'd heard a lot of horror stories about the Russian mafia. But they all seemed to take place in

Moscow. It wasn't hard to make bad jokes to Harry when the bad guy was probably in Moscow. But if he was in Manhattan, and I could, in fact, take the fight to him . . . I swallowed hard and looked at the small, folded piece of paper in my hand. Paul Vidal's reaction to my naming Bezukhov had shaken me. If he was worried than I had a lot to be worried about.

I opened the piece of paper. Vadim Bezukhov didn't live in some swanky Manhattan address. He didn't even live in New York City. He lived at a swanky suburban address in Westchester County, immediately north of the city. Vadim Bezukhov, Russian mafiosi, billionaire, and killer lived in Bedford Hills.

*   *   *

After leaving the precinct house, I walked down Lexington Avenue until I found a discount electronics store and bought a burn phone, which is only a prepaid cell phone with a cool name. Since the phone's airtime is paid in advance, the telephone provider doesn't keep any identifying information on the user. I assumed that Vadim Bezukhov's gang was sophisticated enough to trace my phone if I called those numbers I'd found in Trench Coat's phone.

With my new, anonymous phone in my jacket pocket, I took the 6 Train downtown to 14th Street, transferred to a crosstown L Train, then the uptown 1 Train to West 72nd Street. Inside the 72nd Street station, I crossed to the downtown track and took the 3 Train all the way back to

14th Street. I didn't really imagine that there was any way Bezukhov knew where I was or what I was doing, but I wanted to make sure I wasn't being followed. I wasn't.

Eventually, in late afternoon, I emerged from the subway at Seventh Avenue and West 14th Street. From there I walked to the Meatpacking District and Tom and Judy's loft. Entering the loft, I saw Tom, Judy, and Donna watching a news report on TV. There was a scroll at the bottom of the screen: BREAKING NEWS: Wall Street Killer Speaks Again.

The news anchor, a young Asian woman with long black hair and a very serious expression was speaking, " . . . the NYPD Task Force on the Wall Street killings has confirmed that they believe the latest note to be genuine—it is from the same writer as the first note. It is yet to be determined if the killer wrote the note, or if this is a bizarre attempt to use the publicity from the killings to force Wall Street CEOs into changing the way they do business."

Behind the anchor, the first few lines of the note were visible on the graphic being displayed.

The anchor continued, "The note reads:

To Law Enforcement,

You continue in your failure to punish the Wall Street thugs

who ravaged the economy for their own gain and who have

been a plague on the common man.

I continue to make things right. I am punishing the Wall Street criminals. Charlene Mercier has now joined Edmond Garner and

Bernard Abel in paying a debt to society. She will not be the last."

In justice, the Real Lawman

The camera returned to center on the anchor, who said, "Police had no comment other than to confirm the existence of the note."

A picture of the Golden Gate Bridge appeared on the screen, and the anchor said, "In San Francisco, the mayor has—"

Tom clicked off the TV and looked at me. Donna followed his glance and asked me, "Did you hear that?"

"Enough of it."

"What are you going to do about it?"

Judy was surprised by Donna's question, "Are you working on those killings?"

"No," I said as quickly and reassuringly as I could. "No, uh . . . that's not what Donna meant." I turned to Donna, "Could we talk? Maybe on the roof? It's beautiful out, and there's a great view."

"Sure." She stood up and followed me to the roof. We looked west, past the High Line and toward the Hudson River. The late afternoon sunlight was dazzling.

"It is a very nice view," Donna said. "Why did you

lie to your cousins? Don't you trust them?"

"They're safer if they don't know what's going on."

"Oh, sorry." She leaned against the railing and let the sun warm her. I hesitated to begin the conversation I needed to have with her. After a few moments of silently appreciating the view and the June weather, Donna turned to me. "Harry said it was safer if I didn't know where Richard was."

"Oh? Did Harry come here?"

"A couple of hours ago. He took Richard to a therapeutic community. Harry said he'd be safe there and that Richard would be in touch soon."

"Good."

"Do you trust Harry?"

That was an interesting question, and I shocked myself by saying, "Absolutely. Believe me, if you can't trust Harry, you can't trust anyone."

"Really?" She sounded surprised, but I didn't know if my answer or the conviction in my answer was the surprise. It wouldn't help if I admitted I was surprised by my own response.

"Yes." I said it firmly. Not argumentatively but positively. "Don't you?"

"Yes, I do. But *you* seem a lot more . . . *suspicious* of people."

"Thank you for the vote of confidence."

We both chuckled.

"Sorry, I didn't mean to insult you. But you don't strike me as the kind of man who takes anything at face value. You always try to see what's going on underneath."

"Isn't that your job? You're the shrink."

"Yes, it is my job. But it seems to be yours, too."

"What's the difference between us then?"

"I do it to help people."

"Me, too." I protested. I was desperate to help her.

She chuckled again. "I help people by getting them to understand themselves. You're after the truth—sometimes that helps, sometimes not."

"I thought the truth shall set you free."

"Freedom can be extremely painful."

"My wife used to say that when therapy is working, it can be very painful. If I remember correctly, she said it's usually painful when the patient's doing really good work."

"That's been my experience with patients."

I waved my right hand across my chest, palm out as if brushing something away, "Enough soul-searching. At least for me." I gazed at her face and saw her smile. "You seem better."

"I am better. You've been a Godsend. My brother is safe and getting help. Thanks to you and Harry."

"My pleasure." I returned to the Hudson River view. "I'm curious: How did you meet Harry?"

Donna paused as she tried to remember. It was such a long pause, I turned to look at her. She was shaking her head, "I . . . I don't know." She first looked down as if the answer might be on the deck and then up at the sky. "This is ridiculous. I handed over my brother to a man, and now I can't remember how I met that man."

The eerie strains of the *Twilight Zone* theme played in my head. "Probably stress. When you've relaxed a bit more, it'll come to you." What I told myself was: When this whole thing gets resolved, you won't remember Harry at all. Or me.

"How did you meet him?" she asked.

"Oh . . . my wife introduced us."

"How did she meet him?"

"Don't know. Maybe he works in the therapy area?" I grinned mischievously, "I bet he was a patient."

"No way he was a patient. And you damn well know it."

I shrugged. "Speaking of not knowing how we met people . . . "

"Yes . . . ? Where is this segue going?"

"How would you feel about disappearing? You and Richard. Leave New York and begin new lives."

"Are you out of your mind?"

"That's a particularly insensitive remark from a therapist."

"My apologies," she didn't sound contrite, "but what the hell are you talking about?"

I exhaled and said, "I think a Russian mafiosi named

Vadim Bezukhov used Richard to kill a couple of people in the hopes of scaring the ever-loving hell out of a whole bunch of other people. It was Bezukhov's guys who chased us out of your apartment the other night. Bezukhov is very well connected and extremely dangerous. He knows who you are and where you live. I honestly think the safest thing you could do would be to go into hiding."

"How could I possibly hide from someone like that?"

"Well," I thought it over for a second, "I have some pals in the Marshals Service, folks who handle Witness Security. They can hide you from anybody."

"But we'd have to give up our lives, leave behind our friends—" she paced several steps away and then came back, "—I'd be abandoning all my patients. I can't do it."

"It's the only way to be truly safe. Unless . . . " my voice trailed off; I didn't want to make promises I couldn't keep.

'Unless what?"

"Unless I can figure a way to stop this guy once and for all. But a lot of people have tried to shut down Bezukhov and failed. There's no reason to think I'll succeed. In fact, the odds are heavy that I'll fail—and get killed in the process."

"Sounds like you have good reason to be afraid."

"Damn straight."

She leaned on the railing again and stared at the

Hudson. "If we don't go into hiding, what will you do?"

I sighed, "I'll use all my persuasive skills to convince Mr. Bezukhov to leave you alone."

"But you said that might get you killed."

"Well, I might have exaggerated for the sake of a nifty turn of phrase."

Her eyes focused on me with glittery hardness. I felt as if I were being scanned by some kind of sci-fi device that could perceive my thoughts and emotions. "Were you exaggerating?"

"Maybe a little."

Her head dropped, and her voice was racked with pain, "It's not fair to you, but I don't want to give up everything . . . to leave my patients . . . I'm not sure Richard can start over . . . "

I reached out and rubbed her left shoulder. "Look, we don't need to make a decision, yet. You're safe here for the next few days. I'll reach out to Bezukhov and start negotiations. Who knows? Maybe he'll be surprisingly reasonable."

"You don't believe that."

"When it comes to negotiating with Bezukhov, I'll burn that bridge when I come to it."

She chuckled again. "Okay."

"Good."

She reached for me and hugged me around the waist, burying her head against my shoulder. I put my arms around

217

her, hugging her back. Her hair was lightly perfumed by her shampoo. Not to mention how smooth and soft it felt against my chin. I hadn't held a woman that way since Maggie . . .

We stood together for a long time. If it were possible, I would have stayed that way forever. But eventually, Donna gave me a squeeze, let go, and stepped back.

"Thank you," she said, a tear running down her cheek. "For everything."

"All part of the service, ma'am."

She smiled.

"I don't mean to chase you away," I said, "but I need to make a phone call."

She reached out, stroked my forearm, then walked off the deck and down the stairwell. I stood, rooted to the spot, staring at the stairwell doorway for a ridiculously long time. I finally snapped out of my reverie, dug my burn phone out of one pocket and my smart phone out of another. I found Bad1 in the contacts on my smart phone but dialed it on the burn phone. I took a deep breath, attempted to relax, and pressed "Send" to start the dialing.

"Hello," answered a Russian-accented voice with husky softness. "I was wondering when you were going to call, Mr. Tyrrell. This is Mr. Tyrrell, isn't it?"

"Yes. Good guess, Mr. Bezukhov. As for calling you, I've been busy."

"Yes, you have. My men speak very highly of you."

218

"I find that hard to believe."

"They may not use the most positive or polite terms when they speak of you, but they acknowledge your competency."

"I wish I could say the same for them."

"Oh, now really, Mr. Tyrrell, I expected more from you than petty insults."

"What did you expect, Vadim?"

"Courtesy, for one thing, Jack. But since that is not to be, I hope we can discuss what happens next in a rational way."

"Sure. Why not? What are you hoping happens next?"

"I want Richard."

"Yeah, well, that's not going to happen," I said. "Sorry to disappoint you."

"I am not disappointed. I expected that. You are protecting Richard. Saving him from me. That is how I know you are not recording this call, because it would incriminate him by tying him to the killings. But you will give me Richard, one way or the other."

"Was that a threat? 'Cause if that was a threat, you were being too subtle for me. The obvious approach works best."

"Deliver Richard, or I kill his sister."

"Now there's the Bezukhov I've come to know and love."

"Deliver Richard, or I kill his sister and you. I will not send the men you have already met. The man I send will be a different . . . caliber altogether."

"Very clever. Well, since we're having a pissing contest, it's my turn: Leave us alone, or *I'll* kill *you*. What do you think?"

"Very amusing."

"If you know anything about me, and I'm guessing you do, you know I can do—and will— what I say."

"Yes, your resume is quite impressive. But I do not think you have ever tried to kill a target with my . . . resources."

"Vadim, believe me, when you've been in the shit in Afghanistan, someone with your resources isn't all that big a deal." If only I believed that. Harry, you'd better back my play with this Russian mobster, or I am a dead man. A dead man who was killed with extreme violence and abundant pain.

"I had hoped you were above bravado. But, like many of your countrymen, it seems to be your main characteristic."

Was I imagining it, or had Vadim said "your countrymen" the way people usually said "cockroaches"? Putting that aside, I had to admit he was right about the bravado. But it was one thing to admit it to myself, and a very different thing to admit it to Bezukhov.

"Vadim, you and I may have gotten off on the wrong

220

foot. Instead of trading insults, we should talk seriously and respectfully. Let me try this again, from the beginning: With all due respect, if you don't leave us alone, I'm going to take you and your operation apart. Piece by piece. You'll be finished in the United States. As for Russia, I'm guessing some of your lieutenants will fight it out to see who takes over. Do I make myself clear?"

He was chuckling. "You know, when you play cards and you bluff, you better be prepared to have your bluff called. And I am calling your bluff. Either you produce Richard or you can attempt to make good on your threats. Either way, I will get what I want. I will find Richard, and you will be dead."

"I guess we have nothing left to talk about."

"Nothing to talk about? You amaze me. Is that your final offer? You make threats and I make threats and it ends in a draw? When you negotiate with me, you need a lot more than that."

Given that Bezukhov was as dangerous as a man can be, I really didn't want to hear what his idea of a final offer was. On the other hand, putting my hands up and surrendering was out of the question.

"I'm waiting," I said.

"Since a simple threat of death did not move you, I am escalating. If you do not deliver Donna *and* Richard to me in twenty-four hours, I will kill twelve people on Wall Street on Monday morning. They will be regular people who work in the financial markets. Not the CEOs who are all hiding behind multiple layers of security. No, these targets will be the everyday people who will be easy to kill as they leave the subways and step down from buses. I repeat, give me Donna and Richard in twenty-four hours, or I will kill twelve people from Wall Street. Now you know how I make a final offer."

My brain was whirling in shock. There was no way I could protect twelve random people. Especially if Bezukhov had more than one man carrying out the lethal work. I inhaled deeply and spit out my retort.

"Hey, you want to kill a dozen people, go ahead. You'll have a difficult time selling that as the work of the Real Lawman, the lone killer seeking justice for the people from the financial titans. But, if you want to throw away all your work at setting up Richard as your patsy, go ahead."

"Richard as my . . . patsy, hmm, I like that word, . . . is a small part of my plan. If I have to let him go, I will. To use a phrase of your language, I will cut my losses. Are you willing to cut yours? Are you willing to watch twelve people die?"

Bezukhov hadn't just called my bluff, he'd chewed it up and spit it in my face.

"Vadim, hear me when I say this: If you hurt Donna or Richard or twelve innocent people, I will kill you."

"Same threat as before, only now with a minor variation. I am going to give you some bonus time and make this easy: The deadline is tomorrow—Sunday—at midnight. That's a little more than twenty-four hours. If I do not have the Krugers, twelve people will die on Monday morning during the rush hour. You have my number when you decide to do things my way."

"Don't hold your breath." I disconnected and said to the sky, "Holy shit." I looked down at the phone then up to the sky again. "Harry? Couldn't you make Vadim see reason?"

There was no answer. No sudden appearance by Harry.

"Harry, are you going to back my play with Vadim? Even if I have to kill him?"

"Yes, I will give you the help you need," Harry said, suddenly at my side.

"Couldn't you make a normal entrance?"

"That was normal."

"Yeah, sure, that was normal," I scanned his stony face for a clue to what he was thinking and found nothing. "Did you hear my conversation with Bezukhov?"

"I'm aware of what was said."

'You're *aware* . . . ? Never mind. He's going to kill a lot of people. There's no way I can handle this alone. Do you have more guys like me who work for you? Could we put together a team to go after Bezukhov's people?"

"No. That's not the way it works. You have to decide if you're willing to be completely selfless. If you are, you will be willing to sacrifice yourself for others. Are you willing to sacrifice yourself?"

"Are you crazy?"

His right eyebrow shot up into a cynical arch, but he said nothing.

"Am I willing? I've been willing all along. I've taken a bunch of chances that could have gotten me killed. But going to war with Bezukhov, going all by myself, isn't willingness to sacrifice. It's guaranteed suicide, which means it's just plain stupid."

"Nothing is guaranteed with the Chairman."

"Nothing—?" I exhaled in frustration then took a deep breath. Counted to ten in my head. Only made it to six. "Is this one of those faith moments?"

"What do you think?"

"You are *really* pissing me off," I said.

"Much as I wish I could avoid making you feel that way, I can't."

I was sure there was a smirk on his face as he uttered that last statement, but I couldn't see it. "If I do sacrifice myself, and I'm killed, will I see Maggie?"

"I'm not the final judge of these things. The Chairman decides."

"This sucks. Really and truly."

"I can see how you would feel that way."

"No team?"

"No."

I walked around the deck for a moment, trying to get loose and avoid hauling off and belting Harry. I had a feeling that I would never land the punch if I tried.

"The second note from the Real Lawman," I asked, "is it a decoy? Or a scare tactic to keep the Wall Street community terrified?"

"What do you think?"

I shook my head and muttered, "I hate it when you—" I took a breath, "yeah, it's both a decoy and a scare tactic." I stared directly into Harry's eyes. "Are you going to help me kill this guy? Assuming that's the only way to keep Richard and Donna safe?"

Harry clearly was unsure how to respond to that question. His eyes went skyward, and after a long moment, returned to me. "I don't know. I'm sorry."

"Killing's not in your usual repertoire?"

"No."

"It's not the way the Chairman does things?"

"If He has used killing, He hasn't used me to do it."

"Doesn't the Bible have an avenging angel story? Maybe the holy smiting the unrighteous?"

Harry didn't reply. The confused expression was gone; the stony face was back in place.

"I'm pretty sure there's at least a wrestling angel— didn't Jacob wrestle with an angel?"

If it was possible for a stone to become denser and harder, then Harry's face was like that. "Do you want specific help, or are you satisfied giving me a hard time?"

"I want to be sure you're going to help me with Bezukhov."

"You'll get the help you need."

"Could we define 'need'? Could we reopen the discussion about a team?"

"What about Richard?" Harry asked, ignoring me.

"What about him? You've got him someplace safe, right?"

"Yes. Do you need to see him?"

"No, no. And I don't want to know where he is, either. What I don't know won't hurt him."

"What you don't know is rather voluminous." Harry said, still giving me his stone face for a few seconds. He *whooshed* away without another word.

I stared at the spot he'd vacated, dug in my pocket, and pulled the paper out with Vadim Bezukhov's address. I read it and thought, no time like the present for a visit to Bedford Hills.

8

"Could I borrow your car tonight?" I asked Tom as I joined him, Judy, and Donna at the kitchen island.

"Sure. Would you mind gassing it up?"

"Isn't that kind of a necessity for it to run?"

Tom grinned in response. "We still park it over near the river in the West 40s."

"Ah, yes, I remember it well."

Like many New Yorkers, the Corcorans did not pay to park in their neighborhood because the cost would be the equivalent of the annual budget of a small corporation. My cousins parked in an open lot, exposed to the weather, convenient to nothing. But it was cheap by Manhattan standards. (It was extreme by the standards of, say, the *entire* state of Iowa.)

"Going for a ride?" Donna asked.

"Yes."

"Can I come?"

The idea of a night's drive with Donna was very appealing. On the other hand, the idea of being shot up with Donna next to me was not appealing at all.

"Better not."

"Are you sure?"

"Unfortunately, yes."

She smiled but she was disappointed. My cousins were wonderful people, but it was only natural that Donna had at least a mild case of cabin fever. And . . . maybe . . . she wanted to spend some time with me.

Stop it, Tyrrell, I told myself. I was very firm. Commanding, you might say.

"When are you going?" she asked.

I noticed that Judy gave Tom a knowing look, and that he winked back in affirmation. I ignored them and focused on Donna. "Not until after dinner."

"Just wondering."

After dinner, Tom walked me to the front door. "I called the guy at the lot. Show him your driver's license, and he'll get the car. Please tip him. And please don't take this the wrong way, but you're not going to put any bullet holes in my car, are you?"

"Try not to."

"I hate it when you get bullet holes in my car."

"That only happened once," I protested, keeping my voice down so that I wouldn't frighten Donna. "Don't make any jokes like that in front of—"

"—No, of course not. But I needed to make a joke to you. You're as tight as a guitar string. Loosen up. Stay safe."

"I will." Unspoken was my next thought: I hope.

When I got to the street, a cab was dropping people off at one of the current, hip restaurants of the area. I climbed in without hesitation and gave the driver directions. We were about to pull away when I heard a woman shout and a hand pounded on the passenger side door. The taxi jerked to a stop, and Donna climbed in.

"Okay, you can go," she said to the driver.

"No, hold it," I said loudly to the driver and then to her, "What the hell is this?"

"Take me with you?"

I could imagine Harry looking over her shoulder and shaking his head at me. Not to mention how he would feel about the prospect of her being killed by Bezukhov's men. "I can't."

"Why?"

"Well . . . uh . . . it's not how I work. I'm a solo act."

"Bullshit." She spoke to the driver, "Go ahead!"

"Hold it!" I shouted. Given that the way men define a shout is different from the way women do, a woman would have told you I shouted. Whether I shouted or not, the taxi driver halted in the middle of the street. "Pull over and wait, please," I said in a reasonably moderate tone of voice. The cabbie did what he was told—no loss to him, the meter was still ticking over.

"You don't want me to come because it's dangerous," Donna said.

"Yes . . . kinda . . . " The word "kinda" might have

229

been the grossest understatement of my life.

"But if I come, you'll be more careful. Please."

"Donna, you didn't hire me to be careful."

"I didn't *hire* you. And please stop with the cavalier tough guy routine. It's bullshit."

I had hoped that my "cavalier tough guy routine" was charming. Oh well. And it wasn't calming my fears, either. "Let's not argue semantics. You asked for my help, and I'm giving it. You don't need a person with my . . . skill set if there isn't danger involved. I'm okay with it."

"But *I'm* not okay with it. I can't ask you to risk your life."

"You didn't. This is on me."

"Why?"

I thought that over for a second and told her the truth: "My wife wanted me to help someone."

"But . . . your wife . . . is gone."

"She is, but—" this was hard. I took a deep breath and continued, "—believe me, I know she wanted me to help people. And she wanted it even though she knew the risks."

"She sounds like a great lady."

"She was." I forced a smile, "You need to get out of this cab and let me get to work."

Donna nodded, leaned across the seat, and kissed me. A brief, tender nothing of a kiss. It rocked me to my toes. She was out of the cab before I knew it, the door closing behind her with a thunk.

I said to the cabbie, "Okay, let's go."

*   *   *

I drove Tom's car, a blue Ford Fusion, up Twelfth Avenue, onto the West Side Highway. On my right, Riverside Park was backed by a line of pre-war buildings. On my left, the Hudson River stretched westward to the Palisades of New Jersey. I shot under the George Washington Bridge, past Fort Tryon Park, and the medieval Cloisters. Within minutes I was over the bridge at Spuyten Duyvil, the northernmost tip of Manhattan Island, and into the Riverdale section of the Bronx. Most of the highway's route in the Bronx was through dense woods and by the time the road crossed into Westchester County and changed names to the Saw Mill River Parkway, there was almost no difference between the supposedly urban Bronx and suburban Westchester.

As I continued north, the road became hillier and the curves sharper, forcing me to drop speed a bit. Much as I wanted to race along it, I decided that caution was the better part of valor. Especially since it was very possible that I might end up with a bullet hole or two in the car—it seemed too much to ask my cousin to accept a crashed car that was also had bullet-holes.

I exited the Saw Mill Parkway in Bedford Hills and drove east, up and down a winding road that went past the Bedford Hills Correctional Facility, which was set far enough back from the road that it didn't disturb Bedford

Hills's bucolic beauty. I wondered if there was an inmate anywhere in the facility who approached Vadim Bezukhov in terms of sheer evil. I shook my head: no way.

Driving deeper into Bedford Hills, I found the road continued to snake through the countryside, with trees overhanging the road. Occasionally, I could make out the lights of a big house sitting well back from the road. The yards for these houses seemed to have been carved out of the woods. It felt as if I was hundreds of miles north of New York City instead of thirty or so.

Bezukhov's house number was carved onto a small sign hung on a split-rail fence post at the end of his driveway. The house was set back too deep into the woods to be seen from the road. The only thing visible was a short stretch of blacktop winding off into the dark and the trees.

I drove about a half-mile past the driveway, pulled over on a tiny sliver of shoulder, and parked with my passenger side wheels off the pavement. There was very little traffic so I hoped the parked car wouldn't cause problems. I grabbed binoculars borrowed from Tom, locked the car, and jogged back to Bezukhov's. I slowed as I neared the driveway. Good thing, too. I was only about twenty yards away, when I saw the red glow of a cigarette. You just can't get good help, I thought. Smoking was a great way to give away your position. And ruin your night sight.

Then again, maybe the security guard was wearing infra-red goggles so his night sight was fine, thank you. And there were probably more guards nearby, with interlocking areas of patrol, limiting the vulnerability of any single guard.

It seemed like a good idea to get off the road before I went any nearer to the guard. I worked my way into the trees at my left. I wondered if these trees were on the border of Bezukhov's property or within it. I could barely see the path of the driveway to my right and moved roughly parallel to it, stealthily approaching the house. Staying undetected is one of the tricks of the Green Beret trade, and I was eternally grateful to Uncle Sam for training me how to do it.

There was a noise to my left, the very slightest footfall. I stopped. Stopped breathing, while I was at it. I scanned the dark, turning my head in the tiniest increments possible. I wasn't the only one slinking through the trees. A doe was picking her way through, too. Her appearance could prove to be providential. I dropped to the ground and crawled in super slow motion, reaching out with both hands for a stick or rock. I found a rock about the size of an egg and tossed it near the deer. It made a tiny thud, but she sprang through the air and leapt away from where I lay. For an animal in escape mode, she didn't make a lot of noise, but it was plenty to draw the attention of any nearby guards.

Two sets of human footsteps, one on my left, the other on my right, quickly and quietly rushed past me following the deer. I pushed off the ground and sprinted in the opposite direction. I hoped I was close to the house. As luck would have it, the house was only about 30 yards away.

I ducked behind a tree at the edge of the yard and gave the place a thorough once-over. It was a wood-sided colonial home, and it was pretty damn big: probably five or six bedrooms. The structure had been added to twice—its original lines were good, but the newer additions were less successful. It was white with black shutters. Maybe they were dark green. I couldn't tell in the harsh glow of the floodlights mounted under the eaves. It seemed as if every corner of the house had a pair of floodlights mounted under the eves, and the entire yard for fifty or sixty feet was bathed in light. Kids could play catch in that light. Hell, I could read a book in that light. A book with really tiny print.

What I couldn't do in all that light was get any closer to the house.

I spent about an hour circling the house, staying in the dark outside the lit perimeter. It took the whole hour to circle the abode. But it was worth it. There were four guards. Each had night vision goggles—I had seen one of the guards silhouetted against the floodlights, and I saw the goggles, making him look like a giant praying mantis out of some '50s sci-fi movie. The other thing, I noticed was that each guard carried an AK-47 assault rifle—a nasty piece of work, capable of spraying lead at a devastating intensity. Not the most accurate of weapons, but the damn things were as close as can be to jam-proof, and when a weapon spews 10 rounds a second accuracy is a secondary factor. I'd survived my share of firefights, but the idea of going against four AK-47s with my Ruger made my stomach queasy. Very queasy.

Despite my fascination with the guards' night-sight goggles and lethal AK-47s, I did manage to observe a few other things about Bezukhov's compound. There appeared to be no security cameras. If there were, they were teeny weeny ones that I couldn't spot, but I was 99.9999% sure there weren't any. My buddy Vadim was counting on old-fashioned security: guards on their feet, making the rounds. And there were no dogs. If there had been dogs, no way I could have skulked around the house undetected. A dog would have sniffed me out within a minute.

As I made my way around the house, I used Tom's binoculars to scan every inch of house. Alarm sensors placed on every door and window. Four or five guys, all dressed in dark slacks and pullovers, all wearing sidearms in hip pistols, clustered in a room near the kitchen. Probably back-up for the guards outside. If an alarm sounded—either electronic or human—the backups would be bringing more firepower to bear in moments.

I completed the circuit of the house and headed back through the trees for the road. I thought I was getting close to a point where I could relax, when a cigarette glowed in the dark about ten feet in front of me. I was in a crouch, very low to the ground, next to a tree, but became motionless as the cigarette burned more brightly as the guard inhaled. I saw his praying mantis face in profile; the night-vision goggles were facing away from me. The good thing about night-vision eyewear was that you can see in the dark, directly in front of you. The bad thing is the way the goggles wrap around your head, pretty much eliminating peripheral vision. I was in the guard's blind spot.

The guard exhaled and the smoke reached me about a second after the sound of his exhale. The smoke reached me so fast it made me think the guard was walking toward me. If the guard was moving around and scanning in all directions, he was bound to see me. The smoke was at its most intense to my left, and I crept to my right, remaining hunched over in a crouch. I silently pulled the Ruger from my holster. If I had to use my un-silenced weapon, I might be successful and take down the guard, but success was likely to be short-lived. Unfortunately, I was likely to be short-lived. The other AK-47 toting guards would be on me long before I could escape.

There was a muffled crunch, a dull little nothing of a sound, as a tiny branch cracked under the smoker's foot. He *was* on my left. I continued circling to my right, keeping the tree between me and the guard. The soft pad of footsteps continued to move away from me. It seemed as if it were taking this guy about ten minutes between footsteps, but I knew it wasn't any more than ten or twenty seconds. Eventually the sound faded completely. I waited five minutes then resumed my stealth trek to the road.

Once there, I jogged back to my cousin's car and opened the car door, slid behind the wheel, shut off the lights, and started the car. I pulled a U-turn and headed west toward the Saw Mill River Parkway.

When I passed Bezukhov's driveway, I glanced up the blacktop lane but still couldn't see a thing. I realized I was breathing fast—I was out of practice in scouting out the enemy location while surrounded by hostiles. As my breath returned to normal, I thought about what I had seen: Bezukhov's house was a private, secure place to live. But not what I expected for his main base of operations. No, Vadim's criminal headquarters would have even more guards. It would definitely have cameras. And tall fences with barbed wire at the top and steel gates at the entrance. Steel doors and barred windows. Bezukhov's criminal headquarters would be a fortress. Strong enough to stop the competition. And tough enough to give Bezukhov and his associates time to destroy evidence if the law-enforcement folks ever came a-calling. Or kill any hostages they might happen to be entertaining.

My guess was a warehouse somewhere in the five boroughs of New York. And taking the battle to Bezukhov in a place like that would be brutal.

The dashboard clock said 11:03 PM. Less than twenty-five hours to go on Bezukhov's countdown to killing twelve innocent people. That would be more brutal than anything I faced going up against Bezukhov.

*   *   *

I exited the Saw Mill at Interstate 287, known as the

Cross Westchester Expressway in this part of the world. Not surprisingly, at the Tappan Zee Bridge where 287 crossed the Hudson, the "Westchester" designation was dropped. I drove east toward White Plains, exited, and made my way to a 24-hour coffee shop on Mamaroneck Avenue. One of those Greek places with everything on the menu from moussaka to Roumanian steak to ridiculously great cakes and pies. I grabbed a parking place close to the the entrance, went inside, took a booth, and ordered coffee and a piece of three-layer chocolate cake.

The waitress went off to place my order; I used my burn phone to call an old friend from my time in Afghanistan. Alex Cranston had been my primary CIA contact.We had spent time doing some very challenging things with some very interesting people. Shortly after I had left Afghanistan, Alex had been rotated back to Langley to a desk job. He wasn't the desk-job type, but his wife slept a lot better these days.

"Alex? It's Jack Tyrrell. Sorry it's been so long. And I'm sorry about this late call. "

"I thought maybe you were dead."

"Kinda. I've been resurrected."

"And you're calling me for help."

"Yes, I am."

"Is this on the up and up?"

"Absolutely. You'd be proud of me if you knew what I was doing."

There was a pause. "But I don't want to know what you're doing, do I?"

"No. But I'm helping a fellow vet from Afghanistan."

"Really?"

"Yes. On the level."

"Good to know you've returned."

"Thanks. Feels good," I said, realizing that I *did* feel good about what I was doing. Even when I was crawling through the dark, hiding from AK-47s. "Sorry to bother you, but I don't have anyone else to call."

"Okay . . ."

"Vadim Bezukhov. I need to know where and what he's doing in the New York City area."

"Bezukhov is a singularly lethal guy. Someone you do not want to mess with. No how, no way."

"If I'm going to help this vet I was telling you about, I have no choice."

"Wow, when you return to the fight, you go straight for the heavyweight belt."

"Like I said: I had no choice. What about him?"

"He's an FBI problem; you know that."

"Yes, I do. But I told you, I have no one else to call."

"I start poking around in FBI business, and I may not be worth calling."

"Look, with a guy like Bezukhov, I need everything

I can get. I wouldn't call if I weren't desperate. Bezukhov wants me to turn over two people to him—two people who will die within minutes when they're in his custody. If I don't turn them over, he's going to kill twelve innocent people at random. Well, not exactly at random, they'll all work on Wall Street."

"I thought you said they were innocent."

"Really? A Wall Street joke at a time like this?"

"Sorry," he said. "All right, you're in an extremely tight spot. Is this connected to the Real Lawman killings?"

"Yes."

"Oh . . . shit." He hesitated, "You *really* should go to the FBI and tell all."

"I haven't got a single piece of evidence. Nothing. If I bring in the FBI, Bezukhov will probably smoke the twelve people."

"That sounds like him. Okay, I'll make a call and get back to you in an hour."

I gave him the burn-phone number, "thanks."

"You're welcome. But giving you the skinny on Bezukhov isn't going to help you. What you need is an armored division."

I thought about Harry Mitchum. Was he as good as an armored division? "I have what I need. Believe me."

"Okay." He clicked off.

I drank my coffee, accepted a refill from the waitress, and started in on the chocolate cake. It was good. I had to force myself to eat slowly—my usual speed is like a steam shovel in constant motion. But I wanted to savor every bite.

As good as the cake was, it didn't distract me from the unpleasant possibilities in my life. The way I figured it: with or without Harry's help, going up against Bezukhov was a great way to get killed. No, let me change that, it was a great way to get *destroyed*.

But I didn't have a choice. Not if I wanted to earn the chance at redemption that Maggie had gotten for me.

It was almost midnight, and many of the tables amidst the mirrored walls and chrome-trimmed counters were empty. I let the waitress refill my cup—with decaf because there are limits to what a man can handle—and stoically resisted the urge to order another piece of cake. Getting hopped up on caffeine and sugar wasn't the best way to tackle Bezukhov's forces.

The decaf was long finished when Alex called back. "Are you sure I can't talk you out of this?"

I sighed. I wasn't sure at all. But I was going to trust in the chance Maggie had gotten for me. That meant I was trusting Harry . . . and the Chairman, whom I hoped I wouldn't be meeting anytime soon. "No, you can't talk me out of it. What have you got?"

"Bezukhov has a bunch of 'businesses'"—Alex's tone of voice made it obvious that he had a low opinion of Bezukhov's businesses,—"in the metro New York area.

Couple of offices in downtown Manhattan and another couple in Jersey City. But if you're looking for his operational center, I'm guessing it's a warehouse at 25 Commerce Street in Brooklyn. A couple of blocks from the waterfront, a bit north of Coffey Park in Red Hook."

"I have a vague idea where that is—I can find it."

"It's nothing fancy, a rectangular building with the short end at the sidewalk, and the long side stretching away from the street. There's a narrow parking lot running along side it."

"Parallel?"

"Yes."

"How tall is it? And are there any vantage points in the neighborhood?"

"Almost everything is two stories out there, including Bezukhov's building. There are a couple of buildings across the street that are about the same height."

"What about adjacent to it? I know the parking lot is on one side, but what about the other?"

"There's an overgrown alley between 25 Commerce and the next building. And Bezukhov has an eight-foot high, electric fence on the roof on that side. You could get past it, but not easily."

"And if I break the circuit the alarm goes off."

"That would be my guess."

"Shit." I mulled over the challenge and said, "What else?"

"Thought you'd never ask. All doors are steel. All open outward, impossible to push in. No windows on the first floor on the street side. Cameras everywhere. And at least six guards on the premises at all times."

"Gee, I see why you think this is the place."

"You got it."

I stared into my empty coffee cup. The waitress happened to be walking past and gestured toward it, silently questioning whether I wanted a refill. I covered the phone's microphone and said, "Yes, please, decaf."

"Are you there?" Alex said.

"Yes, I'm here. Thinking suicidal thoughts." The waitress refilled my cup, and I nodded my thanks. "I don't suppose there are any sewer tunnels or anything like that going into or very near this building?"

"There's the sharp guy I worked with in Afghanistan. I was wondering when you'd get around to that idea."

"Does that mean there is one?"

"Yes."

"Has Bezukhov done anything to secure it?"

"Don't know, but probably not."

"Why probably not?"

Alex said, "'Cause he doesn't have the resources that we do to find sewer tunnels." I could hear the satisfaction in his tone. "Maybe he does, but I would be willing to bet he doesn't."

"Yeah, well, you're not the one who's betting."

"I could be talked into taking that bet."

I couldn't believe what I had heard. "Really?" I asked.

"Yeah, really."

"You've been telling me I'm crazy, and now you're willing to be crazy, too?"

"I wouldn't be here if not for you," he said. "I haven't forgotten what you did for me in Afghanistan. If you want help, you've got it."

"I . . . I don't know what to say."

"Try 'yes.' I'll hop a plane in the morning. I'll bring the complete plans for Bezukhov's place on Commerce Street. What do you think?"

"Uh . . . yes, thank you, Alex. Thank you."

"You're welcome."

"I had no idea what a deeply disturbed individual you are," I said.

"Why do you think I work for the CIA?"

*   *   *

A few minutes after 1:00 AM, I returned my cousin's trusty Ford to its parking lot. The attendant was semi-conscious when I handed him the key and thanked him. He mumbled something in response, something that sounded like, "sirh . . .bah." No clue what language that was or what the possible meaning could be. I smiled, shrugged, and walked out to the street. When you're in the West 40s close to the Hudson at the hour of the morning, taxis can be impossible to find. I considered going back to the attendant's tiny shack with its single, overhead light bulb casting a glow over the cars to see if there was a phone number for a taxi taped to the wall next to last year's calendar. The calendar's untimeliness was not important—the photo of the bikini-clad, extraordinarily well-endowed young woman was. If I had to guess, I would have said that the calendar would still be there a decade from now. I looked up at the midtown towers, most of which were still lit, and thought, what the hell, I'll walk. It was about a mile and a half to Tom and Judy's loft—might as well burn off some of the chocolate cake.

I reached Eleventh Avenue and turned right. I was going to walk down to West 23rd Street, then east to Tenth Avenue, and downtown again on Tenth, which would bring me almost directly to my cousin's door. Eleventh was not the most scenic place in Manhattan, but I figured I could make pretty good time. Traffic was light, and there were no pedestrians, I could cross almost every street at will, regardless of what color the traffic lights were.

The late hour and the empty streets would have made Maggie very nervous. She believed I could take care of her, but she would have sweated every moment until we were close to our own neighborhood. Poor Maggie, none of our occasional forays into neighborhoods like this had been a problem. But she had been killed on her own front stoop, in the soft daylight before evening. The thought of Maggie dying because of my anger and venal stupidity knotted my stomach. I wondered if the day would ever come when I would be able to forgive myself. I could hear her say, "I forgive you. And now you have a chance to work through this and forgive yourself." I hope you're right, Maggie, I really do.

My tolerance for feeling grief, even after five years, was very low. Instead I turned to analyzing the job at hand. A check of my watch followed by a quick bit of arithmetic produced a frightening result: twenty-three hours to go before Bezukhov killed the innocent dozen. For what seemed like the kazillionth time, I realized that the only way to stop Bezukhov was to do such immense damage to his operations that he couldn't possibly kill all those people. And a frontal assault, well, frontal through the sewer system, was probably the only way to proceed. There was no time to recruit a bigger team: Harry had said "no" to a team, I couldn't call in enough favors, and there wasn't enough evidence to justify the forces of law and order descending upon Bezukhov like the wrath of God. Alex's building plans had better be damn good, or we were going to end up as *kotlety*, or Russian meat patties.

I was completely wrapped up in planning the assault on Vadim, and as a result, the mugger caught me by surprise. I heard a foot scrape on the sidewalk behind me and felt something hard press into the small of my back. If word ever got back to my mates in the Marshals Service, I would never hear the end of it. Fortunately, this guy made a stupid mistake: he had pressed the gun against me. Before he uttered a word, I spun 180 degrees instantly, my left arm knocking away the gun. At the same time, he fired—he was an amateur but he was a really fast amateur—and the shot flared in the night as the bullet whined off into the distance. As the gun went off, I kept wheeling around, my right fist slamming upward into his Adam's apple and his jaw. He was a big boy, almost my height and twenty pounds heavier, but the force of my fist lifted him off his feet and sent him unconscious to the sidewalk. The gun clattered on the sidewalk, bouncing to a stop against the steel base of a street light.

I gave the mugger the once-over and shook my head. He wasn't going to find a lot of people to rob in this part of town at this time of night, but he probably had thought that anyone he did find would be ripe for the picking. He was dressed in blue jeans, work boots, T-shirt, and a denim jacket. Nothing fancy, but nothing dirty or ragged. I patted him down and found a stiletto, which I pocketed, and another magazine for his gun, which I also pocketed. I picked up the gun, an old .45 automatic. The ammo would have made a hell of a mess if he'd hit me. I ejected the magazine from the weapon, shoved it into my pocket with the first, and walked away, leaving my would-be mugger asleep on the sidewalk. Okay, he was unconscious, as in knocked unconscious, but asleep sounds better. Gentler.

A few blocks down Eleventh, I dumped the two magazines in a sewer grate, and a few blocks after that, I dumped the gun itself and stiletto. I hoped my gun-dumping career was at an end.

At 23rd Street, I made my planned turn to the east then downtown when I reached Tenth Avenue. A couple of young women staggered out of a club down the street from Tom and Judy's loft and bumped into me, but that was much more pleasant than my experience with the mugger. Although one of them was wearing too much perfume, and her brushing against me transferred a bit of the faux French aroma to me.

It was almost 2:00 when I reached the street door for Tom and Judy's. I let myself in, stepped into the elevator, and quietly pulled the old-fashioned elevator gate shut behind me. The elevator clanked up the several flights to their floor, and I trudged down the hall to their door. I twisted the key in the lock as quietly as possible, but the bolt thudded back with a metallic *thwack*. It seemed enormously loud to me, but maybe I hadn't woken anyone. There was no stirring in the direction of my cousins' room. A single lamp was on in the living room, where Donna was lying on the couch. She yawned and stretched sleepily as I walked in, pulling off my now-perfumed jacket and dropping it over the back of a chair. She was wearing a long-sleeve, white T-shirt, and her stretching pulled the cotton fabric tight over her breasts. Not that I had needed reminding, but Donna was a very attractive woman. I decided that now was a propitious time to study the floor given that sexual stimulation was more than I could handle at the moment.

She smiled, "I'm glad you're home safe. Is everything all right?"

"Fine, thanks. No problems. No bullet holes in my cousin's car."

"I'm sure he'll be happy to hear that."

"Probably." I collapsed into a chair facing the couch.

"Come sit with me," she said.

I was tired, but not that tired. When a beautiful woman asks you to sit with her, you sit.

She leaned over and kissed my cheek. "I was worried about you."

I shifted away from her and said, "I'm sorry about that."

"Why did you just move away?" She really was a therapist, reading every word I said and every bit of body language. On second thought, maybe it wasn't a therapist thing. Maybe it was a woman thing.

"This is . . . complicated," I said. "It's best if we don't confuse things."

"Maybe once this situation is settled? I'd like to see you."

"That would be nice," I said. What I thought was: Once this is settled you won't remember me.

"That would be *nice*? Is that the best you can do?"

"I don't mean to be such a loser, but I . . . I . . . don't know . . ."

"Is this because of your wife?" her voice invited me to answer.

"Partially. I guess. I'm . . . not sure."

"You are one articulate guy." Her tone was warmer than her words.

"Look, right now I'm trying to make sure your brother is safe, and that you're safe, and I'm dealing with Harry's issues—"

"—Harry's issues?"

"Uh, yeah, well, I kind of work for him, and he's got these rules. Or, I guess you could call them guidelines, well . . . I don't really know. Anyway, I'm trying to make sure you and Richard are safe and that Harry is happy. And . . . and you're right, probably, about my wife. I miss her, and—" I looked into Donna's blue eyes, which was a mistake "—and I feel guilty that I have . . . "

"Feelings about someone else?"

"Yes," I said quietly.

"I didn't mean to push."

I smiled, "You didn't. I'm such a mess that I would be equally inarticulate if I were talking to Sigmund Freud."

"You'd be better off with Jung."

I grinned, "I think you're right about that."

Donna stood up and walked to the windows

overlooking 13th Street. She watched the last vestiges of night life trickling along the sidewalks below. "Are you doing something dangerous tomorrow?"

"A little bit."

"That's bullshit."

I joined her at the window, watching the street and sidewalks. The city that never sleeps was pretty close to nodding off.

Donna took my right hand in both of hers and asked, "Why?"

"Because we were right," I said reluctantly. "Because Richard *did* kill Edmond Garner and Bernard Abel. Your brother was manipulated by a ruthless gangster, who wants to use your brother as the patsy for all the Wall Street killings."

"But he didn't kill the woman in the Hamptons! Richard was here with me and your cousins."

"I know. But the man behind this can probably make the first two killings stick to your brother. I think a professional was brought in to handle Charlene Mercier, and that means law enforcement won't find a thing. The police suspect that there's a conspiracy at work here, but they won't be able to find anyone other than Richard."

"He can give evidence against the man behind all this, he could cut a deal—"

"Your brother will go to prison for a very long time or end up in some mental institution."

"But Harry can keep Richard safe, can't he?"

"Probably. But . . . there's another problem."

She squeezed my hand. I squeezed back, and she relaxed her iron grip. "Unless I figure out a way to stop this guy, he's going to kill a dozen innocent people in," I checked my watch, "about twenty-two hours."

"Oh my God." Donna let go of my hand and raised her right hand to her mouth, covering her lips. Her eyes were wide with fear. She said, "You're going to stop him?"

"I have to."

"You're not going alone, are you?"

"No, I'm not Gary Cooper in *High Noon*."

"Never saw it."

"Cooper plays a sheriff who has to face the bad guys—and these are *very* bad guys—by himself. Completely alone."

"The loner hero. It's an archetype."

"That's not much use to Gary Cooper. Or me, but like I said, I'm not going alone."

"Should I ask who's helping you?"

"No. The less you know, the better. For what it's worth, my helper is very good. He and I worked together in Afghanistan."

"Can I do anything to help?"

I thought her offer over for a minute. "You could make breakfast in a few hours."

She laughed, "Done."

9

My old CIA buddy, Alex Cranston, arrived at 9:00 AM at LaGuardia Airport the next day, Sunday. He was about five foot nine, but appeared shorter because he was lean and wiry. Maybe he seemed short because he was almost a half-foot shorter than I am, and a half a foot seems short. Despite the Anglo last name, Alex had brown eyes, dark brown hair, and a heavy, dark beard. He could pass for an Arab or Afghan, and had a number of times. His facility with a dozen languages didn't hurt.

Alex was walking out of the terminal toward the passenger pick-up area as I was pulling to the curb in Tom's Fusion. Alex slung his small duffle into the back seat and climbed in next to me. We shook hands.

"It's good to see you," he said. "Really good."

"Thanks. Good to be seen." I put the car in drive and pulled away from the curb, following the "Airport Exit" signs. "Where to?"

"The Peninsula Hotel on Fifth."

"Are you kidding me?"

"No. We're going to do a bit of shopping."

"At the Peninsula? Little rich for our price range, isn't it?"

"We're not staying there, and the goods are being offered pro bono. A favor from the friend of a friend."

Driving back into Manhattan a few minutes after 9:00 AM wasn't easy. There was plenty of rush hour traffic left. What should have taken twenty minutes took about twice that. I drove west on the Grand Central Parkway, over the Robert F. Kennedy Bridge (although most New Yorkers still called it "the Triborough"), and then downtown on the FDR.

"I should know better than to ask," I said, "but how did you make the necessary arrangements for our little project so quickly?"

He twisted in his seat to face me, "I told a couple of people I needed to help you, and they practically fell over themselves trying to be of service."

I didn't know what to say. "Oh . . . " I swerved to avoid a van that was taking portions of two lanes on the Triborough. ". . . wow."

"You remember Joanne Agar?"

"Of course, Army intelligence."

"Yeah, well, Joanne seems to feel she owes you big time. Something about saving her life over there."

"She exaggerates."

"She's not the exaggerating type. Anyway, she works for the FBI now, she's the one who gave me all the

254

info on your buddy Vadim. Including blueprints and schematics for his building."

"I'll have to thank her."

"You should. She'll be glad to hear from you. She was happy to know that you were pulling yourself together after all this time."

"Is assaulting Vadim Bezukhov's headquarters pulling myself together?"

"Of course. It's like starting a stamp collection or taking yoga."

We came off of the Triborough onto the FDR, a nasty little entrance that required way too much traffic to merge into way too little space, but I navigated the merge without collecting a single dent in my cousin's car.

"Do I owe a thank you to anyone else?"

"Marty O'Connor."

"Don't tell me he thinks I saved his life."

"No, but he said that you pulled him out of a house of ill repute when it was raided by MPs. Given his record, it probably would have cost him rank."

"What's Marty up to now?"

"He works for my company."

"Ah," I said. "Is he the one who set up our meeting at the Peninsula?"

"Yes. How'd you guess?"

"He was a great scrounger in Afghanistan. Why would anything change?"

"Well, he was really glad to hear—"

"—that I'm pulling myself together. I'm beginning to get tired of that."

"Tough shit. A lot of people missed you these last few years. We were all sorry when Maggie died, and it was hard watching you go to hell afterward. Now we get the chance to help you—"

"—pull myself together!" I laughed. It was hard to take offense when a bunch of people cared for you and were working to help you.

"Okay," I said, "do I need to write thank-you notes to anyone else?"

"No one comes to mind. But I'll let you know."

I exited the FDR at 63rd Street, drove west on 63rd until I reached Fifth Avenue, and turned left to go downtown to 55th Street and the Peninsula. We pulled up in front of the Peninsula, Alex grabbed his duffle out of the back seat, and I let a hotel valet whisk Tom's car away to a parking lot. Inside, we declined an offer for help with Alex's puny little bag and headed to the elevators and a room on the seventh floor. Actually, calling it a room did not do it justice—it was a full-fledged suite, with thick carpeting, good quality reproductions of art on the walls, and a full bar in the living room. A room service trolley filled with fruit, toast, croissants, and a silver pitcher of what I hoped was coffee was positioned near the bar.

We were met by a pair of older gentlemen in well-tailored business suits and old-school ties. One was Asian, I thought probably Chinese, short with a thick shock of black hair. The other was Latino, and had short, gray hair and a bristling mustache. We all shook hands but didn't bother with names.

"How can we help?" the Asian asked in accentless English.

Alex said, "We're going visiting and need a lot of firepower."

The Latino grinned and said in equally accentless English, "By 'a lot' do you mean enough to take on a squad or enough to invade a small country?"

"Small country," Alex replied.

The Asian smiled, "You do know how to have a good time."

The Latino walked into another room then returned wheeling in a very large, black trunk. Large enough to fold a corpse into with room to spare for a couple of six packs. A moment later, he was back with another equally large, black trunk. He snapped open one trunk and then the other. "We'll start with these. If you don't see what you want here, we have more inventory for your consideration."

I couldn't speak for Alex, but I liked what I saw. The Asian asked if we'd like some coffee, and I said I would help myself. Alex joined me.

I whispered, "I'm guessing that I shouldn't ask what these guys are up to?"

257

"Let's say they're international businessmen who operate at the fringe of the law."

"Yeah? Inside or outside the fringe?"

"Let's not go there."

"Why are they doing this?"

"They believe I am collecting a favor on behalf of the agency for which I work. I am not disposed to clarify."

I nodded with understanding. We returned to the two trunks, coffee cups in hand, and did some window shopping. I guess, to be accurate, it was trunk shopping, but window shopping has a lot much more cachet. And we did have the necessary Fifth Avenue address for cachet.

Within a few minutes we had what we needed. M16 assault rifles with 60-shell banana clips, Uzi machine pistols, a light mortar with high-explosive rounds, concussion grenades, and smoke grenades. I wasn't sure if we had reached the "invade a small country" standard, but we were good to go for an assault on a New York City fortress.

Our arms dealers consolidated our selections into one of the trunks. The Latino asked if we would be interested in accessories.

"Yes, please." replied Alex.

He disappeared and came back with another trunk. We selected multiple pairs of dark coveralls, night-vision goggles, breathing filters, duffle packs, and a nice assortment of other goodies. These were all tucked into the two duffle packs.

Alex said, "Thank you."

"You're welcome," said the Asian. "Have fun."

*   *   *

MANHATTAN, WALL STREET AREA:

HENRY WILCOX HAD GONE TO HARVARD FOR HIS BA, THEN TO THE BUSINESS SCHOOL FOR AN MBA, THEN TO COLUMBIA FOR A LAW DEGREE. He had started in his father's wealth-management firm in Boston, moved the firm to New York when his father died, and built Wilcox, Dunaway & Rigano into one of the major powers in the global financial markets. He had served as Secretary of the Treasury of the United States for five years, then returned to his family firm as chairman. Henry Wilcox was quoted by the business press almost as often as Warren Buffet. Sometimes, more often.

Wilcox was tall, patrician—the ultimate WASP. His full head of silver hair was carefully cut and combed with the part on the left, his forelock artfully brushed to the right across his forehead. His suit was a navy blue, bespoke two-piece. His tie was Italian silk, his shoes black, Italian leather. After the Real Lawman began his killings on Wall Street, Wilcox was the only Wall Street executive who refused to be driven to work in some kind of armored vehicle. He refused to have defensive additions made to his office. As Treasury Secretary, he was accustomed to traveling with security personnel, but he now refused to allow his firm's security chief to increase the size of his personal detail, and

259

he refused to allow them to carry more firepower than previously. As Wilcox had been quoted in the press, "I am not going to allow some pathetic, anonymous bully to frighten me. If my time is up, it's up. If it's not, I will not allow some thug to make me change the way I live."

Sunday morning, Wilcox's Bentley Flying Spur sedan glided to a stop at the curb in front of 44 Wall Street, only a few hundred feet away from the entrance to the New York Stock Exchange. It wasn't the newest, tallest, or flashiest building in the financial district, which is exactly what you would expect for Henry Wilcox. The chauffeur stepped out and stayed by the driver's door, scanning in all directions. A bodyguard stepped out of the passenger door, checked the sidewalk up and down in front of 44 Wall Street, and reached for the handle of the rear, passenger-side door. As he did, a group of five men emerged from a Ford E-Series Van that had pulled up behind the Bentley. When Wilcox stepped out of the Bentley, he was in a cocoon of men, all slightly taller than he, all wearing the body armor he refused. Wilcox was far from invulnerable, but he was a lot safer than the Sunday-morning tourists on their way to the 9-11 Memorial on the west side or to the South Street Seaport on the east.

Wilcox was coming to the office directly from the Sunday morning service at the Church of the Heavenly Rest at Fifth Avenue and East 90th Street. His firm was handling the merger of two tech companies (a social media company was buying out a privately owned app firm), and he was playing the good leader—showing up to roll up his sleeves on a deal that his people had been working on non-stop for the last week. While he had been at church, most of his team was eating cold, leftover Chinese food and pizza for breakfast.

The second Real Lawman, the short man who had blown Charlene Mercier into a million pieces, watched from further east on Wall Street, a couple of blocks from the security barriers and personnel at the Stock Exchange. He stepped out of the back of a van with a sign on the side that read: "New York Steam Systems." Below the company name was a slogan: "We Keep The Heat On!" and a 212-area-code phone number. There was no such company. The man had placed several bright-orange traffic cones on the street ten minutes before Wilcox's Bentley arrived. He'd pulled aside a manhole cover and placed a small, three-sided metal barrier around the open hole. Any casual walker-by would assume he was one of thousands of workers dealing with Manhattan's intricate, crumbling infrastructure. Exactly what he wanted.

When Wilcox began crossing the sidewalk to the entrance of his building, the man was standing on the ladder in the manhole. He waist was at street level, and he was mostly hidden by the three-sided barrier around it. The fourth side, the open side, gave him visual access to Wilcox. The man shouldered a small, thirty-inch-long canister onto his left shoulder. He pulled the caps at each end of the canister, flipped up a small sight, aimed, and pulled the trigger as Wilcox's group arrived at the front door of 44 Wall Street. The grenade arrived a half-second later and blew out the entire revolving door entryway. Two dozen people were scattered on the sidewalk and inside the entrance to the building, bleeding, groaning in pain, and dying. Or dead already.

The man calmly dropped the canister into the manhole, then scrambled out of the hole, shouting, "Holy shit! Did you see that?" to anyone who was listening, and joined the running crowd. Many people were running from the blast scene. A few others, including the man responsible, ran toward the blast, as if trying to help. The man knelt beside one of the guards, realized he was dead, glanced every which way, and spotted Wilcox.

Wilcox was staring at the sky, gasping, bleeding out. The man knelt by him, grasped one of Wilcox's hands with his left hand, and released a knife from a sleeve harness into his right hand. "It's all right," he said, "help's coming. You'll be all right." Wilcox didn't seem to hear, didn't seem aware of his presence. Wilcox gave one final, tight squeeze on the killer's left hand and was dead.

There had been no need for the knife. Dropping Wilcox's hands, the man stood up and surreptitiously slid the knife back into its sheath on his forearm. He knelt beside one of the security men and then another. When he was done with the pretended kindness, he slowly walked back to his van and climbed in. He drove away from the crime scene as NYPD units came swarming in.

He drove through the Brooklyn Battery Tunnel into Brooklyn to Commerce Street. He made a brief call on his mobile phone as he neared Commerce Street, and when he arrived, another man was opening the steel gates that protected the narrow parking lot that ran parallel to the building. The man parked the van, climbed out, peeled the New York Steam System signs off both sides of the van, took off his coveralls, and gave all of it to the other man, who took it inside to burn.

The Real Lawman, second incarnation, didn't smile. He brushed dust off of himself—dust that no one else could have seen. Then he walked inside to confirm to Bezukhov that it was done.

*   *   *

Alex and I drove my cousin's car, with its trunk full of military mayhem, out to LaGuardia Airport to a rental car agency. I drove, and Alex checked our back constantly. If we were being followed, the person following us was a wizard, because Alex saw no one, and he was as good as it gets. I parked at the curb and waited in the car as Alex went inside the rental agency.

Alex rented a plain, dark-green van, no windows on the sides. He paid for it using a driver's license and credit card under the name of Joseph Monet. "Hey, my company makes really great, phony IDs," he explained, shrugging. He drove the van out of the rental-car parking lot and stopped a few hundred feet away, out of sight from the rental place. We transferred the lethal merchandise from Tom's Fusion to the van, and threw an old blanket over it, just in case someone tried to inspect the van's contents through the rear door windows.

We formed a two-vehicle caravan to Manhattan's west side, where we returned my cousin's car—still without a single bullet hole—to its regular parking spot. Then we drove back to Tom and Judy's neighborhood and were lucky enough to find parking about a block away from their apartment. We locked up, hoping like hell that no one would steal such a nondescript van, and went to the loft.

Tom and Judy were both out at work, but Donna was there. I introduced the two of them, using Alex's real name, which he knew meant she was a friend. A real friend.

"Can I make you some coffee?" she asked.

"Yes, please," Alex said.

We followed her into the kitchen, and she set right to work, filling the carafe with water and pouring it into the coffee maker, dumping the appropriate number of scoops of coffee into the filter, snapping it into place, and starting the drip.

"You've made yourself right at home," I said.

"You've placed me under house arrest. What did you expect?" Donna smiled.

"You're in hiding, not house arrest."

"Hiding—house arrest, those 'h' words can be confusing." She directed a question to Alex, "Are you helping him?"

"Yes."

"Do you know how dangerous that is?"

Alex raised his eyebrows in surprise. "Wow, she's blunt."

"Do you understand your life is at risk?" Donna asked insistently. "Jack is helping me, but I don't want anything to happen to anyone else."

"Which means if it happens to Jack," I said, "it's okay."

She shot me a hot glance that was angry but didn't completely conceal the beginning of a smile. To Alex she said, "Do you understand?"

"Yes, and I'm fine with it," he jerked his thumb in my direction, "this guy saved my life in Afghanistan. I wouldn't have come home and seen my family again if it weren't for him. If he needs help, *any kind* of help, he's got it."

Donna regarded me with new appreciation.

I said, "Hey, I also help old ladies cross the street and can do entire scenes from *Monty Python and the Holy Grail* in the original voices and accents. I'm extremely talented."

Alex shrugged, too. "I wouldn't say 'extremely,' but

he does do large bits from that movie pretty well . . ."

"You know that neither of you is funny, don't you?" Donna asked.

"That's shockingly insensitive," I said, "coming from a therapist."

"You'll get over it," she said without a trace of concern. She poured my coffee, asked Alex how he liked his and poured it black as he requested. We both sipped coffee and said it was good. The three of us stood around the kitchen in an awkward silence.

After a moment, Donna said, "I guess you need to work. You'd probably like it if I left you to it."

"That would be helpful," I said.

Donna took her own coffee cup to the living room. After a minute, we heard the sound of the TV coming on and what sounded like a news anchor.

I said to Alex. "Should we get to work?"

"You've got a seriously good-looking client there," he said.

"Yes. And it's seriously unproductive of you to point that out. Could we get to it?"

Alex put his brief case onto one of the kitchen stools, pulled out some papers, and spread them over the island. There were architectural drawings, blueprints, and even some below-street, cross-sectional diagrams for Commerce Street and environs. There were photos of the street from several angles.

"This is good stuff. Really good," I said.

"Like I said, when Joanne heard it was for you, she couldn't do enough."

"I will have to write one hell of a thank-you note."

We spent a few minutes poring over all the information in silence, soaking it in. We didn't get past the soaking stage—Donna shouted at us from the living room, "Come here, you need to see this!"

Both of us hustled into the living room in time to hear the male anchor intone, "The New York Police Department is confirming that there has been a fourth Real Lawman killing. Henry Wilcox, former Treasury Secretary and Chairman of Wilcox, Dunaway & Rigano, was killed in an explosion at the entrance to his building this morning as he was about to enter. Also killed in the blast were three members of Wilcox's security detail and four others all believed to be innocent bystanders. Another dozen people sustained injuries and were taken to NYU Langone Medical Center."

As he spoke, the screen filled with video of the post-explosion scene. Blood covered the sidewalk, and teams of EMTs were carrying people on stretchers. From one camera angle, the front of the building, blown open like a meteor crater, was visible. From another angle, the street filled with ambulances, police cars, and fire trucks. The Real Lawman, acting on behalf of Vadim Bezukhov, had stepped up his efforts big time.

The anchor, a fortyish man with an impeccable coiffure and what appeared to be an artificial tan, continued, "Sources at the NYPD are now saying that another note has been received from the Real Lawman, once again claiming responsibility." A graphic of the note came up on the screen as the anchor said, "The note reads:

'To Law Enforcement,

'I will continue to make things right as you continue to fail in punishing the Wall Street thugs who pillaged the economy for their own gain and who have been a disaster for the common man.

'You must punish the Wall Street criminals, now. If you do not, Henry Wilcox will not be the last of the dead.'

'In justice, the Real Lawman'

The camera cut back to the anchor "The NYPD, which is directing a joint Task Force investigating these killings, issued a statement along with a copy of the note that it is doing everything it can to bring the so-called Real Lawman to justice as swiftly as possible."

The anchor continued, shifting to a story about the latest tensions in the Middle East. Donna clicked the remote and shut off the television. She asked, "Will they blame my brother for this?"

I hesitated, completely unsure what to say to her.

"Will they?"

"I . . . I don't know. Probably."

"Can you stop them?"

"That's what Alex and I are trying to do." This didn't seem to be the moment to explain that her life was also on the line, as well as the lives of a dozen innocent people who worked on Wall Street.

"When?" She was struggling to fight down hysteria, and she was losing.

"Tonight."

She stepped over to me and threw her arms around my waist, hugging me close, burying her head against my shoulder. I glanced at Alex, who quickly and quietly walked into the kitchen. I put my arms around her and held her. She was crying. I still didn't know what to say so I kept quiet. I held her and let her cry.

After a few minutes, her crying subsided, and she whispered, "I'm afraid."

"Given the situation, that's a natural reaction."

Through her sniffles, she asked, "You playing shrink with me?"

"I wouldn't dare."

Still in my arms, she leaned back, smiled through her tears, stood on tip-toe, and kissed me. "Thank you," she said.

Thank me after tonight, I thought. I also thought it would be nice if Harry had somehow missed that kiss. But he probably knew about it the millisecond that it happened.

"Excuse me," Donna said after another minute. We let go of each other, and she walked toward the bathroom. I went back to the kitchen to resume planning with Alex.

"Don't say anything," I said before he could come up with a remark.

"Not me."

I pulled out my burn phone and dialed Bezukhov's number. He answered on the second ring. "I thought I might hear from you," he said with husky silkiness.

"I still have ten hours. What happened to your deadline?"

"Nothing. My deadline never included the activities of the Real Lawman and his targets, who are all much bigger criminals than I am."

"Vadim, I can't believe you'd ever say that anyone was bigger than you. As for your deadline, you're splitting hairs."

"What? I am doing what?"

I realized the American expression didn't translate for him. "What I meant is that you are full of shit. Do you understand?"

He chuckled, "You should be more careful. I fully understand when you say I am 'full of shit.' That could make me angry. I could kill a lot more people."

"But you won't. You kill anyone else—and I mean *anyone else*—you'll never see Richard or his sister."

Alex, who could only hear my part of the

conversation, had his eyebrows approaching the top of his forehead. I wasn't sure if he was skeptical about my negotiating or amazed.

"That was not what we discussed," Bezukhov replied.

"It's what we're discussing now. No more Real Lawman killings or you won't get Richard and Donna. Take it or leave it."

There was nothing on his end. I looked at Alex, whose eyebrows dropped to their normal positions, and his hands went out, palms up, in a "who knows?" gesture.

"All right," Bezukhov grunted, "I will take it. But your deadline is the same."

"What a surprise."

"Contact me when you are ready to deliver, and I will give you instructions."

"No," I said. "I will contact you *if* I decide to deliver, and then *I* will give *you* instructions."

"Oh," he laughed, rather unpleasantly, "now *you* are in charge."

"No, *I* have what you want. When the time comes, we'll do it my way."

"What if we say that we shall see what we shall see when the time comes?"

"Fine."

"Good," he disconnected.

"Fuck you," I said into the phone.

"Did he agree to your terms about the deadline and delivery?" Alex asked.

"No, but I didn't think he would. He agreed to talk it over later. Sort of. But I had to try to renegotiate to protect others and set up the deal for delivering Donna and her brother."

"Because Vadim would expect you to renegotiate?"

"Wouldn't you in his shoes?"

He nodded. "Well, given the givens, you played that reasonably well."

"Reasonably?"

"I would have done better, but . . ."

I waved him off, poured myself some more coffee, and leaned over the island to study the plans and diagrams. Alex joined me. For a long time, we reviewed every piece of paper and photo in silence. Then we began to map out our attack on Bezukhov's operations center in Brooklyn.

An hour later, Alex was taking a nap on the sofa. I'd been on a dozen ops with Alex, and he always took a nap before. It always made me crazy that he could sleep. I needed to pace. Or stare at the scenery (whatever that happened to be). But go to sleep? I went to the rooftop and stood on the deck, gazing past the High Line toward the Hudson. There were no answers for me in Jersey City's skyscrapers on the far side of the river.

"Harry," I called. "Harry, I need to speak with you."

"You *need* to speak with me?" His flat tone of voice

managed to suggest a huge dose of cynicism. "You might be overplaying the 'need' card."

He had magically materialized on my right, wearing the same suit, shirt, and tie as always. Actually, I didn't know for a fact that they were the same. For all I knew, Harry had an inexhaustible supply of identical suits, shirts, and ties. I allowed my mind to wander and consider the possibility of Harry in a bright-red, tropical-flower print Hawaiian shirt. While I was at it, I imagined him with a wide-brimmed straw hat. And a gigantic cigar . . . no, that was too much. I'd gone too far. My imagination failed me, and I confronted the reality: Harry in the same suit, shirt, and tie I'd seen him wearing every single time I'd seen him.

"Need is need," I said. "Right now I need to get into the latest Task Force meeting on the Real Lawman killings."

"Why?"

"What if they've found something related to this latest killing? What if they have new suspects? What if Bezukhov has dropped clues that set up Richard Kruger for any or all of the killings? What if they found definitive proof that there was no second shooter on the grassy knoll in Dallas?"

"Excuse me—Dallas?"

"Just making sure you were paying attention."

Harry responded with his usual, stone-faced silence.

"Are you going to get me inside the Task Force meeting?"

"Yes. Twenty minutes—"

I had been looking right at him and didn't see him go. No dissolve, no fade out, no sudden blip out of my line of sight. Gone. Without any time to process his disappearance, I realized why he had gone so swiftly on this occasion.

"Jack?" I heard Donna call through the open door to the roof.

"Up here."

She appeared a second later and crossed the wide deck. "I thought you might be up here. Alex seems to be waking up. I thought I'd make a fresh pot of coffee—do you want some?"

"Sure, thanks."

She made no move to go.

"I'm guessing you didn't come up here just to take my coffee order."

"No, I did," she smiled, "but not *only* to see if you wanted coffee."

"What else?"

"I don't want you going tonight. I don't know what you have planned, but I'm afraid."

"Aw, shucks, Ma'am. Weren't nuthin'."

"What the hell was that?"

I shook my head, "Forget it. Bad attempt at a Gary Cooper moment."

"This isn't some movie. You're going up against the

Russian mafia. I checked Vadim Bezukhov online. He's a really, *really* bad guy."

"Look, if your problem was easy, Harry would have introduced you to someone else. But he introduced you to me. That's because he knows I can handle this."

"What makes Harry so knowledgeable?"

"Uh . . . " how to explain Harry? "Well, Harry has seen just about everything there is to see. He gets around, and he's a lot older than he looks. His background is so complex that there's no way I can explain it to you. But if he thinks I'm the man for your job, I am."

"Am I supposed to buy that bullshit? He vouches for you, and you vouch for him?"

I shrugged, "Sorry, but that's the way it is."

The knuckles of her left hand were white from gripping the roof railing. I reached for her hand and stroked the back of it. She pulled away from me.

"You could get killed," she stopped, wiped a tear away, and said angrily, "you probably will get killed."

I used Harry's method and kept quiet.

"You feed me all that happy bullshit about being the man for the job, but I think you're trying to convince yourself as much as you are me. You know you shouldn't go."

"You and Richard will never be safe if I don't go."

"We'll run away," she said. "You can come with us."

"You can't run far enough away to hide from Bezukhov."

"I don't believe you. This is all about some ridiculous macho code of honor. You're trying to prove something to yourself. Well, I don't want to be responsible for your death. Richard and I will run away and hide. We'll take our chances."

I reached for her hand again. She pulled back, but I held on, firmly enough to keep her hand in mine, gently enough not to hurt her. "I'm not trying to prove anything to anyone. I've proved myself over and over for years. This isn't about me. Not about my emotional needs or psychological needs. Nothing. It's . . . about . . ." My voiced faded. I hadn't the faintest idea how to explain this to Donna.

"What?" she asked, insistently. "What is this about? Why are you doing this?"

I collected the few stray thoughts I had, took a deep breath, and plunged ahead. "It's about . . . a promise I made."

"To your wife?"

I nodded. I wanted to explain my wonderful wife to Donna. I wanted to tell Donna that I had been a pathetic, shameful loser. That I had caused my wife's death with my greed and selfishness and anger. And that my wife had loved me so much that she had forgiven me for my part in her death. That she had secured a second chance for me to make things right.

There were tears in the corners of my eyes, and my throat was tight. I managed to croak, "I promised I would help others."

"Even if you got yourself killed?" Donna asked in disbelief.

"Even if."

"Your wife wouldn't have wanted you to throw your life away like this."

"I'm not throwing it away. I'm getting it back."

Donna shook her head. I felt a tear roll down my cheek and resisted the impulse to wipe it away. Maggie deserved my honest tears.

"I don't understand," Donna said.

I spoke in a husky whisper, "I can't explain it any better. I made a promise to my wife. I'm keeping it."

"No matter what?"

"No matter what."

Donna stared into the twilight that was falling over New York, looking downtown toward 1 World Trade Center. "Are you running from me?"

"No."

"Are you sure? It feels that way," her gaze returned to me. "Maybe I'm confusing my gratitude with other feelings, but I think there's something between us. But you won't let it happen."

"I can't . . ."

"Because of Maggie?"

I sighed. "Yes. But it's more complicated than that. I can't . . . I'm not allowed . . . "

"Not allowed? What does that mean?"

After what seemed like an eternity, I admitted, "I don't know how to explain what's going on with me. I'm sorry."

"You're a mess," she said, sympathetically.

"That's for sure."

"And I'm too involved to help."

I didn't know how to respond to that.

Donna waited for a moment for a reply then walked off the roof. I heard her footsteps as she went downstairs.

*   *   *

Harry and I materialized into the Task Force meeting after the preliminaries were done. I probably shouldn't use the word "materialize," it makes it sound as if we appeared over the course of five to ten seconds. In fact, one second we weren't there, and then one tiny micro-second later, we were. And I realized that stone-faced though he might be, Harry had a flair for the dramatic. We had cut into the meeting just as it was getting interesting.

The atmosphere in the Task Force conference room at One Police Plaza was unpleasant to say the least. The group had been working too hard, eating too little, probably consuming way too many cups of coffee, and smoking way too many cigarettes. They were tired and tense. And no doubt, frustrated at their inability to stop the Real Lawman. For all I knew, they were pissed off at his chosen name. I would have been if I were a member of the Task Force.

Hall and Beirne were reviewing the details of the latest killing. Beirne said, "Unfortunately, Wilcox was an easy target. Very easy. He refused to take any extraordinary security measures, and a well-placed grenade took out his normal security detail."

Someone from the back of the room interjected, "Why no extra security? Couldn't he afford it?"

There was some bitter laughter, and Chief Hall answered, "He said publicly that he was not going to be bullied by the killer. He would not change his life to give the killer any satisfaction."

"Yeah, and how is that working for him?"

More bitter laughter, which Beirne waved down. "Look, it doesn't matter. Wilcox said 'no,' and the killer took advantage. The M.O. was different than the previous Real Lawman killings, but he apparently had knowledge of Wilcox's routines and his resources suggest that this is no lone assassin working off a personal resentment. We're pretty damn certain that these are murders for hire." He scanned the people at the table and stopped when he saw the FBI's Mancini. "Special Agent Mancini, can you brief us on what you've found out about the organized crime angle?"

Linda Mancini stepped to the podium. Her hair was clasped in its usual ponytail, and she was still wearing the librarian glasses, but no suit. Today she was dressed in tan slacks, a white blouse, and a dark blazer. I thought that the blazer was probably navy blue, but since I was at the other end of the room and the fluorescent lighting was harsh, I couldn't tell. Maybe black. What the hell, she was still the most attractive FBI agent I had ever seen. Once again I had to scold myself to focus on what she was saying and stop focusing on her looks.

"We've reviewed a number of the Russian groups that we know operate internationally, groups with commodities connections in Russia, mainly oil, groups that might benefit from intimidation through murder. The three top suspects are Vadim Bezukhov, Dimitri Golubkin, and Oleg Muratov. It's believed all three have killed as part of normal operating procedures in Russia. Our profilers believe that all three are aggressive enough and confident enough to use murder as a tool to expand their businesses in the United States."

Mancini paused and frowned. "Unfortunately, even though we've put these three through a microscope, there isn't a scrap of evidence any of them are involved in the Real Lawman killings."

"Oh . . . shit," I muttered to Harry as people around the room began asking Mancini questions. "How the hell could they find nothing on Bezukhov? Nothing? After all, the guy is guilty."

"Why don't you tell Agent Mancini what you

know?"

I mulled that over for a second. "I'm getting confused is why. The law-enforcement part of me wants to bring down Bezukhov. But the mankind is my business part of me worries that if this Task Force finds Bezukhov, he'll do some kind of plea bargain and give up Richard for the first two murders. Richard goes to jail for those two killings, and the others go on the unsolved pile. Maybe someone pursues them, maybe people shrug and say, 'we got the guy, let's not worry about it.'"

On the podium, Mancini was wrapping up, "We're going to continue looking into the big three, and into other possibilities, but at the moment we've got nothing."

Hall stepped back to the microphone, "If there are no other questions . . . Okay, let's talk about increased security in the Wall Street area . . . "

I said to Harry, "We can go. I don't need to hear this."

He whooshed me to the front of One Police Plaza. "You're bothered that Bezukhov isn't more of a suspect."

"I guess. If he was, there's more danger that he'd reveal Richard, but . . . I can't help feeling that it might be good for us if he were in trouble. I'd like it if there were pressure on him from another direction." I looked up at the squat red bulk of One Police Plaza and then at the gracefully tall Manhattan Municipal Building. I exhaled, "What the hell . . . for now, I'm going to leave it alone. I can change my mind later."

"After your attack on Bezukhov?"

"Yes."

"What if you don't survive?"

I didn't know how to reply to that. Didn't make the attempt.

"What if you can't halt Bezukhov's operations?"

No answer for that, either.

"Don't you have a Plan B?" Harry allowed his right eyebrow to arch and display surprise at my lack of foresight.

"I kind of assumed that you were my Plan B."

"Excuse me?"

"I figured if I gave it my all and died in the attempt, it was reasonable to assume that you would watch over Richard and Donna. Isn't that how the Chairman handles things? Don't you act as people's guardian?"

"Guardian? No, I'm your supervisor."

"So . . . you wouldn't take care of them?"

He hesitated then said, "If the Chairman wants me to take care of them, I will."

"And does the Chairman want you to do that?"

"He has not informed me of his plans beyond this moment."

"Keeping you on a short leash, huh?"

Harry's frown appeared and disappeared into his stone face with lightning speed. "The Chairman has Plans A, B, C, and on and on."

"Can't make up his mind?"

A raised eyebrow was his only response.

"Oh, I get it. This is free will again, right? The Chairman makes multiple plans. Regardless of what we choose, He's prepared. Is that it?"

"That's a very rough approximation of what happens. You can't really understand the fullness of the Chairman's thinking and planning."

"That's why people spend a lifetime trying to figure Him out, huh?"

"Yes." He waited for me to make a wise-ass remark. But when I didn't respond, he took the conversation in a new direction. "What are you doing with Donna?"

"I'm helping her."

"Don't think I don't know what's happening. I told you when we first met that you could not become emotionally involved with Donna Kruger."

"How the hell do I help a woman as beautiful as Donna and not become emotionally involved? Do you even know what it's like to have feelings for a woman? Or is that beyond your experience or knowledge?"

"My feelings aren't like yours . . . I mean like any human being's. But I know what it is to have feelings for another being. I understand that when you help someone, you care more for them. I even have a fond feeling for you, difficult as that is to believe."

My eyes widened in disbelief. "Me? Wow . . ."

"Yes. But I told you from the beginning, you can't get involved with someone you're helping. You spent five years in indulgent self-destruction. Now you have to help others selflessly."

"You also told me that Donna won't remember me. Why not give her a bit of joy now, and let her forget me later?"

"That's selfish manipulation, not selfless help."

I realized he had me in a box. "What about Linda Mancini?"

"Who?" For once, Harry was completely bewildered. "The FBI agent?"

"Yes. I'm not trying to help her. And she's sexy as all get out. Can I get involved with her?"

"I . . . suppose that would be all right . . ." Harry was genuinely puzzled.

"Could you arrange to introduce me?"

"That's not funny. Even by the standards of what you call humor."

"Why not? Whoosh me into a hallway upstairs," I jerked my thumb at NYPD headquarters, "at an opportune moment. I'll introduce myself and hope she likes me."

"Do you think I'm some sort of matchmaker?"

"No, I think you have a great skill set that could be very helpful."

"How is what you're proposing not selfish on your part? Or are you saying all this to provoke a reaction from me?"

I grinned. "Got me. Actually, it's a win/win for me. If you said 'yes,' I get to meet Agent Mancini. If you said 'no,' I'd be entertained by your response."

His Mona Lisa smile made the briefest possible appearance. "Sorry to disappoint you."

"Yeah, me, too."

10

A pall hung over dinner at my cousin's—the danger Alex and I were going to expose ourselves to later that night made the meal very uncomfortable. Tom and Judy shifted in their seats and threw knowing looks at each other every few minutes. Alex was in his pre-op mind set, quietly gearing up for the action ahead.

Donna was angry. I could almost see steam emanating from her. She stared straight ahead, chewing her food like some kind of grinding machine. Whenever she wanted salt or pepper, she reached for it rather than asking anyone to pass it. After sharing a couple of meals with her, I knew these table manners were not like her at all.

I had tried a few conversational gambits when I first sat down but gave up when my comments crashed like the *Hindenburg*. I choked down my pasta and salad, drank a lot of water, and gratefully cleared my plate.

As Alex and I were headed toward the front door, I said to Tom, "Don't wait up for us."

"I'd tell you to behave, but I have a feeling that's not on your agenda," he replied.

Judy added, "Be careful. Please."

"We will."

Alex was out the door, and I was about to follow him when Donna called for me to wait. She rushed to me, threw her arms around my neck, and kissed me. It was a long, lingering kiss on the mouth. Then she went down the hall to her room before I could say anything.

Tom and Judy smiled. But their expressions were bittersweet.

Outside, Alex and I walked to the van in silence. We each had a backpack with the plans of 25 Commerce Street, water bottles, and some face paint to give our faces that genuine commando appearance. Alex climbed behind the wheel and headed to Brooklyn. It seemed fitting that Alex was driving since we had used his fake ID to rent the vehicle.

Alex went west, then downtown on Lincoln Highway, which became West Street, past 1 World Trade Center. As we approached Battery Park where I had met Joe, the homeless veteran pretending to be Richard Kruger, we dropped below the park's ground level into the Brooklyn Battery Tunnel. The Tunnel was nowhere near as iconic or scenic as the Brooklyn Bridge, but it emerged in Brooklyn a few short blocks from our destination.

As we drove under the yellowish lights of the tunnel, I said, "I have it on good authority that the FBI was checking out several of the Russian mafiosi who operate in New York, including our buddy Vadim, in regard to these Real Lawman killings."

"Oh? Did they find anything interesting?"

"Not the tiniest scintilla of evidence."

"Hmmm. Are you worried you're chasing the wrong bad guy?"

"No, he's the right bad guy."

"You're sure?"

"Yes."

"How sure? Sixty percent? Seventy?"

"About ninety-nine percent."

"That's close to an absolute certainty. Why not one hundred percent?"

"Not sure I believe in absolute certainty." I wondered what Harry would make of my qualified belief.

"You know that Vadim is the right bad guy," Alex said. "But the Feds don't. And I'm guessing that you're unhappy about that. Why can't they figure it out—is that what you're wondering?"

"Yup."

The tunnel was beginning to rise, leading us to street level.

"Does this have any impact on what we're about to do?" Alex inquired.

"Not a bit."

"Then we're a go."

"We are."

Alex drove out of the tunnel and made a few turns toward Commerce Street. We finally turned right on Commerce, headed east, and parked behind an aged, bright-blue panel truck, which was bigger than our van and screened us from Bezukhov's headquarters.

The June evening was slowly fading to nighttime black. I climbed out of the van, edged to the front of the panel truck, and scouted the Commerce Street area around No. 25. The surrounding buildings were occupied by plumbing suppliers, electrical suppliers, and small construction companies. No young couples were out strolling the sidewalks, hunting for mochachinos. Bezukhov's building, a squat warehouse, was on the other side of the street from where we were parked. The parking lot that ran along its side was close to us. Opposite 25 Commerce Street was another squat, nondescript warehouse. The neighborhood was exactly what Alex and I had seen on Google Earth when we planned this mission. So far, no surprises. That was a good thing.

I walked back to the van, climbed into the front, then slid between the seats into the cargo area in back. Alex had opened the duffles with our "accessories" and our armaments and had taken off the casual shirt and slacks he had worn at Tom and Judy's and put on dark-gray coveralls. He'd applied face paint in diagonal smears across his face, and topped everything off with a black baseball cap. I began to dress in the same fashion. Alex holstered his many weapons, seemingly over every inch of his body: handguns in underarm holsters, M16 assault rifle slung diagonally across his back, Uzi hanging from a strap under his right arm, bandoliers with grenades attached, and coverall pockets bulging with ammo clips.

"The Rambo look works for you," I said.

He grinned, "Blow me, clown."

"Maybe later."

I finished dressing and packed a second set of coverall and boots into a doubled-up black trash bag, cinching the bag tight to make it waterproof. I reached into the weapons duffle, choosing fewer grenades and more handguns than Alex. Grenades are not the weapon of choice for extreme short-range assaults, and our plan called for me to get up close and brutally personal.

Once I was finished arming myself, Alex spread a map on the floor of the van. It was a customized map of our target. Alex had drawn it with information compiled from the architectural drawings and infrastructure schematics we'd used in our plans. But this map was simple enough for quick use and detailed enough detail to keep me from getting lost or surprised by obstacles. Alex pointed to parallel lines that crossed Commerce Street from a starting point near where we were parked and ended under 25 Commerce.

"This is a very old sewer line, at least a hundred years old. You access it from the manhole ten feet behind this van. It's approximately fifteen feet below the street."

Alex paused. "I don't envy you this. God only knows what you're going to find. Grease plugs the size of icebergs . . . rats the size of small dogs . . . odors that would topple the pyramids—"

"Brooklyn Dodgers fans—yeah, I get it. Very ugly."

"Just wanted you to know that I will be thinking about you."

"That's a big help. Really."

"Okay then. You'll enter 25 Commerce Street place through a manhole into the basement at the front of the building. Total travel will be about one hundred feet. One hundred, disgusting, repulsive—"

"—thank you."

He grinned. "Given the age of this tunnel, I doubt that Bezukhov has any security on it. He probably doesn't know it exists. So you don't have to worry about alarms when you enter the basement. Which doesn't mean you shouldn't check to make sure."

"I'll check."

"Other than that, your only worry is human security. Could be as many as a dozen, well-armed men in place. And, of course, once you reach the main level of the building there is bound to be an electronic alarm system, but that's for internal purposes only, no connection to NYPD."

"And you'll make the alarms superfluous with your show."

"Yup. Speaking of which, it's unlikely that Bezukhov has a fire alarm, either."

"Rather have the place—and whatever evidence—burn down than have the fire department save the building and anything incriminating inside it?"

"That's my guess. Anyway, you're going through one hundred feet of disgusting, rat-infested sewer tunnel into a building defended by a dozen armed men."

"Maybe more."

"Maybe more."

"Got it." I said. "But you are going to do your best to whittle down the armed men?"

"Of course. I'll be in position in twenty minutes. But it won't be dark yet. Should we say fireworks at 9:15?"

I synchronized my watch to his. "Let's make it 9:30 just to make sure it's plenty dark."

"9:30 it is." He opened the side door of the van and climbed out. I slung my backpack over my shoulders and, trash bag with clothing in one hand and crowbar in the other, left the van directly behind him. He led the way to the manhole. We checked both directions on the street. No sign of activity.

I stuck one end of the crowbar into a notch on the manhole cover and stepped down on the curved end with my right foot. The manhole popped open; Alex crouched down and shoved it out of the way. I stepped down onto the first rung of the ladder and climbed down until my head was below street level. The aroma was already fierce, even with the night air coming in. I slipped a breathing filter over the lower part of my face, imagining that I looked like a high-tech version of a stagecoach robber in an old western. Instead of using night-vision goggles, which I find uncomfortable, I snapped on a flashlight that was clipped to my pack's shoulder strap and inspected the sewer floor. Well, I assumed there was a floor under the dark, muddy ooze.

"Good luck," Alex said. I twisted upward and gave him a thumbs up.

He shoved the manhole cover back into place, sealing me inside the sewer. I stayed where I was on the ladder, a few feet above the oozing mess on the floor, and poked around with the beam of my flashlight. Even through the breathing filter, the air was foul. There was no sign of life, other than the invisible bacterial soufflé that I assumed was in the ooze. No dripping water. It was quiet and clammy. My back was sweaty in the coveralls.

I stepped down the final few rungs then paused when the next step would put me into the mud. I preferred to think of it as mud. Mud was dirt and water, right? I sure hoped this was a shallow layer of mud. I took as deep a breath as I could manage through the filter and lowered my left foot. It sank into the mud for three or four inches and stopped, well below the ankle-covering top of my boot. Not too bad. I lowered my other foot, and it also stopped about three inches deep. With a bit of luck, it wouldn't get any worse. I took a few seconds to orient myself—I was facing the direction of that went under Commerce Street to Bezukhov's operations center. Another deep breath, and I was off, striding very slowly, taking one step and planting my foot before beginning the next step, making sure of my footing before moving again. A couple of times the mud rose all the way to mid-ankle but never hit the top of my boots.

Alex had said the distance was only one hundred feet, but when you are walking through a stink so thick it permeates a breathing filter, and when each step has to be taken distinctly and carefully, one hundred feet seems like a very long distance. Twice tunnels opened off of the one I was in, one to my left, one to my right. Ledges just above the surface of the mud ran along the sides of these offshoots. And the ledges were chock full of little gray bodies with eyes that sparked red in the beam of my flashlight before my rodent companions ran away in the other direction, crowding each other on the narrow ledges. I'd guess that a couple of dozen rats were knocked off those ledges and forced to swim in the mud. Better you than me, I thought. And thank God you're running away. I wasn't quite sure how I would have handled being stampeded by frightened sewer rats.

The phrase "thank God" made me wonder if Harry would join me in the sewer if I called him. What if I said I needed him? If he appeared, would he be in his suit? Would it—magically?—stay clean and neat? Or would he be in some kind of hazmat suit with thick rubber boots protecting him from the sewer environs? Tempted as I was to call Harry, I stayed focused and kept going. One agonizing, aromatic step at a time.

After five minutes, I heard a deep, low-frequency rumbling coming toward me. The sewer tunnel was vibrating and shaking—I felt as if I was trapped in an earthquake. Then the rumbling was all around me, the vibration grew more intense—and a second later, it was gone. A truck. A damn, huge truck. Earthquake, yeah right. Get a grip, Tyrrell. Get a grip.

A few minutes after the truck had rumbled by, I came to a very tall shaft, about fifteen feet above me. I remembered from the map that there was a manhole immediately in front of 25 Commerce Street. This was it. I was only about twenty feet away from my entry point. I started moving much faster but remembered that there could be a muddy deep awaiting me; I really didn't want to discover an oozing abyss the hard way. I slowed down to my original painstaking pace.

The tunnel narrowed by a couple of inches, and a few feet later, I felt a draft of air on my brow, the tiny part in between my baseball cap and breathing mask that was exposed to the sewer atmosphere. About four feet above me was the manhole cover in the floor of Bezukhov's basement, approximately ten feet below street level. I climbed the first two rungs of the ladder, switched off my flashlight, pulled night-vision goggles from my pack, adjusted them over my eyes, and waited a few seconds as I adjusted to the weird greenish image the goggles produced. I ducked my head, climbed up one more rung, wedged my upper back and shoulders against the manhole cover, and straightened my legs under me, pushing up. The heavy metal cover lifted, and I shifted my body toward the edge of the shaft, moving the cover sideways a few inches. I turned to face the cover, reached up with my right hand, gripped the cover's edge, and shoved it farther to the side. The cover slid out of the way with a soft metallic rasp against the concrete floor.

I checked the room through the night-vision goggles. This space could only be called a storeroom by the most euphemistic real estate agent: cinderblock walls, rusting metal shelves, and cardboard boxes of all shapes and sizes, filling the shelves and covering most of the floor. Some of the boxes had burst open—due to age or being overstuffed— and cascaded paper all over the floor. I climbed up the ladder quickly and quietly then pulled the manhole cover back into place. I pulled the breathing filter down so it hung loosely around my neck and inhaled basement air: the smell of musty paper and cement was like perfume after the sewer. Diagonally across the room from where I stood was the only door in the room. It appeared to be metal, but I guessed that it was a wooden door with thin steel sheeting. Not that I cared if it was solid steel or not. The only concern I had was if the door was locked, and the quality of the lock. I had many talents, but picking locks was not among them. I grasped my Ruger in my right hand and checked my watch; it was 9:04. Plenty of time before, as Alex had said, the fireworks began. Plenty of time to deal with the lock.

The door wasn't locked. I discovered this by the simple expedient of turning the knob. There was a click, and the door opened toward me. I let it swing until there was enough space for me to stick my head through. It was dark beyond the door, and, at first, I only inched forward enough to see around the outer part of the door frame. Night-vision is a wondrous thing: I was looking into a hallway that stopped a few feet on my right, on the street side of the building, but on my left it disappeared in a darkness that my goggles couldn't pierce, probably all the way to the end of the building.

I pulled the door shut and checked the time again: 9:06. I stripped out of my reeking coveralls and boots, swapped them for the clean ones in the trash bag. I tied up the trash bag and hid it behind shelves farthest from the door. I felt so much better in clean clothes and shoes.

A couple of boxes on the floor near the door seemed solid and dry. I pushed and pulled on them, and the boxes *were* solid and dry. I sat down on one of them and contemplated my gun. Thought about the wonders of the Brooklyn sewer system. Thought about the armed men at large in this building. Contemplated my gun again. Wondered if I called Harry would he come now that I had emerged from the sewers? Although sitting around killing time before I killed something else hardly qualified as "need." I reviewed the times when Harry had appeared to me in the last few days and realized that it probably wasn't driven solely by need. On the other hand, there was no way in heaven or hell that Harry was going to sit in a dark basement with me for the singular purpose of amusing me as I whiled away the minutes.

Did Harry ever get bored? Did the Chairman? When I thought about it, I realized it terrified me to think the Chairman could be bored. I hoped not. What would happen to all of us if He got distracted in his boredom and stopped paying attention? I decided that no, He could *not* be bored.

Well, Tyrrell, does this mean you believe in the Chairman? After all, you're sitting here having a philosophical debate with yourself. Why bother, if you don't believe?

Just passing the time.

Really?

I flipped up the goggles and stared into the blackness, into the absolute dark. No answers in that dark, but no nagging questions either.

*   *   *

BROOKLYN, COMMERCE STREET: ALEX SLID THE MANHOLE COVER OVER TYRRELL AND WALKED TO THE CORNER, MOVING AWAY FROM BEZUKHOV'S BUILDING. He found an alleyway between two buildings that was blocked at the sidewalk by a tall, steel-mesh gate with barbed wire at the top. He wasted no time attempting to pick the lock, instead he placed a small explosive charge against the lock's faceplate and blew the lock clear out of the gate and into the alley beyond.

He passed inside the gate and closed it behind him. At the rear of the building a metal awning stretched over the back door. He dropped his duffle pack on the ground, unzipped it, pulled out a quarter-inch nylon cord, and tied the cord from one of the duffle's shoulder straps to his wrist. He jumped and grasped a brace on the awning and swung himself on top like a circus acrobat. Not bad for an old field agent, he thought. He pulled on the nylon cord and hauled the duffle up next to him. From the awning it was a short jump to the coaming along the top of the roof. Within seconds he was standing on the building, hauled the duffle up, made his way to the edge and stepped across a narrow alley to the next building and then the next after that. When he reached the building that was almost directly across Commerce Street from No. 25, he stopped. He didn't want a straight-ahead shot; he wanted an angle. Shooting at an angle wouldn't be any more difficult for him, but it would make things more difficult for the defenders inside 25 Commerce Street—they'd have to shoot up *and* at an angle.

Alex crouched behind the roof's short wall and unpacked his gear: M16 assault rifle, bipod, multiple ammo clips, a dozen grenades of different types. Last but not least, he unpacked a 51mm light mortar, once popular with the infantry of the British Army. It weighed less than fifteen pounds and could deliver shells with great accuracy. He smiled, yes, he was going to throw a party for the Russian mafiosi.

He set his M16 on a bipod, sorted his grenades into the order he thought he would use them, readied the mortar, and took note of the time. 9:26. If he smoked, he'd have enough time for a quick one.

*   *   *

In my head, I'd gone round and round about my belief in the Chairman. Or even Harry. For crying out loud, I could see Harry. But still, the guy whooshed me in and out of police meetings and all over town. Wasn't Harry's being real less likely than my talking myself into some delusional state? Convincing myself that I was playing the hero because I felt intense guilt for getting my wife killed? I wouldn't be the first guy who went around the bend because of guilt.

I shook my head and broke out my equipment. I clipped a couple of grenades onto my belt and slipped into crossed shoulder holsters for my two Rugers. Finally, I draped an Uzi submachine gun from my right shoulder—it hung an inch above my right hip, perfect for firing. I slipped extra ammo clips into the several large pockets of my coveralls. The weaponry and ammunition was bulky as all get-out, but I had a feeling that once the action started, I wouldn't notice my unfashionable bulges.

My watch read 9:27. I adjusted my night-vision goggles, pulled my breathing filter up over my lower face, stepped to the door, and opened it a crack. I wished I could see Alex's fireworks display, but at least I'd probably be able to hear it. However there was a reason that missions operated on synchronized time pieces. Maybe I wouldn't hear Alex's work. But I would know it was 9:30 regardless of what I could hear. Starting the mission at a set time eliminated uncertainty. I hated uncertainty: Would the Dodgers ever return to Brooklyn? Would Harry take this last moment to show me I was making a fatal error by attacking Bezukhov?

God, I hoped I wasn't making a huge mistake . . .

*   *   *

BROOKLYN, COMMERCE STREET: ALEX LOADED A HIGH EXPLOSIVE SHELL IN THE MORTAR, SCRUTINIZED 25 COMMERCE STREET THROUGH RANGE-FINDING BINOCULARS, ADJUSTED THE MORTAR'S ELEVATION SETTING, checked his watch a final time, and fired. The high-explosive shell arched high through the air, reached the peak of its trajectory, and nosed downward. A split-second later, the roof of 25 Commerce exploded in flames.

The second shell was on the way even as the first detonated. The second explosion occurred inside the building—the shell had passed through the hole ripped in the roof by the first round. Walls and windows shattered, wreaking havoc inside Bezukhov's operations center.

Alex broke down the mortar and left it on the roof to cool. He grabbed a concussion grenade and walked several paces from the front edge of the roof. The low wall would largely shield him from the street-level windows of 25 Commerce. He gauged the distance, pulled the grenade's pin, and tossed it as if it were something he did once a week instead of once upon a time in Afghanistan.

The grenade glided through the large hole in the roof and exploded. The concussion grenade was designed to kill or at least to stun. Anyone who had survived the mortar shells was unlikely to be in effective fighting condition after the grenade. But Alex didn't believe in half-measures. If two was a good number for mortar shells, it was a good number for concussion grenades. The second exploded about 30 seconds after the first.

For an encore, Alex tossed two smoke grenades through the hole. Smoke billowed throughout the building. He had two more close at hand. If the air inside the building cleared, he could toss more grenades and create more cover for Tyrrell inside. He put the assault rifle's bipod on the rooftop wall and sighted through its scope, scanning every foot of B25 Commerce. If anyone showed at a window or doorway, Alex would take him out. Tyrrell would be safe because he knew better than to stick his head out an opening.

But Alex wondered how long he'd be safe on this roof. It wouldn't take Bezukhov's people very long to figure out from where the attack had been launched.

*   *   *

Punctual as an atomic clock, Alex's first shell rocked the building at 9:30. I heard it and felt it. Seconds later, the next round landed, and it was formidable. The walls and floor shook in the explosion. Dust drifted down from the ceiling and up from the shelves and floor. Pistol in hand, I stepped through the door and walked to my left down the long part of the hallway, heading toward the back of the building. I needed to find a stairway to get to street level. I heard and felt another pair of quick, banging shocks. Concussion grenades. For a one-man band, Alex put on a helluva show.

By my guesstimate, I was more than halfway toward the back of the building when I found the staircase. It wasn't in the middle of the building's footprint but on a side wall. That way the staircase's footprint wouldn't occupy valuable floorspace in the center of the ground floor. I holstered my pistol and unslung the Uzi. If I ran into anyone still on his feet on the ground floor, I didn't intend to spend a lot of time taking careful aim. It occurred to me that I had a cavalierly disrespectful attitude toward the lives of Bezukhov's people, but I'd always found that in a firefight, he who hesitates is lost. And I had absolutely no intention of becoming lost. If Harry wanted to correct my thinking or readjust my moral compass, he could now appear and set me straight.

Of course, my experience of Harry was that even if I

needed setting straight he wouldn't do it. He would want me to puzzle it all out. I could feel the Free Will Express making its way through my brain again. I was supposed to make choices. But I didn't really have the time for an in-depth moral assessment of this situation. Bezukhov had already arranged to kill about a dozen people under the guise of the Real Lawman. He'd probably killed dozens in his native Russia. And he was threatening to kill more, lots more, here in the United States. And he wanted to get his hands on my client and her brother to do God knows what.

The way I sized-up the situation was: I had to stop Bezukhov and anyone and everyone who was helping him. Killing them as fast as possible seemed like a positive outcome when viewed this way.

Now I knew that "Thou Shalt Not Kill" was one of the Ten Commandments, and it was pretty hard to argue with it. But even the nuns who'd taught me as a little boy said that self-defense was not precluded by this commandment. Given the level of hostility in this environment, there were going to be a large number of kill-or-be-killed moments. Until and unless Harry told me I *needed* to chose the be-killed option, I was going to kill.

I looked at the Uzi in my hands and clicked the safety off. As I stared at the weapon and listened for the sounds of my enemies on the floor above me, I wondered: Where did the Chairman stand on all of Harry's free will stuff? Or maybe the real question was: Is Harry representing the Chairman correctly on free will? I had a feeling that free will was really the Chairman's schtick and not Harry's. Either way, I was supposed to make an informed, moral choice about what I did.

Smoke from one of Alex's grenades drifted slowly down the staircase, reminding me that I had business to attend to. Okay, Tyrrell, there are some very bad, very lethal people upstairs. They will kill Donna, Richard, and you if they get the chance. This is self-defense. Period. I took a deep breath, well, as deep as I could manage through the breathing filter, and slowly crept up the stairs until I was able to see the ground floor. I pressed against the staircase wall and turned, checking every angle.

Smoke billowed through the large, open space—it must have been a hundred feet long, thirty wide, and twenty-five feet to the ceiling. Most of the ground floor of 25 Commerce was a single, big room. The street end of the building had a double-height garage door and a few feet away, a small steel door for people. Inside the small door were two metal desks with steel shelves and a couple of very old, very battered filing cabinets shoved up against the walls. The desks probably functioned as the receiving area for whatever legitimate business Bezukhov might be running here.The long wall to my left had no windows, but the other on my right had six windows, each about three-feet high by four-feet wide, each with heavy steel bars over them. A catwalk ran several feet under them. Metal stairs near the desks ran up to the catwalk. I knew from the quick-check map Alex had done that the windows overlooked the parking lot parallel to the building.

When the smoke wafted away a bit, I could see two single-storied, windowed offices in the rear corners of the building, about ten-feet square and eight-feet high. A small hallway was centered between the offices—probably more offices off of that. The roofs of the offices were a storage space that went up to the building's ceiling. The storage area was reached by the catwalk. Given the distance you'd have to carry anything to store it, I guessed nothing heavy was up there. That probably ruled out any dead bodies.

Almost all of the ground floor's space was taken up with wooden packing crates big enough for refrigerators or coffins, two forklifts, and two Audi A6 sedans. At a quick glance, the place gave the impression of a busy enterprise. But I could see footprints in the dust around the packing crates. The appearance of business was all for show. No one had done any honest labor here in a very long time.

The smoke had cleared substantially and I saw two men's bodies almost directly below the hole in the roof. Other than that, no sign of the enemy. I quietly crossed the ground floor, took a quick look through the desks, the shelves, and the filing cabinets, then headed toward the offices in the rear. No one popped up from behind a car or crate. I was a few feet away from the hallway between the two offices when I heard the softest footfall imaginable above me. I stopped and swung the Uzi upward.

It was my old friend Trench Coat, pointing a sawed-off shotgun at me. I fired instantly, hitting him at least three or four times. The shotgun went off a second before his body rocked backward and blew a hole in a crate a few yards behind me. At the same time, I dove forward, rolling against the wall of one of the offices. I was on my back, looking up. When Curly made an appearance, leaning over the top of the office wall, I fired again. Curly toppled to the floor beside me.

I scrambled into a combat crouch and ran to cover behind the nearest Audi. No one was shooting at me. No one appeared who seemed hostile. I plucked a smoke grenade off of my belt, pulled the pin, and sent it spinning away from me. It hit the floor with a thunk, and smoke gushed out of it. I waited a few seconds for the grenade to create enough smoke for me to run to the hallway between offices. I kicked open a door on my right, searched the desk for any evidence of Bezukhov's illegal activities, hurried back into the hallway, and kicked open the other office door. Nothing incriminating in this office either. From what I saw, there was nothing anywhere in all of 25 Commerce Street that hinted of illegality. Except for the presence of a lot of armed men. I was about to exit the office when a heavy automatic weapon opened up. Sounded like an AK-47. Whatever it was, it tore through the office walls as if they were tissue paper. I dove behind the desk and got as flat to the floor as I could. The AK-47 shells would chew up the desk almost as easily as they had the walls, but it was the only possible cover in the office.

The gunman was emptying the damned clip into the office. The shells, bits of drywall, and shards of desk flew everywhere. I felt a tugging on the back of my coveralls at the shoulder blades and hoped that it was flying debris and not that I'd been shot and wasn't feeling the pain. Yet. I reached down to my belt and grabbed my last grenade, a concussion grenade. I rolled onto my back, pulled the pin, and hurled it through the shattered office window.

The boom blew out the few bits of glass that had remained in the window. The AK-47 went silent. I jumped to my feet and ran through the door, firing to my left and sweeping right with my finger on the trigger. The Uzi clicked empty. I switched clips fast and continued firing until it was empty again. I ducked behind a crate and waited. Listened. No sound. My breathing filter was hanging loosely around my neck—the strap or the clasp must have been damaged when I dove for cover.

After a few minutes, I edged around the crate and found a dead man still gripping an AK-47. The grenade must have landed within a few feet of him; he was not a pretty sight. I slowly reconnoitered the entire ground floor. The grenade had been effective: the total body count was now seven dead.

On a whim, I went to the end of the office hallway

and found what I had hoped would be there: another metal staircase to the storage area above the offices. I slowly climbed the stairs, and when I could stretch my arms over the storage area floor, raised the Uzi over my head and blindly emptied another clip into the space. Then I climbed up the last of the stairs and searched through the storage area. No evidence of any wrongdoing. And nobody there.

*   *   *

BROOKLYN, COMMERCE STREET: ALEX HAD LISTENED TO THE FIREFIGHT INSIDE 25 COMMERCE STREET AS HE WATCHED THE BUILDING THROUGH HIS TELESCOPIC SIGHT. His job was to pick off anyone who strayed from the building or who tried to flank Tyrrell by going outside and then re-entering. But there were no targets. From the sound of things, Tyrrell was doing one helluva job in there.

He noticed a black Audi A6 drive down the street and park directly outside Bezukhov's building. Three men emerged. All carrying AK-47s. Alex was about to fire on them when he heard a thud next to him. He turned and saw a gas grenade rolling across the roof toward him. It went off as he jumped to his feet and began to run. His eyes were burning and his legs were weak. He staggered and felt his knees buckle under him. Jack wasn't going to like this, he thought, as he fell forward onto his face, unconscious.

*   *   *

It was tempting to take the catwalk from the storage

area to the front of the building, but I resisted. The idea that I might get stuck up there like a target in a shooting gallery was very unpleasant. Instead, I went back down the stairs and walked stealthily up the hallway toward the open space on the ground floor. I scurried from crate to crate to Audi to crate, giving myself as much cover as possible. I didn't think there was anyone in any condition to give me trouble, but the last thing I wanted was to be shot and proven wrong.

As I closed in on the front of the building, I heard a car stop outside the garage door. The engine went dead, followed by doors opening and thumping closed. Reinforcements? I knelt behind the car nearest the garage door and waited. I heard metal scraping on metal, coming from the side of the building next to the parking lot. Probably the gate to the lot being opened. From Alex's quick map, I recalled that there were no doorways on the parking lot side of the building. Whoever was in the parking lot could have themselves a fine time trying to gain entry as far as I was concerned.

But Alex was supposed to deal with anyone outside, and that clearly had not happened. I ran for the basement stairs, but I was way too late. Three of the windows over the catwalk shattered as grenades came through and clattered onto the cement floor. Three more grenades followed quickly and then three more . . .

Gas grenades—and my breathing filter was still hanging uselessly around my neck. My eyes burned, and I staggered toward the basement staircase. I reached the top of the staircase and stretched my hand for the railing, but I sank to my knees, toppled sideways, and was out. . . .

11

Every part of my body hurt. I felt as if I had been pummeled all over. As I slowly became conscious, I realized that my wrists, arms, and shoulders were the worst—as if they were being torn from my body. Something heavy was pulling at them and had been pulling for a long time.

A splitting pain sat directly behind my eyes. Probably because an intense, white light was shining on me, burning through my closed eyelids.

I was standing. Actually, "standing" was too strong a word for what I was doing. I was vertical, but my toes were touching the floor, my feet were not planted under me, and my legs were not supporting my weight. Without any deliberate thought, I put my feet down flat on the floor and wobbled into an upright stance. The instant my feet were firmly on the ground, the torturously painful pressure on my wrists, arms, and shoulders eased. I tilted my head back and opened my eyes in a squint. Even with the glare of the white light partially blinding me, I could see that my wrists were manacled to chains attached to the ceiling.

"Ahh, are you awake?" said a husky, Russian-accented voice.

"Hello, Vadim."

"Oh, I did not know that we were on a first-name basis, *Jack*."

"Whatever works for you, Vaddy." I couldn't see him. A pair of lamps with single light bulbs and the lamp shades had been positioned to focus all of the light into my eyes. I figured that Vadim was behind the lamps, probably centered between them and probably not alone.

"Jack? Are you paying attention?" Vadim asked, breaking into my pain-infused thought process. "Jack, I want you to answer my questions."

"No, thanks."

"I do not think you understand your situation." He was amused by me. "Take a moment. Take in your surroundings. Take in your . . . ah, what is the word in English? . . . ah, predicament."

Since I didn't have anything better to do, I took him up on his suggestion. I realized I was cold. I glanced down and saw that I was naked. There was a momentary flash of humiliation followed immediately by anger. Anger is much better than humiliation. I can use anger to drive myself to escape this ugliness. Still squinting, I examined the room, which wasn't easy since my arms being pulled up past my ears restricted my view. The floor was cement and the walls were cinderblock. I guessed we were in the basement at 25 Commerce Street. I twisted to my right and was unpleasantly surprised by what I saw: Alex was hanging in chains, naked, next to me. He was still unconscious.

"Okay," the American word sounded funny with a Russian accent, but it wasn't the time for a smile. "Now, you are aware of what kind of trouble you are in." Bezukhov said something in Russian—I thought it was "go ahead."

My old friend Buzz Cut stepped from the dark behind the lamps and placed the barrel of a Ruger automatic against Alex's chest, directly over his heart. I had the sinking feeling that it was my Ruger. It was certainly my friend the gun was pointed at.

Vadim said, "Tell me where I can find Donna and Richard Kruger."

"I don't know and before you threaten me or him," I jerked my head toward Alex, which hurt hurt like hell, "please believe me, my partner doesn't know a thing."

"He did not have a need to know?" The amused edge in Bezukhov's voice was damn annoying.

"No, he didn't. If you let him go, I might cooperate."

"I doubt that." Again something short was spoken in Russian.

Buzz Cut pulled the trigger and fired into Alex's heart. I screamed but couldn't hear my own voice over the sound of a second shot that went under Alex's chin and blew out the back of his skull. His body hung limply in the chains, as the shots echoed in the tiny cinderblock space.

I was breathing heavily with anger. "You . . . you

son of a bitch."

"Not very clever. Even by your poor standards. Now that we have dealt with the man who knew nothing, we will deal with you. Where are Donna and Richard Kruger?"

"I don't know."

"Very brave. Very stupid."

"I guess this is where things get really ugly for me." I managed to keep my voice even-toned and firm.

"You could say that." Again the Russian for "go ahead."

A cadaverously thin man stepped out from behind the lamps. He had a pair of small alligator clips attached to electrical wire. He stooped to put the clips on my toes—I yanked myself up on the chains and brought my right knee into his jaw as he bent down, slamming him across the room out of sight in the dark.

"Was that necessary?" Vadim said. His tone was untroubled.

"It was for me."

"I could have you beaten unconscious and then attach the clips. Or you can cooperate."

"Well, given that choice, I'll cooperate."

The cadaverous man stepped gingerly out of the dark, rubbing his jaw with one hand and holding the wires and alligator clips in the other. He bent down again and attached one of the clips to the smallest toe on my left foot.

I jerked up again, bashing my left knee into his jaw

315

and sending him sprawling on the floor. I looked down and saw that his legs weren't moving.

"Is that what you consider cooperation?"

"Yup."

Buzz Cut came from behind the lamps and hammered me with a brick-like fist, catching me above the jawline, in the center of the cheek. The blow knocked me off my feet and sent me swinging at the end of my chains. He stepped close to me, tugged me upright, and kneed me viciously in the balls. I collapsed, my arms snapped taut at the end of the chains, my shoulders in agony. I panted in pain and hung at the limit of the chains. The cadaverous man rose from the floor, stepped over to me, and attached another alligator clip to the middle toe on my left foot.

They could have been sadistic jerks, flipped the switch, and jolted me with electricity while I was still recovering from Buzz Cut's kneeing me savagely in my special place. After all, they had killed Alex without a trace of mercy or concern. Not to mention four Wall Street tycoons. But this time around, they decided to behave like gentlemen and give me a few minutes to recover from the punishment they'd dished out.

No one spoke during the next five minutes. As my breathing became regular, I was able to get my feet under me again, which eased the pain in my shoulders and arms. I was acutely aware that I was naked and attached to electrical clamps. This was going to be a very long, very unpleasant night.

"The three of us have been having a discussion," Vadim said, the amused tone back in his voice. "A disagreement really. My workers feel that you will tell us what we want to know after one shock. Maybe only two."

"But you don't agree with them," I replied.

"No, I think it will take several more. I would not be surprised if you black out once or twice. In fact, to get you to tell us what we want to hear, I think we'll have to move the clips from your toes to your genitals."

"I could save you the trouble and take the birth-control pill."

He actually laughed at that. "Thank you for the offer, but I think not. No, my guess is that even when we attach the clips to your genitals, we will have to shock you three or four times before you finally tell us what we want to know."

My stomach was knotted in fear, but my voice was firm, "I'm happy to provide you with entertainment."

He chuckled and then said, in Russian, "Go ahead." Buzz Cut stepped forward and raised a rag to jam in my mouth.

I leaned my head away from him and called out, "Harry!"

Vadim said, "No one here is named Harry."

"I know," I replied and shouted again, "Harry! It would reflect well on you to respond."

Vadim was chuckling. Buzz Cut looked to his boss, and Vadim repeated the Russian for "Go ahead." Buzz Cut shoved the rag so hard into my mouth—he did it so hard I was afraid I might lose a tooth. He stepped away from me.

A switch clicked in the dark.

I felt as if I were burning and exploding all in the same instant. The electric power shook me like a rag doll. My body jerked savagely at the end of my chains, racking my upper body as it jolted at the chains' limit. I could barely breathe, thinking was impossible . . . everything was burning and more burning . . .

It stopped.

The electricity had probably been on only for a few seconds but felt as if it had been coursing through me for hours. I was utterly exhausted; the burning pain had swept my entire body and my legs below the knees had no feeling at all. I hadn't fallen unconscious, but I was dazed. I really didn't know what was going on. There was a burnt flesh odor, and I was dimly aware that the burnt flesh was the skin of my toes.

Vadim waited for a few seconds, making sure I could concentrate enough to answer his questions. "Tell me where they are." Buzz Cut tugged the rag from my mouth.

I took a deep breath and gasped, "Fuck you."

The rag was jammed into my mouth, and I heard the switch click . . .

*   *   *

I lost count of how many times the switch clicked and the electricity swarmed through me. I don't think I ever passed out, but I was barely conscious—I was so confused I couldn't have read *The Cat in the Hat* by Dr. Seuss. At some point in the proceedings, I stopped trying to stand up after they jolted me, allowing myself to hang in the chains. Compared to the pain of the electricity, the strain on my shoulders and arms was nothing.

The burnt flesh odor grew stronger, and they switched the clips to the toes on my other foot. Not sure why they didn't go for the genitals, not that I wasn't grateful they hadn't. I assumed they were saving them for something special. Maybe when they figured I was one jolt away from telling them all they knew, they'd go for my balls . . .

The rag was pulled from my mouth again. Vadim said, "Tell me," again.

Much as I wanted to tell him to fuck himself, I couldn't do it. Instead, I grunted, "No."

The rag was re-inserted. The switch clicked. The pain finally overwhelmed.

*   *   *

It was quiet and dark when I woke up. Not completely dark, one of the lamps was lit, but the shade had been pointed to throw the light down onto the table the lamp was sitting on. I was still hanging in chains. Still naked. I struggled to stand and looked down at my feet. No alligator clips attached anywhere. And maybe it was the dim light, but my toes didn't appear to be badly burned. In fact, they didn't appear burned at all. I also realized that all the soreness in my upper body was gone. It was great not to hurt anymore, but I had a feeling that the pain was simply masked by numbness from all the electrical shocking.

To my right, Alex was hanging in his chains, his chin resting on his chest. He had bled very little—once the first shot destroyed his heart there was nothing to pump out the blood. I couldn't see either the entry wound or the enormous exit wound on the back of his skull.

"I'm sorry," I whispered.

I turned away from my friend and said, "Harry?"

No response, no whooshing. If I ever got out of this and saw Harry again, he and I were going to have a very long conversation about what constitutes "need."

Since poor Alex was beyond talking, and Harry wasn't deigning to make an appearance, I studied my surroundings to see if there was any opportunity for me to change my situation. I noticed that all of my and Alex's gear was on the floor in the corner farthest from me and the door. Good to know if I ever managed to get out of these chains. The chains were fastened into the cement ceiling with a steel bolt. The light wasn't the greatest, but the bolt looked to be two-inches thick and probably six- to eight-inches deep in the cement. It would take a jackhammer to get me out.

Because I had nothing better to do, I stood on my tiptoes, grasped the tiny bit of slack in the chains, tucked my feet up, and let my weight swing on the chains. After a minute, I lowered my feet and stood. And felt something touch my forehead and cheeks. It was feathery light and dry. Had I loosened the bolt? Was I being powdered by cement dust? I tucked my feet up again, swung back and forth as long as I could, until . . . there was definitely powdery dust coming down. And . . . maybe I was hallucinating because I was desperate, but it appeared that the bolt was the tiniest bit loose. It was a microscopic shift, but I was pretty sure it had shifted as my weight swung on the end of the chains. I considered the electric cables and the alligator clips and wondered if when Vadim's boys hit me with electricity, my body had jerked and yanked at the bolt like a whirling Dervish. Maybe the bolt had been pre-loosened. Maybe there was a tiny bit of hope . . .

I spent the next ten minutes tugging, pulling, and swinging on the chains. I put every bit of muscle I could muster and every ounce of my body weight into it. I was exhausted and panting like a marathoner at the finish line. Every time I stopped to take a breather, more dust sifted down from the ceiling through the gray light of the room. Cement dust wafting through the air can be surprisingly beautiful.

My timing was perfect—while I was waiting for my breathing to return to normal instead of swinging around like Tarzan—a key turned in the door lock. The door opened, and Buzz Cut walked in. He was grinning. It was the ugliest grin I had ever seen.

"Who's Harry?" he asked. His accent was more Brooklyn than Russian. It was comforting to think that Bezukhov was creating employment for Americans. "Who is Harry?" he asked again.

"He's . . . my guardian angel."

"Really? Your guardian angel? He's done one fuckin' great job of guarding you today, hasn't he?"

I smiled. "He's not perfect. But he's better than whatever you have."

Buzz Cut's grin twitched down at the corners of his mouth. After a few seconds, it reappeared. "Want to know why we stopped torturing you?"

"Sure. If you want to tell me."

"We found the woman. We had taps on all her phones. She got a message from her office about some crazy woman who needed to see her on an emergency basis. The woman was begging. Donna is now meeting with her. As soon as they're finished, we'll be waiting."

I didn't say anything. I was too busy trying to control my anger. And my fear. Surrendering to those feelings was pointless in this moment. Buzz Cut wanted me angry and afraid. I finally said, "Your mother must be proud of you, kidnapping a woman. What a son you are."

His lips compressed to a thin, tight line across his face. Then he forced a new grin, and began pacing up and down the room, careful to stay out of reach of my feet.

"You know what I like about this?" he waved his hands to encompass the room we were in. "You got yourself electrocuted over and over. For what? Nothing. Nothing at all. 'Cause we got the girl anyway."

"Like I said: Your mother must be proud."

He stopped pacing for an instant then resumed. "You think you're clever, but you're not. You got shocked to shit for nothing. We're going to get your girl soon. And then I'm going to hook you up and shock you some more. Just for the fun of it. Don't worry—I'm only going to do it until you die. I'm going to turn on the juice and let it run through you until you're burnt from the inside out."

"Nice."

"I don't believe your tough guy shit."

"What difference does it make? Is there anything I can say that will make you change your mind about killing me?"

He paused in his pacing again, as if he couldn't think and walk at the same time. When he responded, he began pacing again, "Nothing. There's no way."

"Since I'm going to provide you with entertainment in a bit, would you mind doing me a small favor?"

"Maybe. What?"

"Where did you come from? I thought I had this place locked down and all of a sudden you guys appeared with grenades. What happened?"

He snorted, laughing. "We don't have an alarm

system hooked up to the police."

"I figured."

"But we got one hooked up to an apartment maybe three blocks away." He was pacing closer to me, forgetting to keep his distance as he toyed with me. "There's always a shift of guards there and a couple of cars. You know, just in case."

"Thank you. Now I can die happy."

He grinned his ugly grin. "I . . . don't . . . think . . . so. You're going to die bad. It's going to hurt like hell. You'll be begging me to stop."

"Don't hold your breath."

"I forgot, you're a tough guy." He stepped a little closer. Not quite in range but almost . . .

"Tough enough for you."

"Maybe I should hook you up to the juice and we'll see." He took a step toward the cables, farther from my feet.

"Maybe you should suck my cock first." Above my head, my hands were tightly clasped onto the chains.

He jerked around, frozen in place.

"Come on, you homo-phobic shit," I said, "I'm dangling here. Go ahead. Drop to your knees and take a good, long suck on my—"

Buzz Cut growled and charged me. I pushed off the ground with my right foot, hauled up with both arms, and slammed my left foot into his oncoming face. My heel caught him flush on the jaw, staggering him. His eyes glazed over, and he sidestepped a couple of times, trying to stay upright. I pushed off the floor again, hauled on the chains to pull my body up, and slammed him with my right foot this time. He arched backward, hit the table, knocking it and the lamp over, and plunging the room into darkness. His body crashed to the cement floor.

I pulled up on the chains and swung my feet straight for the ceiling as if doing a jackknife dive in reverse. I planted the bottoms of my feet on the ceiling, holding all of my weight in my hands. I straightened my legs and pulled down on the chains. The muscles in my entire body ached with the effort and breathing was almost impossible.

There was a cracking noise above me, and I fell, twisting to avoid landing on my head. I dropped onto Buzz Cut, who was a hell of a lot cushier than the cement floor beneath him. He grunted when I hit but did not wake up.

I stood up, pawed around in the dark, found the table, and put it upright. Found both lamps, tried both, and was lucky that one still worked. I went over to my gear and pulled on underwear, coveralls, socks, and boots. I searched Buzz Cut's pockets and discovered his keys. A long, black one fit my manacles, and within seconds I was free. Then I placed the chain on Buzz Cut's belly, rolled him over so the chain encircled his waist, and locked the manacles on each of his wrists behind his back. I rolled him to his back, partially undid his belt, and relooped it through the chain to keep the manacles at his waist. I sorted through our packs, found some nylon cord, and trussed Buzz Cut's ankles with it. Then I bent his legs at the knee and tied another piece of cord between his ankles to the chain around his waist. This cord was behind him, and it was tight so he wouldn't be able to straighten up.

I repacked my duffle with an M16 assault rifle, most of the grenades, an Uzi, a couple of Rugers, and, of course, ammo clips for all the guns. Whatever I didn't take was staying here. I used the rag that had been jammed in my mouth to wipe down everything that I had touched. Even the stuff I *might* have touched. There was no way there weren't traces of my DNA in the basement, but I wasn't going to leave my prints. No point in gift-wrapping myself for law enforcement.

I nudged Buzz Cut with my left foot. "Wake up, Sleeping Beauty."

Nothing.

I nudged again. Okay, I kicked him with enough force to drive a football through the goal posts at forty-three yards. He groaned. Maybe he needed a bit of energy to get going. I attached the alligator clips to the thumb and pinky finger on his left hand. The clips were attached to cables that were plugged into a heavy-duty socket in the wall. There was a toggle switch about four feet above the socket. I flipped the switch, heard the all too familiar click, and watched Buzz Cut's body shiver and shake. I flipped it off.

"I'm sorry," I squatted next to him, "I forgot the rag.

You bit yourself."

He was bleeding freely from his lower lip. His eyes were wide with anger. And fear.

"I need to ask you something," I said. "But first, a bit more juice to wake you up completely."

I stood up and flipped the switch. He was in absolute agony. Can't say it bothered me in the slightest. I cut the power, and he lay perfectly still and sobbed from the pain.

"I'm not sure, but I don't think I cried. Huh? Did I?"

He couldn't answer. He was blubbering too much.

"When are they going to get Donna Kruger?"

"11:30," he gasped.

I checked my watch: already 11:22. "Where are they kidnapping her? Where's her office?"

"89th Street . . . and Madison . . . Avenue," he panted.

No way I could get there in time to stop them. "Where are they taking her?"

"Bedford . . . Bedford Hills . . ."

Off to Bedford I would go. I undid the clips and tossed them to the far side of the room. "Open your eyes," I said.

He was very frightened.

"Look over there." I pointed at Alex. "You killed that man. He was a very good man."

"It wasn't me . . . it was . . . Vadim . . ."

"I'll take care of him later. But you pulled the

trigger. I saw you. Remember?"

He was terrified.

"Do you *remember*?" I asked loudly.

He nodded his head amid more sobs.

I had a Ruger in my hand. It wasn't the one Buzz Cut had used on Alex, that was lying on the floor a few feet away. I placed the barrel against Buzz Cut's chest, the same way he had done to Alex.

"This is for my friend," I said and pulled the trigger.

*　　　*　　　*

The Brooklyn night air was cool and crisp after the confines of the basement. I let myself out of the small door at the front of 25 Commerce, crossed the street, and walked to the van Alex had rented. I dumped my duffle pack on the passenger seat, sat behind the steering wheel, started the engine, and drove across the Brooklyn Bridge into lower Manhattan. I found a bit of open curb near the South Street seaport. It probably wasn't a legal parking spot, but I didn't really care. I wiped down all the surfaces I had touched inside and outside the van, grabbed the duffle full of weapons, and walked away to the end of one of the South Street piers. It was pretty quiet at this time of night, despite the bars and restaurants in the area.

Looking at the East River flow south, I used a burn phone to call the New York City office of the FBI. "I want to report multiple homicides at a warehouse on 25 Commerce Street in Brooklyn. The warehouse is owned by

Vadim Bezukhov, probably through a shell company or two."

I stopped for a few seconds and focused on the river. "One of the homicide victims is Alex Cranston of the CIA." I disconnected and threw the phone into the river. It made a tiny splash.

I checked my watch: 11:35. If Buzz Cut had been correct, by now Vadim's people had Donna and were taking her to his place in Bedford. I needed to get there and get there fast.

"Harry?" I said conversationally.

He stood near the railing with his back to the river.

"Where the hell have you been?" I asked.

"You killed people."

"I wouldn't be talking to you now if I hadn't." I considered that comment. "Maybe I would be talking to you somewhere else."

"Maybe." He continued to look at me. "You killed people."

"It was self-defense because I was in a kill-or-be-killed situation."

"Not the last one. He was chained."

"Yeah, *his* victim was chained, too. I'm not sorry I killed him. He deserved it."

"Are you the one to judge?"

I took a deep breath and said, "I don't know. But I saw what I saw, and I killed without thinking or judgment. It seemed right and it still does." I leaned on the railing and gazed over the water. "When I was little and learning about sin from the nuns, what I learned was that a sin is doing something wrong when you know it's wrong. Committing an evil act consciously. There was nothing evil in avenging Alex."

"You're sure?"

"Yes."

Harry said nothing but was nodding. "You're right."

"I don't need absolution?"

"No, you don't."

"Okay, speaking of absolution, shouldn't you ask for mine? You left me to be tortured."

"You had the resources you needed."

"They shocked me until I passed out. Until they'd burnt the flesh on my toes. You couldn't help me out? The Chairman couldn't have intervened?"

"You didn't tell them what they wanted to know. Where do you think the courage to resist came from? Before you put your boots on, did you notice that there were no burns on your feet? Before you were tortured, you had immense pain in your arms and shoulders, but when you woke up, none. What happened to the pain?"

"I was numb from being shocked," I muttered unconvincingly.

"You think you were numb? Is it possible that the pain was lifted from you?"

"Uh . . . I . . . guess . . ."

"What about the strength necessary to pull the chain out of the ceiling and free yourself? How could you have that kind of power after you had been tortured?"

He waited a long moment for me to answer. "The Chairman . . . ?" I asked.

"What do you think?"

"I don't think I'm ever going to like it when you answer a question with a question."

He smiled. No Mona Lisa routine—a definite smile.

"Wow . . . if I'm hallucinating, this is the weirdest, longest hallucination in history. Okay, the Chairman intervened." I took a deep breath, unable to believe that I had just admitted what I did. "Enough of this," I said roughly, "You have to do two things for me."

"I *have* to?"

"Yes, *have* to. If you don't want any trace of me connected to what's happened, you need to clean all my DNA evidence out of the warehouse and the van."

"Done. What is the second thing I *have* to do for you?"

"I've got to be in Bedford Hills and very quickly." As I spoke, I was rearming myself from the duffle pack, putting Rugers in my holsters, slinging an M16 diagonally across my back from my right shoulder to my left hip, and magazines in easy-to-reach pockets. Whatever I wasn't carrying on my person was left inside the duffle.

"Bezukhov's guys are taking Donna there now. They'll arrive in about thirty minutes. You have to get me there now, Harry."

"If I don't?"

"I don't care if you're an angel or an illusion or whatever, I will kill you if you don't get me to Bedford *NOW!*"

Whoosh.

12

We were in the trees about ten feet from Bezukhov's driveway. The house was lit up by brilliant floodlights. Two guards were walking along different parts of the inside edge of the light's perimeter. I gently grasped Harry's sleeve and guided him behind a tree.

"Are you going to help me with this or am I on my own?" I whispered.

"I've already helped you," he whispered in reply. "You're here, aren't you?"

"Damn it, Harry, are you going to help me take out these guys or not?"

"Not. I don't *take out* people."

"Are you going to do anything?" I reached for his left arm and grabbed it.

"No," he tried to pull away from my grip. He may have been an angelic being, but I'm a big guy with a mighty firm grip.

"You're not disappearing on me, not yet," I said. "Look, in a military engagement where one force is invading another's territory, it's axiomatic that the invader needs to outnumber the defender by a large margin or have overwhelming superiority in firepower. I'm the invading force here, and the defenders, Bezukhov's boys, outnumber and out-weapon me."

"But you have the element of surprise."

I arched an eyebrow in appreciation of his comment. "Someone's been auditing classes at West Point."

"Excuse me?"

"Surprise will be a huge help, but I don't have complete surprise. They don't know when I'm coming or how much help I may bring with me. But they know I'm coming."

"That makes sense."

"With these odds, do you think you could play the Avenging Angel? Even up the firepower equation?"

Harry's response was to glare at me without blinking and tug his arm.

I kept my grip. "All right, then help me with intelligence."

His eyes widened and for the briefest second, I thought he was going to make a joke about my intelligence. But he didn't. "I can help with that."

"Bezukhov hired someone, we'll call him the Real Lawman No. 2, to kill Charlene Mercier and Henry Wilcox. That someone is a professional assassin. If I were Bezukhov, I would have Real Lawman No. 2 positioned high, somewhere he could watch most of the approaches to the house and kill any potential attacker with a high-powered rifle. Kill the attacker before he ever got near the house, before he ever got close to Donna Kruger. I want you to show me where the assassin is. And keep me safe while you do."

Harry didn't answer. He wasn't squinting in disbelief or glaring in anger. He was considering what I had requested. After a moment, he looked up and then down at me so quickly that if I hadn't seen it before I would have thought I had imagined it.

"I'll show you."

He whooshed us to the base of a very large oak tree at the side of the driveway, almost where it joined the road. I still had a firm grip on Harry's arm. He shook me off, and I let him. He pointed straight up the tree.

"The assassin is about forty feet up in this tree." Harry pointed in both directions along the road and then toward the house. "Commanding views of the road and the driveway. And he can see most of the front yard through an opening in the trees."

"Thank you."

"You're welcome. Good luck." Harry disappeared right in front of my eyes.

"Man . . . I wish I could do that," I said and looked up at the tree. It was unlikely that the assassin could see me; there were too many branches full of leaves in between his position and mine. But if he couldn't see me, the reverse was also true. I should have had Harry whoosh me to a branch ten feet above the killer. But I guess that would have been too much help.

I could burn the tree down, but whatever element of surprise I had would literally go up in smoke. I needed something subtle and lethal. I dug into the duffle, found the suppressor for my Ruger, and screwed it onto the barrel of the pistol. It was a customized silencer, courtesy of Alex's weapons dealers. Since the Real Lawman No. 2 was protecting the house and its occupants, I guessed that he was on that side of the tree, standing sentinel above Bezukhov's home. I paced five steps out from that side of the tree, aimed with both hands at what I estimated to be a forty-foot elevation, and fired fast and almost continuously, moving back and forth under the tree. I ejected the spent magazine and rammed home another. The bullets sounded as if they were tearing through paper as they ripped through the leaves, and I could hear some of them thud into the tree trunk.

Then there was a different thud, two actually. Then another sound altogether: a heavier ripping sound as something dropped through the branches and banged into the ground: a sniper rifle with telescopic sight. It was followed by the very heavy crash of a man's body slamming into the dirt a few feet to my left. There were bullet holes in his right thigh and his upper left chest—the second bullet might have killed him, but if not, the fall had done the job. I dragged the body and the gun into the trees away from the road. I searched his pockets but found no identification. I snapped on a mini-flashlight, careful to hood the beam of light, and examined his face. After all, I had never seen the Real Lawman No. 2. He wasn't much to look at, especially after the fall he'd just taken.

The house was about five hundred feet away, and although the assassin's fall had sounded loud to me, it didn't seem to have raised an alarm at the house. I recovered my duffle and M16, slung the rifle onto my back while carrying the duffle, and carefully walked toward the house, staying in the cover of the trees all the way. When I was within ten feet of the floodlights' glowing perimeter, I stopped and observed the guards' movements for a few minutes. They didn't seem to have a set pattern or timing to their patrols around the house, which was going to make it extremely difficult to predict the best time to take them out. Distasteful as Harry found the notion of taking out.

I went deeper into the trees, away from the driveway, and toward the rear of the house, keeping well beyond the glare of the floodlights. My Special Forces instructors would have been proud: I moved like a ghost but like one helluva fast ghost. It was 11:56. I might only have minutes before Bezukhov's people arrived with Donna. At the rear of the house, there were two more guards. Like the pair at the front, they were erratic, but either they both headed to my left or to my right. When one of them was directly in between me and the guard room near the kitchen, the other was at the extreme end of his range. I had the Ruger in hand, with a fresh magazine. I also took four grenades out of the pack and clipped them to my belt. I edged toward the house, and when I was just outside the perimeter of the floodlights' glare, I stashed my duffle and M16 behind a tree, and continued the last ten feet with only my pistol and grenades. I waited behind an oak tree, using it for cover in the artificial twilight created by the backwash of the powerful floodlights.

The guard on my right hand was approaching his stopping point directly opposite the guards' room in the house, only about twenty feet in front of me. The guard on my left was about a hundred feet away. The guard near me stopped and looked toward the front of the house as headlights flashed through the trees. The team that had kidnapped Donna.

The guard tilted his chin so he could speak into a microphone clipped to his shirt just below the shoulder, "Everything okay?"

"Just back from New York . . ."

"Okay." His chin lifted away from the microphone, and I shot him. He fell as the *phffft* of the bullet was still in the air.

The other guard went into a combat crouch, his AK-47 at the ready. He reached for his microphone. I fired; the *phffft* caught him before he could say a thing and he, too, fell to the ground.

I studied the guards' room. No one seemed to have noticed, but it was unlikely that would be true for long. I hurried back to my duffle pack, pulled out the night-vision goggles and put them on my head, lenses up, slung the duffle over my shoulders, grabbed the M16, and ran toward the house.

One of the men in the guards' room had his face pressed against the window, looking out into the yard. He'd seen at least one of the downed guards; he turned and shouted to the others inside. There was a scramble of action in the guards' room. A couple of them burst from the back door, AK-47s held high. My first concussion grenade landed a few feet in front of them and swept them both off their feet. The second grenade went through the window of the room and exploded inside, blowing out the lights and eliminating any more guards inside.

I knelt, took aim, and fired the M16, knocking out all of the floodlights on that side of the building. It wasn't a difficult piece of marksmanship, but I wasn't trying to impress anyone. I just wanted the back yard plunged into darkness.

I lay on the ground, flipped down my night-vision goggles, and waited. The two guards from the front came around the sides of the house, approaching from both directions. They had night-vision goggles, too, but I was lying flat in the grass and presented a tiny target. The guards were relatively easy targets at the short distance, and I had a good weapon. Of course, these two targets could be counted on to return fire, so this mini-battle wasn't an easy proposition. I snapped off three shots at the guard on my right, and he collapsed backward instantly. I rolled to my feet as soon as I had fired my third shot, lunged away from where I had been lying, rolled to the ground, stopped, and looked to my left.

The other guard was firing away, but he'd lost sight of me. His bullets tore up the lawn but didn't get any closer than six or seven feet from me. I got off three shots and dropped him. I waited for a few seconds to make sure no one else was about to pop up and shoot at me. Then I jumped to my feet and ran to the house's back door, kicking it in and diving head-first into the black interior.

I was in a mud room, with a wooden bench on one side and coat hooks on the wall above it. Dim light radiated down a hallway running from the front of the house. To my left was a cracked doorframe—the doorway into the guards room. I peered inside, there were two dead men in a tangled heap on the floor. Turning to the front of the house, I wondered how many people were there, how heavily armed they were, or how exposed Donna was. I did have a clear idea that anyone going down the hallway toward the front door would be trapped in the narrow corridor. No thanks. I pulled the pin on a smoke grenade and tossed it down the hallway. It began to smoke with all of the effect I could have hoped for. There were shouts and a couple of shots. AK-47 shells ripped through the house's plaster walls, but none came anywhere close to me.

I snuck out of the back door as quietly as I could; given that I was still functioning in Ghost Mode, I was very quiet. Outside, I slowly crept to my left, to the corner of the house. Using the Ruger with the silencer, I took out the floodlights on that side. As I was returning toward the back yard, I heard AK-47 shots from inside the house, shattering windows and tearing through the walls near where I had been standing when I shot out the lights.

When I reached the far right corner of the house, I used the Ruger again and plunged the side yard into darkness. I heard feet pounding inside the house and then a firestorm of bullets poured out the windows and walls into the yard I had blackened. I waited until the shooting had stopped, inhaled deeply and exhaled slowly, and crawled on my belly to the front corner, staying as close to the house as possible. Anyone looking out a window wouldn't be able to see me, or more importantly, shoot at me. They'd have to lean out the window to do that, and I'd have a chance to shoot first. That was my plan, anyway . . .

At the corner, I edged forward enough to scan the front of the house. There were no guards in sight. I'd taken out the four guards patrolling the grounds and probably had taken out an equal number with the grenade into the guards' room at the back of the house. How many were left? Another four? And Bezukhov? I thought it was a safe bet that I was facing *at least* five guns. Probably four AK-47s. And a pistol pointed directly at Donna from can't-miss range. I sighed: the closer I got to her, the harder this rescue would become.

Parked in the driveway were three Audi A6 sedans. They were far enough away from me and from the floodlights that I wasn't completely sure of the colors. At a guess, one silver metallic and two dark grays. They were parked in a single line along one side of the driveway with enough room in the driveway for another car to pass. Just sitting there, ready for Bezukhov to make a quick escape and get away with Donna forever. Or . . .

I crawled away from the front of the house to the back yard and straight to the body of one of the guards I had shot. He was face down. I pulled an extremely sharp knife from my pack and cut both of the long sleeves off his dark shirt. I found a second body and did the same thing. Tucked the knife and all four sleeves into the pack and crawled straight out from the house into the trees.I scurried all the way around the house to the driveway, rushing as fast as I could while staying silent. I crept to the car farthest from the house, found the gas cap, pried it open, knotted two of the sleeves together into one long rag, and shoved it down into the gas tank. I had to find a stick under the trees and use it to push the sleeve/rag all the way in.

At the middle of the three parked cars, I repeated the process. I took a lighter from my pack—Alex had done a stunningly thorough job in equipping us—and lit the rag. I ran back to the last car and lit that rag. Then I took off through the trees, making a lot more noise than on my previous forays.

A shot cracked in the night and another—shells whizzed by me and snapped off tree branches and bark. There were more shots, more misses, thank God, as I lunged behind an oak tree. I gulped air for a few seconds as at least two AK-47s continued to fire in my general direction. I hoped they didn't hit my sturdy oak; I wasn't confident in its bulletproof properties.

The middle Audi exploded with a loud *BOOM* and a small fireball. About one second later, the last Audi exploded with a huge noise and another small fireball. I was extraordinarily pleased with my improvised pyrotechnic display. Understandably, Bezukhov's men were not.

There was a tremendous amount of shouting at the house, and four men came running down the driveway. Two of them had fire extinguishers; their assault rifles slung over their shoulders. Their night-vision goggles were flipped up—otherwise the fire would have created a blinding flare in the goggles. The other two men were holding their AK-47s as if they meant to use them and had their goggles in place. They ran in formation, the two with the extinguishers in the lead and tight together. The other two trailed in a spread formation.

I knelt behind the tree and targeted the men through

343

my assault rifle's sight but decided to wait until they had a chance to get the fires under control. I didn't want the blaze to spread into the trees anymore than they did—we could all be barbecued. I kept completely still, because the two guys with night-vision goggles would pick up any movement and kill me without hesitation.

As the two with goggles scanned the night, looking from one side to the other, I took aim at the one closest to the house. I checked the other guard briefly, pre-targeting him for my second shot. Then I focused on my first target and fired. The shot caught him high, above the heart, in the shoulder, and slammed him into the still-burning car. He bounced off the front door and fell to the ground.

As he was slamming into the car, I had already targeted his mate. The second target was aiming his AK-47 right for me. I didn't flinch; I didn't hesitate. I squeezed the trigger as I had been trained to do.

He fired at virtually the same instant. My bullet caught him in the forehead. His got me in the right thigh, burning a line down the outside of my leg and knocking me sideways into the tree. I pushed back into my kneeling position and aimed again. The two men with extinguishers had dropped them and unslung their AK-47s. Their goggles down, they were desperately scouting for some sign of me.

Ignoring the pain in my leg, and it did take an intense, concentrated effort to ignore. I paused, wiped sweat from my brow and eyes, took a breath, re-aimed, exhaled, and fired. The guy at the last Audi pitched backward and crashed to the ground near the rear bumper.

The last guard was scrambling for cover. It was my bad luck, but, before I could shoot him, the guard found a safe place behind the first Audi, the car nearest the house.

My leg was a screaming mess of pain. I slouched behind my oak tree and went into the pack. Alex had had the foresight to pack a highly specialized first-aid kit. I used the knife to cut a twelve-inch-long by six-inch-wide hole in the right thigh of my pants, opened a plastic bottle of antiseptic, and poured the liquid over the wound. To put it mildly, that stung. I followed the antiseptic with a liberal amount of Lidocaine jelly, a local anesthetic that is pretty effective. Finally, I covered the wound with a four-inch by three-inch piece of gauze with a generous application of surgical tape.

When I had finished my field dressing, I took a deep breath. The pain had dropped from a scream to a modest shout. I repacked the knife and first aid kit—and fervently hoping I was done using it—and edged around the oak tree to see if I could spot the last guard. The two cars were still burning, but the flames had diminished to the point where I could have gotten close enough to toast marshmallows. The last guard had taken cover on the far side of the first Audi, the car nearest the house. It had taken a few minutes of surveying every inch of the driveway through my rifle sight to find him, but I did. His feet were visible under the front bumper. That was it. Only his feet.

I aimed for the driveway about eight or nine inches short of his feet. I inhaled and exhaled slowly, and squeezed the trigger. The shell ricocheted off the drive, the last guard cursed, and I heard his body thump to the ground. He'd fallen behind the mid-section of the sedan, where I couldn't see him at all.

The fallen man was still. Was he dead? Or playing dead, waiting for me to check on him and shoot me when I got close? I walked in a circle around the burning cars about thirty feet behind the Audi where the last man had gone down. The hiss and pop of the cars as the flames consumed them, allowed me to move more quickly than my previous sneaking around. As soon as I had circled around far enough to see the Audi where the fallen man had gone down, I found a tree for cover and targeted the side of the car. Through the telescopic sight, I saw that the ground behind the car was bare. My target was on his feet.

Was he sneaking through the trees, playing cat-and-mouse with me? Was he aiming at me right now? Or had he guessed what I was doing and decided to fall back to the house? After all, his three teammates were down. Not to mention all the guards around the house. The classic military move when you've suffered casualties at this rate was to retreat then shorten and consolidate your defensive lines. If that's the decision the fallen man had made, he was on his way back to the house.

I sighted from the Audi toward the house, slowly

shifting the telescopic sight along the driveway and its edges. There he was, about fifty feet from the front door or the house, zigzagging to present a more difficult target, limping, too, as he ran. My ricochet shot under the car must have caught him in the leg but not enough to stop him. I didn't bother taking a shot at him—the distance, his movement, the darkness, the trees, and their branches—it would take a miracle shot to hit him.

Since my enemy was reinforcing his defensive position, I decided to take a moment to regroup. I propped my rifle against the tree and placed my duffle on the ground. I sorted through it, clipped some more grenades onto my belt, and inserted a fresh clip into the Ruger with the silencer and slipped two more into a pocket of the coveralls. Put a fresh clip in the Uzi and one more in another pocket. Slipped the knife into a pocket on my sleeve. I maneuvered to the first Audi and left the duffle and the assault weapon on the ground a few feet from the car behind a tree. The two burning Audis were quieter now, the hissing and popping having subsided substantially. I guess if you really want to set a bonfire, you need wood.

I crept under the trees, moving away from the driveway. Much as I wanted to burst through the front door and begin firing, I couldn't: it was probably the best way to get Donna killed. She most certainly had a gun pointed at her. I needed to get as close to the house as possible, as quietly as possible, to have any chance of saving her.

Near the leftmost corner of the house, I pulled out the silenced Ruger, took careful aim, and shot out the floodlights. I was much farther away from the front lights than I had been earlier with the rear lights, and it took four shots to get the job done. Now there were only lights over the front door and the right hand front corner. That part of the yard was still bathed in a bright glare, but the defensive perimeter of light that had surrounded the house was gone. I had multiple approach paths into the house, which was exactly what I needed. Thanks to my wounded right leg, I limped under the trees, away from the glare of the remaining lights, until I deep in the darkness of the side yard. I crawled across the open yard to the shrubbery at the base of the house and kept crawling to a spot directly below a window. I straightened up until my head was inches below the window sill. I waited and listened.

After five minutes of silence, I felt it was safe to take a look inside. With my night-vision goggles in place, I stood up and looked through the window into the room beyond. Even with the goggles, it took me a minute to realize that I was looking at the dining room. A large, open arch on the far side of the room opened onto a corridor. Across the corridor was a door. Maybe the swinging door into the kitchen. Since I had burnt out the guards' room next to the kitchen and kicked in the back door, my guess was that Vadim and Donna and whoever else was inside were somewhere at the front of the house. I used my knife to cut through the screen and tried to push up the window. No luck. If I was going into the house that way, I was breaking glass and making noise. I thought I'd see what other options I might have.

I crawled through the shrubs along the side of the house toward the front, stopping under another window. I waited and listened and finally stood up. This was a corner room in the front of the house; the remaining floodlights cast a dim backwash through the front windows. It was easy to see this was a den. Big couch, a couple of arm chairs and a huge TV in one corner. The door to the corridor was open. Light spilled into the corridor from the room across the hall. Maybe the room with Vadim Bezukhov. And a gun pointed at Donna. Maybe more than one gun.

I knelt down to avoid being seen by anyone coming out of that room or down the corridor. No matter what happened to me, I had to go inside that house. There was no way to free her from the outside. I had to be close enough that I could threaten Vadim as personally as he was threatening Donna. Shouting through the windows wouldn't do. Then again, maybe making a big noise through the windows would get me inside. I took a concussion grenade from my belt and prayed that I was gauging the risk correctly: Dear God, please don't let me kill her by mistake. With the Uzi in my right hand and the grenade in my left, I pulled the grenade's pin with my right index finger, stood up, smashed the window with the Uzi, and tossed the grenade. I dropped to the ground, and the grenade exploded, shattering all of the windows and showering me in broken glass. I ignored it, jumped to my feet, grabbed a smoke grenade off my belt, pulled the pin, and tossed it all the way into the hallway. I followed it immediately with another smoke grenade.

Running—limping fast actually—back to the dining room window, I broke the glass with my Uzi and tossed in another concussion grenade. The explosion was as devastating as the one in the den had been. I ran for the rear door and ducked inside the house. I flipped up the night-vision goggles; there wasn't much light, but too much to use the goggles. I stalked quietly down the smoke-filled hall, the Uzi ready in both hands.

A man tiptoed into the hall from the front room opposite the blown-up den. His night-vision goggles were down, which meant there would be a second while they adjusted to the darker hallway. I didn't give him the second—a quick burst from the Uzi caught him in the chest and knocked him right through the front door.

Vadim Bezukhov spoke very loudly from inside the room, "Nice work, Jack. You have made a complete mess of my operations. And my home." His voice was a helluva lot less silky when it was loud.

I didn't bother replying but took a couple of silent steps toward the open door.

"Jack, you know that I have a gun pointed at Ms. Kruger. If you do anything to me, she dies."

"Let's look at the reverse of that, Vadim. If you do anything to her, you die."

"Stalemate then."

I had to admit, we were stalemated. This had always been the likely outcome, but since I didn't think there were any other options, I had hoped to create an edge and break the stalemate in my favor.

"Harry," I whispered. "Come on, Harry, where are you?"

No whoosh to the rescue. Nothing.

"Harry, I think this qualifies as *need*."

Still nothing. I took a deep breath, trying to calm my adrenalin-hyped nerves. "Listen, Vadim, this looks like a stalemate, but it isn't."

"Oh? How is that, Jack?"

"Your operations in Brooklyn are destroyed. The FBI has been alerted that you owned the building, and that one of your victims tonight was an employee of the CIA. By the time the Feds and the NYPD are done, you'll be looking at accessory to murder, money laundering, plus all kinds of RICO stuff. Your days of entertaining Vladimir Putin at your Black Sea dacha are over."

"In that case, what have I got to lose by killing the woman? Whether you kill me or not?"

"Right now, you can't be prosecuted for pre-meditated murder. You kill her, you change that."

"I remain unconvinced. It seems to me you are

playing for time."

"Vadim, if you kill her, you'll never find her brother."

"According to you, the FBI and NYPD are already working on my case. It appears that Richard Kruger will be of almost no use to me."

"Okay" I said to myself. I exhaled and called, "Let me explain the facts of life. Or, in your case, the facts of death. If you kill her, I will kill you. But I will kill you very slowly. I learned some horribly interesting ways in Afghanistan to kill a man, and I will happily use all of them on you. The only thing standing between you and a long, pain-filled death is Donna."

"Fascinating," he said. "That is the kind of thing I would say to someone."

I was getting nowhere fast. There had to be something I could say or do to change the balance of power here, something that allowed me to seize the initiative. I shifted down the hallway to the very edge of the doorway into the room, let the Uzi dangle by my side on its strap, grabbed a pair of grenades, pulled the pins with my teeth, and tossed them—the concussion grenade landed near the front door; the smoke grenade just inside the room with Bezukhov and Donna. Smoke poured out of the canister as the concussion grenade shook the front door and porch. I dove into the room with a Ruger pistol in each hand, rolling through smoke as I hit the floor. I crashed into the back of an overstuffed armchair. No one fired any guns. I popped up from behind the chair.

It was a very large room about twenty feet long by fifteen feet wide, probably a sitting room once upon a time. A slightly less formal living room. Donna was tied to a heavy, carved chair—rope at her wrists, waist, and ankles, duct tape over her mouth. Shielding himself behind her was Vadim, pointing a gun at the side of her skull. They were at the far end of the room, about fifteen feet away. With the smoke hampering visibility and Vadim behind Donna, taking a shot at him was impossible. I was still stalemated. But at least I could see Donna. Her eyes were wide with strain. Her hair was undone, her clothes torn and dirty. She was impossibly beautiful, and my heart ached at the thought I might not save her.

"Harry," I whispered, "now, please!"

He whooshed in, only a few feet away from Vadim. The Russian was shocked and spun toward this new threat, his gun coming off of me and aiming in Harry's direction. Harry whooshed out of sight, and I fired four times. Only one bullet caught Vadim, but it hit him in the chest, smashed him against the wall behind him, and sent his gun skittering on the floor. He slid down the wall, collapsing on the floor. I kicked the gun farther away. His eyes stared straight up at me, and he was gasping in pain. He was lying in a puddle of his own blood, and the puddle was growing, although not fast enough for me.

I aimed my Ruger to finish him off but stopped and glanced at Donna. She couldn't speak, but she didn't need words. The last thing she wanted was to watch me kill a helpless man. Even a murderous Russian thug. The look on her face made me hesitate and think, and I realized I still needed him. I holstered my weapon, stepped over to Donna, and gently peeled the tape off of her mouth.

"Are we safe?" she asked.

"I think so."

"Did you . . . did you kill them all?"

"No." I didn't bother to explain that some of Bezukhov's men were probably only wounded. Probably not dead, yet. I used my knife to cut her ropes, grasped her forearms, and helped her stand up.

She stretched, groaned from stiffness, and rubbed her wrists where the ropes had been tied. "I can't tell you how good it is to get out of that chair."

"I bet." I stooped to Vadim, whose eyes had glazed over. If he wasn't in shock yet, he would be soon. It appeared to me that the wound was below his left clavicle and above his heart. I reached behind him and gently rolled him forward. There was an exit wound on his back, and it too was seeping blood. I settled him back against the wall.

"What are you going to do?" Donna asked.

According to my watch, there were less than two hours to go until Bezukhov's deadline to turn over Richard and Donna or he would launch a killing spree. Only about ten hours until the morning rush hour, when twelve innocent people would be killed. "My preference is to let him die."

"But you can't do that," she protested.

"No, I can't. I need him alive, at least for a little bit." I knelt down, almost at eye level with Bezukhov and shook his right shoulder. "Vadim? Vadim?"

His unfocused eyes rolled then fixed on me. As he realized who I was, his eyes sharpened in focus and intensity. "Oh . . . God," he said. "I should have killed you."

"You're not the first person to feel that way. Listen, Vadim, listen," my voice louder, but even a few seconds of conversation was beyond him. "Pay attention to me." His eyes rolled back and focused again. "You threatened to kill more people if you didn't get Donna and her brother."

"Yes," he grinned through his pain. "I did."

"How is that going to happen? Can you stop it?"

His grin widened. "I can . . . but I will not."

"You've lost. You're dying. But I can save you—if you tell me how to stop the killings."

He shook his head. It wasn't much as head-shaking goes, but it was clear what he meant.

"Is the man who killed Mercier and Wilcox going to do it?"

"Ah . . . ? My professional? My . . ." his voice trailed off. Using my left index finger, I tapped his chin and woke him. He peered into my eyes, "I believe you killed my professional on the way in. Otherwise, you would not be here. Am . . . am I right?"

"Who is going to kill the people for you? How is it going to happen? Tell me, and I'll fix you up and save your life."

He shook his head feebly once more, "No, you will not."

I stood up and handed Donna the Ruger without the silencer on it. "Do you know how to use that?"

She held the gun with the kind of distasteful delicacy you reserve for a plate with two-year old Christmas fruit cake. "I'm not sure."

I pointed at the different parts of the gun. "This is the safety, it's in the 'on' position. Push it to 'off,' line up a shot down the barrel, and squeeze the trigger if you have to."

"Why are you giving me this?"

"The conversation with Vadim here is about to become extremely unpleasant." I glanced at him—and saw that he was paying attention to me. I said to Donna, "You should go outside. Wait for me on the porch."

"No."

"Donna, you heard me: this guy is going to kill a dozen people if he doesn't have you and Richard tonight. He's murdered lots of people in the past. He manipulated your brother into killing for him and intends to give Richard to the police as a scape goat for the Real Lawman killings. He would have killed you without hesitation if it suited him.

Believe me, he's going to kill lots more people tomorrow morning. But . . . he's going to tell me what I need to know and I'm going to save those people."

"You're going to torture him to get it?"

"Yes."

There was a long silence. Finally, Bezukhov spoke up, "You should go, Ms. Kruger. This is the way this dance is done. Jack has to go through his steps, and I have to go through mine."

"You could tell him. No torture for you. No deaths of innocent people."

"I could . . ." he was grinning again, enjoying this. "You are a beautiful woman."

She didn't know what to make of that remark, and shifted her eyes back and forth between us. Then said to Bezukhov, very calmly and firmly, "Jack will do whatever he thinks he has to. He won't stop until you tell him."

His grin faded.

"Jack won't stop," Donna repeated.

I wanted to send her outside. The thought of torturing a man while a woman I had grown to care for was listening outside was horrible. But not as horrible as letting those dozen people die. Donna was right: I wouldn't stop.

"Please?" she said to Bezukhov.

He groaned in pain. His eyes went out of focus then back in. He looked at me and then her. "All right," he said. "You are correct about my friend Jack. I know men like him.

357

He will not stop."

"No, he won't."

Bezukhov nodded, his head moving only a fraction, and moaned, "Tomorrow morning . . . a man with an American assault rifle, an AR15, will . . . begin shooting into the crowd at Wall Street. During rush hour as all the traders are hurrying to work. . . . There will be many dead."

"What then?" Donna asked. "Where will the shooter go? How will he disappear?"

Bezukhov coughed and smirked, "He probably thinks . . . he will get away. In reality, he will probably . . . be caught. But he is . . . a fanatic. His family will be generously compensated."

"Is that all?" she asked.

"He has . . . a letter from the Real Lawman. When he is caught . . . or killed . . . the police will think they have their man. . . . They will not be able to trace the killing back to me."

"But you'll make sure that certain people on Wall Street know that the killings will start again if they don't allow you to purchase their firms." I said. "Right?"

Bezukhov's eyes left Donna's face and shifted to mine. He smiled weakly. "Yes." he sighed. "You are tough *and* . . . smart."

"Sometimes," I said. "Where will the shooter be?"

He coughed in pain. His breathing was becoming harsh.

"Where?" I repeated.

"He will be in front of Trinity Church . . . at Wall Street and Broadway. He cannot get too close to the security at the Stock Exchange."

"When? When does he start shooting?"

"You are relentless, Jack. Relentless."

You don't know the half of it, I thought. If you don't tell me when in a couple of seconds, you are going to find out how relentless—and cruel—I can be. "When?"

"8:30 . . ." he coughed.

"Trinity Church, Wall Street and Broadway, at 8:30. Correct?"

He nodded weakly again and groaned, "Yes."

"Donna," I said, "go into the hall for a moment."

Her eyes went wide with fear. "Why?"

I whispered into her ear, "I need to confirm this information. You don't want to be here."

"But he told us," she hissed.

"I have to be sure."

Her eyes held mine for a long moment. Her expression changed from fear to disgust and then resolved into resignation. She walked into the hall, and I heard her footsteps go to the front door and out onto the porch. I glanced through the window but didn't see her.

I leaned in close to Bezukhov and placed the end of the Ruger's silencer against the wound in his chest. He shivered in pain, his eyes tight on mine with the bright energy of desperation.

"Vadim," I said in a low growl, "did you tell me the truth?"

"Yes . . . yes . . ."

I pushed the end of my gun into his wound, and he moaned in pain.

"Tomorrow, 8:30, at Trinity Church . . . Wall Street and Broadway?"

"Yes . . . please stop . . ."

"Are you sure?" I pushed the barrel deeper into the torn flesh.

"Yes . . . please . . . yes . . ." he was sobbing.

I pulled the pistol out of his wound, wiped the bloody barrel on Bezukhov's shirt, stood up, and aimed the Ruger at him. "Time to say goodbye, Vadim."

He grinned. It wasn't a happy expression. "The woman . . . she thinks you were going to let me live."

"Probably."

"But you will not."

"I can't walk away from all of the misery and death you've caused."

"How are we different? . . . You have killed, too."

"I'm in a different business than you. That's how."

He coughed but was still grinning. "You are deluding yourself. Your business is death . . . just as mine is."

"No. Mankind is my business."

"What?" He chuckled, but the laugh was stifled by coughing.

"Someone on the other side will explain it to you."

"The other side? . . . Do you mean . . . heaven?"

"Not in your case." I sighted along the barrel, aiming for his heart.

My finger tightened on the trigger when a woman's voice said, "I need him alive."

I pivoted to see FBI Special Agent Linda Mancini. She had Donna by the arm and was standing slightly behind her. She held a Glock to Donna's head. Mancini's threatening stance robbed her of all her sex appeal. "Give me your gun," she said.

"No." My gun remained pointed at the Russian. "It's really better for everyone if he dies. He's a close personal friend of Vladimir Putin's— if he's arrested there will be an international scandal and diplomatic squabbling. Not to mention whatever complications it would cause for you."

"Sorry, but his death doesn't work for me."

"You're working for Bezukhov, aren't you? You stonewalled the Task Force. You knew this guy was behind the Real Lawman killings."

"How do you know about the Task Force?" she was genuinely puzzled.

"I have a direct line inside it. I know everything." I waved my gun at Vadim. "Are you working for him?"

Her eyes went back and forth from Vadim to me,

assessing, trying to understand.

"Are you working for him?" I repeated.

"I'm *with* him. We're working together." She shifted further behind Donna but continued to hold the pistol about an inch away from Donna's head. "I'm a silent partner in his American business."

"Silent? That's why you don't want me to kill him? You still need him as your front man."

"I need him." She stopped. Thought about what she wanted to say. "The Russian mafia are . . . unenlightened . . . when it comes to women in leadership roles. They won't take orders from a woman. Or an American."

"With a last name like Mancini, maybe you should have stuck with the Italian mafia."

"Isn't that a cliche?"

I shrugged and considered the pool of blood on the floor around Bezukhov. "If he doesn't get medical help soon, he'll be of no use to you."

"I agree," she said. "Put down your gun and stop his bleeding."

Donna said, "You're involved with him, aren't you? Sexually? Romantically? This isn't about money, is it?"

"Shut up," Mancini said then spoke to me, "Take care of him, *now*."

"No."

"I'll kill her if you don't!"

"Listen," I replied calmly, "we both know how this

plays out. You shoot Donna—I shoot you. Then I'll shoot Vadim. Everybody loses but me."

Mancini's eyes were filled with anger. "Fix his wound."

"No."

"Goddamn it! I said—" Mancini was cut off as Donna threw an elbow back into the FBI agent's stomach.

Donna was ducking even as she elbowed Mancini, who fired wildly. The flat cracking of gunfire filled the room as her bullets thudded into the walls.

I shot FBI Special Agent Linda Mancini dead. The three bullets from my gun tossed her back into the wall near the door. Her body slumped to the floor like a rag doll; her head hung loosely on her neck.

I held my hand out to Donna, who grasped it, and pulled her to her feet. "Boy, you read her well."

"I am a therapist, you know. It's what I do."

"And you deliberately provoked her."

"I hoped she would get distracted."

"She did."

Donna nodded, took a quick look around, and stopped at Manicini's dead body. "Oh my God, what have I done?" She buried her face was in her hands and cried like a small child.

I reached for her and hugged her close, letting her cry on my shoulder. I would have liked to stand there forever, but my leg really hurt.

"Donna," I said.

She leaned back in my arms, "Yes?"

"You saved my life. And yours. That's what you did. It was a good thing."

She took a deep breath and nodded. "Okay." She forced a brave smile.

"Could you look around and see if you can find some keys for those Audis out in the driveway?" I asked.

"Are you going to kill Vadim?"

I was, in fact, going to do just that. But as I looked down at him, I realized that job had been taken out of my hands. He was dead, his mouth agape, his eyes wide open— staring at the body of Linda Mancini.

"No."

"Are you disappointed?"

"No," I shook my head, "definitely not. Let's find some keys and get out of here."

13

"I'm not sure how I feel about . . . me," I said. We were driving back to the city in the only drivable Audi left in Bezukhov's collection. I was concentrating on the Saw Mill Parkway's tight curves. "I was so confident that I was right when I was talking to Bezukhov, but now . . . I've thought it over . . . I . . . killed a lot of people tonight. I'm not . . . much different than Bezukhov."

"You're comparing behaviors by the results and finding them equal. That's too simple," Donna replied. "You killed because to protect me. Bezukhov killed out of evil."

"I've killed before. In Afghanistan. I didn't like it, but it was clear to me that it was necessary. Tonight . . . it's not clear . . ."

"But they *were* the enemy. They killed Alex. They would have killed you and me."

"You're right, I know that . . . but . . . "

"You killed because you had to. That's what I believe."

"But Bezukhov—

"—Bezukhov killed because he enjoyed it. He was twisted. He had a murderous spirit."

"And me?" I was afraid to hear her answer but I had to ask, "What kind of spirit do I have?"

"Helpful. Protective. A bit self-pitying at the moment, though . . ."

That made me grin, "Ouch."

We both laughed then rode in silence for a few moments. The pain over the men I had killed had diminished to the point where I could bear it. At least for now.

"Am I crazy," Donna said in what I thought was a peculiar choice of words for a therapist, "was . . . was Harry there for a second before you shot Bezukhov? And then gone?"

I wasn't quite sure how to answer that. Harry had told me that Donna would have no memory of me after I had helped her—what did I have to lose by telling her the truth now?

"Well . . . that's complicated," I said. "Harry is . . ."

"What about Harry?" Donna asked.

"I'm the one who's going to sound crazy, but this is the truth: Harry is . . ." I braked going into another curve, "Harry is an angel. At least, I believe he is."

"He's an angel," she said in a monotone. I heard no judgment, no disapproval. Probably her professional, therapist's voice. "Why do you think that?"

Oh, boy, she did think I was crazy. She was being

kind about it. I sighed, "I think he's an angel 'cause he does things like appear for one second to distract Bezukhov and then disappears."

"He's done that more than once in your presence?"

"Yes."

"You don't strike me as irrational."

"I'm not. And don't you mean 'nuts'?"

I heard her chuckle and felt her hand on my shoulder. Maggie had done that often when we were driving. It was wonderful to feel a hand there again. Wonderful and crushingly sad. I swallowed to get rid of the lump in my throat, took a deep breath, and focused on the road. Focused on it as if I were driving a Mack truck on a circus tight wire instead of a highway.

Maggie said, "No, I meant irrational. I could also say that you don't strike me as delusional. And you seem to handle extraordinary stress quite well."

"It's all the training," I said. It really was largely a function of training. "After the Army Special Forces and the Marshals Service are done with you, you can handle inordinate amounts of stress. At least for a short time."

"What happens after the short time?"

"Oh, I don't know . . . get delusions about angels, I suppose."

She laughed quietly again and rubbed my collarbone through my shirt. "Well," she said after a long pause, "I'm not sure Harry is an angel, but I think *you* believe it."

"Which means I could be nuts."

"Could be."

"Except you saw him, too."

"That is harder to explain . . ."

We sat quietly for a long time, driving south until the Saw Mill crossed into the Riverdale section of the Bronx and the road changed names to the Henry Hudson Parkway.

"I guess I'll have to figure out how to live with the mystery of Harry," she said quietly.

"No, probably not."

"Oh. Why?"

"Because once this is over, probably by tomorrow at lunchtime, you won't remember me."

"That's a terrible joke. Not funny at all."

"Sorry, but it's not a joke. It's the truth."

"Of course, I'll remember you! You saved my brother. You saved me. I'll never forget. Never."

"Just the same . . . you will."

She was thoroughly and completely confused. "Why? How could that be?"

"I don't know. But, I . . . I *believe* it will happen."

"But . . . I wanted . . . I was hoping that we could . . ." her voice trailed off.

"Me, too," I replied.

We drove over the bridge above Spuyten Duyvil and down along the Hudson River all the way to West 13th Street. I parked the Audi a block away from Tom and Judy's loft, next to a fire hydrant, and left the key in the ignition. I wiped down all the surfaces of the car, inside and outside. Then we walked to my cousin's apartment.

Donna slipped her hand into mine. "I don't want to forget you."

"I don't want you to."

When we reached the front door to the building, we kissed for a long moment. It was a clinging kiss; the kind of kiss you experience as a relationship begins to intensify. And it was a sad kiss, a goodbye kiss. I tried to keep my longing for Maggie out of my head, tried to stay in the moment with Donna—my last moment like this with her. It was the sweetest, most forlorn kiss of my life.

"One last night in the old homestead," I said, jerking my thumb in the direction of Tom and Judy's. "Tomorrow night you can sleep at home."

She smiled, nodded, kissed me briefly on the lips once more, and preceded me upstairs.

Tom was waiting in the living room, watching TV with the volume set very low. Donna said good night and went straight into her room.

"You okay?" Tom asked. "How'd it go?"

"We did what we needed to do. There's just one more thing to finish up."

"When?"

I checked my watch and said, "About five hours from now."

"You should get some sleep."

"Yes."

"Will you need help?"

"No thanks."

Tom chewed on that for a few seconds then asked, "Where's Alex?"

I shook my head.

Tom nodded his in acknowledgment. "I'll pray for him." He clicked off the TV with the remote. "You sure you don't need help?"

"No, I'm not. But I could use some prayer, too."

"You got it." He stood up, "No offense, but you look terrible. Should I be worried about you?"

"Probably. But I'll be okay."

"You sure?"

I wasn't sure. But this wasn't the time to explain that I had a guilty conscience because I had killed a dozen or so men. "I'll be okay," I repeated. "Really."

"Get some sleep," He said and patted me on the back as he headed off to his bedroom.

Tom was right—I needed to get some sleep. But I was as tight as a bear trap ready to spring shut. Using every bit of my Green Beret training to move quietly, I let myself out of the apartment and went to the roof. I leaned against the roof parapet and looked at the Empire State Building stretching into the night sky.

"Harry?"

"Is something wrong?" He stood next to me.

"I, uh . . ." I was having difficulty breathing, never mind speaking. "I can't . . . I can't accept how many people I killed tonight. I honestly believe it's what the Chairman wanted, but . . . I killed all those people—"

Harry interrupted me quietly but firmly, "You only killed the man you called Buzz Cut, and Bezukhov, and Mancini."

"What? But I shot a lot of men tonight—"

"Only those three. Each one deserved it."

"What? Really? Just the three of them?" I shook my head in disbelief. I could live with killing Buzz Cut for what he did to Alex. Shooting Bezukhov and Mancini had been self-defense. To be completely honest: I actually felt a grim satisfaction with regard to them. "Only three? Wow, I didn't think I was that bad a shot."

"You're a very good shot."

"But . . . I'm confused, if I'm . . ."

"The Chairman did not want those deaths on your conscience."

I exhaled deeply and felt my entire body relax. I smiled, "This is the best news I've had in a long time."

"The Chairman thought you needed to be released from that burden."

I was giddy with relief. "He was *so* right."

"He usually is."

"Usually?"

"Don't argue semantics with me."

"Okay, I won't. Listen, if all Bezukhov's guys aren't dead, what happened to them?"

"After they are released from the hospital, they will be spending a very long time in prison."

"Thank you, Harry."

"Thank the Chairman, not me." He disappeared as he spoke.

The gut-twisting guilt I had felt ever since Donna and I drove away from Bedford was gone. It was as if a thousand-pound weight had dropped off of me. I walked slowly around the roof, soaking in the panoramas of the Empire State Building to the north, the Hudson River to the West, and One World Trade Center to the south. When I completed my circuit of the roof, I went downstairs. As Tom has pointed out, I needed sleep. The Real Lawman was going to make his final attack in a few hours.

*   *   *

At 8:15 AM the next morning, I was leaning against the ornate, wrought-iron fence at the front of Trinity Church. I had a clear view across Broadway to Wall Street, which opened directly opposite the church and headed to the East River, which was less than a half-mile away. Bezukhov had picked an excellent spot. In military jargon it was a target-rich environment: Rush-hour commuters poured out of the Wall Street subway station onto Broadway. As important for the shooter as the many targets—the heavy security surrounding the New York Stock Exchange was a block away.

The morning news had no reports of the Real Lawman killings being solved, or even a report that Russian mobster Vadim Bezukhov was dead. Since many killings for hire were paid on a half in advance, half afterward basis, Bezukhov's assassin had every reason to give his assignment his best shot, literally. That way he could collect all of the money promised him. Or to have his family collect it, as Bezukhov had mentioned.

Harry appeared next to me.

"Are you going to help?" I asked.

"What do you want?" he gave the word "want" a slight edge.

"I *need* you to point this guy out to me. I have no clue who he is or what he looks like."

"Your ignorance of the killer's appearance does not constitute need."

"Yeah? Then why are you here?"

His eyebrows arched a tiny bit, and his Mona Lisa smile came and went. He scanned the crowd in every direction. "He is coming out of the subway station now. About six feet tall, white, dark-brown hair, wearing a long black trench coat . . ."

"Got him," I said. This guy was the poster child for one of those news stories about a young man going on a killing spree with an assault rifle. Under the black trench coat, he was wearing a black T-shirt, black jeans, and black sneakers. I was sure that under the coat he also had a rifle in a sling that would allow him to start firing the weapon without its leaving the holster. Within the first sixty seconds, he would have emptied his first clip into the rush-hour crowd, resulting in two dozen dead or wounded. He walked south on the sidewalk, stopping a few yards from the station.

"God help me," I muttered, threading my way across rush-hour traffic on Broadway. I wasn't the only person jaywalking, but I was probably the only one wearing an under-the-arm holster with a Ruger under his windbreaker.

The young man in black was looking in every direction, getting a feel for the pedestrian flow, and his hands going under his coat about to fire when—

He saw me coming.

Our eyes locked, we both realized what the other wanted, and both of us grabbed for our weapons. We were equally fast, but since I had to aim, and he only had to spew bullets, I was at a serious disadvantage. We leveled our guns at each other and fired. I missed with my one shot and dove behind a Honda Accord as his assault rifle opened with its staccato flat cracks. The bullets tore through the bodies of several cars around me; tires were shot flat, and cars sagged toward the pavement.

The firing stopped. There was screaming, and the sound of footsteps running in all directions. I took a chance and jumped to my feet. The young man in black was running south on Broadway in the Canyon of Heroes where Dwight Eisenhower, John Glenn, and the New York Yankees had all been celebrated with parades. I glanced around and saw blood here and there, but it didn't look as if anyone was fatally wounded.

I ran south pursuing the killer. I ran as hard as I've ever run in my life. My arms pumped like a performance-enhanced windmill, my legs pounded, and my lungs threatened to burst. The killer was younger than I, of course, but his coat was tougher to run in than my windbreaker, his gun was bigger and heavier, his legs shorter than mine. I was gaining on him. Our headlong rush split the crowds to the edges of the sidewalk. We passed the block-long triangle of Bowling Green Park. He continued furiously south. I continued to gain. I saw the trees of Battery Park ahead. If my lungs held out, I'd catch him there.

He could have turned and fired at me. But I knew why he didn't—the advantage in this situation was with the chaser and not the chasee. He would have to stop, turn, aim, and fire. All I had to do was stop, aim, and fire—not having to turn gave me a half-second edge. He wasn't going to take the chance that a half-second was all I needed. He was hoping the cover of trees or maybe the crowds in Battery Park would give him an edge.

The young man ran off the southern end of Broadway into Battery Park. He ran past the Sphere—a modern sculpture not really to my taste—which offered substantial cover, but it also was thirty or forty feet from the nearest trees and alternative cover. It would be easy for me to pin him there and wait for the police.

He ran down to Castle Clinton and then circled to the north. I raced after him, determined not to stop, praying that my heart didn't explode and that the young man didn't grab an innocent bystander. He was rapidly running out of park, and kidnapping someone and using him or her as a bargaining chip might be the killer's only alternative. A bad alternative for him, but worse for the innocent bystander.

There were too many people in the park for me to take a shot at him. My eyes were watery with the effort of running, and I couldn't have hit an elephant cleanly under the circumstances. We came around Castle Clinton. In front of us, the early crowds for the Statue of Liberty/Ellis Island tours were gathering. I only had seconds to act, before he grabbed someone.

And then I had none.

He grabbed a teenage girl, about 15, held her around the waist with his left arm and shoved the assault rifle under her chin with his right hand. He spun to face me and began backing toward the railing that ran along the Hudson. The girl had been seized from a group of kids, which scattered, screaming as their friend was taken.

"Drop your weapon," he shouted at me.

I could barely speak I was panting so hard.

He shouted again to drop my weapon.

I gulped, "That's not going to happen."

"I'll kill her!"

"And I'll kill you. That's how this goes. You know that."

"Drop your goddamned weapon!"

"No." My panting was slacking off and my eyes were focusing again. But there was no way I could make the dramatic play and shoot over the girl's shoulder and hit him in the head. I wanted to, believe me, I wanted to. But I would have had trouble with that shot under perfect circumstances, and these were not perfect circumstances.

"I'm gonna kill her," he shouted.

"And I'm going to kill you," I shouted back. I knew that he had another option: firing directly at me. I couldn't defend against that, but he didn't see that option. I had to keep him stuck in this shouting match and hope to heaven that the cops arrived soon.

"Your sponsor is dead," I shouted. "There's no more money in this. You haven't killed anyone. You shot up some cars, and you kidnapped that girl, but you haven't killed anyone. If you let her go, you won't be in as much trouble with the law. But if you kill *anyone*, there not only won't be any more money, you'll be going to prison for a very long time. You can't get out of this."

"You're lying!"

"How did I know where you'd be? Your sponsor told me before he died. There's no more money. Let the girl go!"

His eyes widen with panic and anger. Unfortunately for me, the anger dominated. He had realized his other option. His eyes went tight, and he swung the assault rifle toward me. There was no place to go, nowhere to hide, and I couldn't fire back because of the girl. He leveled off the gun. I was staring into the black hole at the barrel's end, the hole that would send death to

me—

A figure hurtled in from the edge of the walkway, slamming into the young man. The two figures crashed into the railing at the river's edge. The girl dropped to the ground, sobbing. I ran to her, pulled her to her feet, and pushed her in the direction of her friends. Then I rushed toward the struggling men.

There was a flash of steel in the young assassin's left hand, and the other man groaned as the knife stabbed into his gut. I dropped to one knee, aimed at the assassin, and fired. The assassin was knocked off of his victim and his body skidded across the ground and stopped at the base of the railing. I took a few steps closer to him and fired again. I was taking no chances.

I knelt by the side of his victim, gently rolling over the man who had saved my life. It was Joe. The homeless veteran who had run away from me when pretending to be Richard. Joe, who hadn't been able to settle down and live happily ever after when he returned from Afghanistan. His stomach was covered in blood, way too much blood. He opened his eyes when I rolled him over and he smiled as he saw me.

"Did we . . . get him?" he gasped. He stretched out his right hand, stained with blood. I clutched it.

"Yeah. We got him. You stopped the Real Lawman, the serial killer."

"I . . . I made . . . a difference?"

"You made a difference."

He pawed feebly at his neck with his bloody left hand; the fingers dug under the shirt and pulled out his dog tags. His name was Joseph Ryan. "Get me . . . a military . . . funeral."

I nodded. "I promise."

His eyes closed, and his head sagged sideways until his cheek lay on the ground. I slipped my Ruger into his bloody hand. "I promise," I said and walked away. Police sirens were screaming and filling the air. When I was almost out of the park, I saw police cars screeching to a halt on the pathway where the dead men lay.

*　　　*　　　*

I went home to my apartment. When I reached the bottom of the stoop, I stopped at the exact spot where my wife had died, felt the tears welling in my eyes, and trudged up the steps into the building.

First, I cleaned Joe's blood off of my hands. Then I made a pot of coffee and powered up my computer. Poured myself a cup of coffee, sat down at the computer, and wrote a long letter filled with details about Vadim Bezukhov, his home in Bedford, his operations in Brooklyn, the murder of Alex Cranston of the CIA, and the involvement of FBI Special Agent Linda Mancini in Bezukhov's dealings. I concluded:

"While nothing in this letter constitutes evidence, if this information is pursued in a thorough investigation, you will close a number of criminal cases and terminate an international criminal organization."

I didn't sign the letter. I couldn't think of anything that wouldn't sound cynical or sophomorically clever. I printed out multiple copies of the letter on my trusty little Hewlett Packard—since there were probably several thousand Hewlett Packard printers in use throughout New York City, I figured the chances of these letters being traced to mine were nil. I addressed the letters to senior officials in the NYPD, the FBI, the CIA, and the U.S. Marshals Service and inserted them into No. 10 envelopes with Liberty Bell stamps. I walked two miles south to the James Farley Post Office building at West 34th Street and Eighth Avenue, the city's main post office, and dropped the letters into the system. Good luck tracing them back to me.

* * *

Staff Sergeant Joseph Ryan was buried with full military honors. The Mayor of New York City attended along with high-ranking officials of the Police Department, the FBI, and, of course, the U.S. Army, and National Guard. His parents were seated at the graveside and were presented with the American flag that had been draped over his coffin. I stood at the back of the crowd, and when the color guard saluted, I did, too.

The media treated his death as a heroic story, which it was. Many journalists also reported on the tragedy of Joe's life and brought attention to the plight of returning servicemen and women. Joe was continuing to make a difference.

*   *   *

Harry later informed me that the CIA buried Alex Cranston with full honors. He didn't let me in on any of the details, and when I asked if he had somehow arranged for Alex's funeral, he gave me the Mona Lisa treatment and answered my question with a question: "What do you think?"

14

I thought of Maggie every day. And hoped and prayed that she'd come to me every night. To be honest, I thought of Donna, too. I told myself that I was fixated on Donna because she was the only woman I'd let get close since Maggie had died. That the similarities between Donna and Maggie were in my head. That the longing I felt for Donna was intense because Harry had told me I couldn't be with her.

The day Joe Ryan died saving my life, Donna had gone home from my cousin's loft. My guess was that she forgot me in the cab ride home.

What I should have done was say goodbye and move on with my life. But I couldn't. I knew I was being stupid, but . . .

In early August, about six weeks after the events in Brooklyn, Bedford, and Battery Park, I was lingering on a sidewalk on a warm summer evening. The sidewalk happened to be outside Donna's apartment building on East 88th. As I waited for her to come home from work, I checked in every direction for Harry. I hadn't laid eyes on him since he'd disappeared just before I shot Bezukhov. The current situation was perfect for him to whoosh in and set me straight on my required behavior when working for the Chairman. But Harry was nowhere to be seen.

Donna walked around the corner at Third Avenue and headed for her front door. I stepped toward her and called her name. She was puzzled as she saw me.

"Donna? I'm Jack Tyrrell, a friend of Richard's."

"Oh."

I extended my hand, and she awkwardly shook it. There wasn't a trace of recognition in her eyes. She was clearly wary and uncomfortable at this out-of-the-blue meeting.

"Richard and I served together in Afghanistan."

"I see." Donna was a very long way from warming to me.

"I thought I'd ask how he's doing."

"He's good, thanks." Still wary. Still at arm's length, maintaining a buffer zone of air between us. "I'm sorry, but I don't know you. I'm not comfortable having a conversation about my brother with a stranger."

"Of course, of course," I said in a reassuring tone. "I'm sorry, I didn't mean to . . . uh . . . scare you."

"What did you mean?" her eyes were hard. And then the therapist in her asked, "What do you want from me?"

What had happened to the woman who had hugged and kissed me? To the woman who'd promised she wouldn't forget me?

"Well, uh . . . nothing. Nothing at all. Sorry I bothered you." Despite Harry's warnings, I wasn't prepared for this.

"I have to go." Donna went inside before I had a chance to say anything else. Given how confused I was, it might have taken me years to say anything at all.

"Are you satisfied now?" Harry asked.

I took a deep breath. "I wouldn't say . . . satisfied."

Harry didn't seem to know what to say but after a long pause, he managed, "I'm sorry."

"Thanks." I began walking west on 88th Street, crossing Third Avenue and heading toward Lexington. Harry fell into step beside me. We were quiet until we reached Fifth Avenue. Central Park, across from us, was in full summer bloom, the trees and bushes impossibly thick with green. I stopped and faced Harry.

"Why did Alex have to die?"

"I don't know."

"No telling me 'it was his time' or that his death is 'part of an unknowable plan'?"

"I don't know."

"How does that help me?"

"It doesn't."

I sighed and said, "Why do *you* think he was killed? Why did the Chairman let that happen?"

Harry watched the leaves in the park as they rustled

in the evening breeze, carefully considering his reply. "I think his death was the next stage of his journey."

"Really? You're handing me some mystical bullshit about journeys?"

"It's not bullshit."

"Sounds like bullshit to me. And since when do you curse?"

"When it's necessary to communicate. If it's bullshit, how do you explain Joe's death?"

"What the hell are you talking about?"

"Joe's life ended when he came full circle. He was a soldier again, he died a hero's death, he made a difference."

I said nothing and stared at him.

"He made a difference. Don't you think it was a good time for him to move onto the next stage?"

"Is that what happened?"

"What do you think?"

"For crying out loud, I hate it when you do—" I stopped, because we were no longer on Fifth Avenue—

We were back on the beach where I had first met Harry.

Once again, it was sunset, once again, red sky at night, sailor's delight. We stood beyond the waves cresting on the sand.

"That's not really fair, is it? Digging into your bag of magic tricks to win an argument."

"It's not about winning arguments. It's about what

you believe."

Turning from Harry, I watched the waves come in. "Donna and Richard have forgotten me?"

"Yes."

"Has Donna already forgotten me after this evening's re-introduction?"

"Yes."

"Will she forget me every time I re-introduce myself?"

"Yes."

"She's really gone." I felt a sharp pang of sorrow in my gut. I wasn't ready to say goodbye. I had known this moment was coming, but no one had prepared me for what it's like to help someone on a life-changing level and then be forgotten by them. Donna had never been mine, but I still wasn't ready to lose her.

"Are you going to report back to the Chairman on my performance?"

"He already knows, of course. He's very pleased."

"Does that mean I'm a bit closer to redeeming myself?"

Harry allowed himself a tiny smile, the merest lifting of one side of his mouth, "A bit."

Neither of us spoke for what seemed like a long time. The red glow of sunset faded into the dark blue of evening. Finally, Harry spoke up. "Are you ready for your next case?"

"What? Now?"

"Soon. There's a young woman—"

"Another woman who needs help? Am I going to have feelings for her, too?"

"I think the Chairman would hope that you have feelings for all the people you help."

"You know what I mean."

"I don't know what, if anything, you will feel toward this woman. But she will need your help. One morning very soon, she will wake up in bed next to a murdered man. She will have no memory of how she ended up there. She will not know if she killed the man."

"I thought you didn't do prophecy."

"The Chairman briefed me on your next case."

"Oh . . . ," I groaned, "Do I have a choice about this?"

"You always have a choice."

"Oh . . . shit."

Harry arched an eyebrow. "Well?" he asked.

"Can I tell you . . . later?"

"Yes."

I watched the waves race toward me and concentrated on the rushing sound they made as they came close to my feet. "Will I get to see Maggie again?"

Harry didn't answer, and after a long pause, I asked again, "Will I see Maggie?"

"I don't know. I'm sorry."

I nodded and concentrated the waves. "I still love her."

"I know."

Harry disappeared before I could say anything else. A tiny fraction of a second later, I was in my living room, standing at the window, looking out at West 76th Street glittering under the street lights.

I walked to my couch, sat down, leaned back, and closed my eyes.

"Thank you, Maggie," I whispered.

When I had told Richard that my wife had helped me, he had responded, "Lucky you."

"I love you," I said. "Come see me . . . please?"

I fell asleep on the couch.

Lucky me.

ACKNOWLEDGMENTS

This book was inspired by the work of three wonderfully creative men: Charles Dickens who wrote the best Christmas and best ghost story ever: *A Christmas Carol*; the dazzlingly inventive Philip K. Dick who wrote the short story *Adjustment Team*; and George Nolfi, the writer-director of the movie based on Dick's story: *The Adjustment Bureau*.

Many thanks to my publisher and editor at Saugatuck Books, Tom Seligson. I appreciate the opportunity to be one of Saugatuck's authors and all Tom's support.

To Alice Siempelkamp, who cleans manuscripts with an obsessive thoroughness. Unfortunately, when it comes to making mistakes, I'm a talented guy. Which means that there will still be mistakes in this book.

And to Ted Berk, who patiently and enthusiastically read what seemed like an endless number of early drafts and made a number of wonderful suggestions.

Thanks to Tom Brennan, who advised me on the experience of returning veterans. And to Fr. Jim Martin, SJ, whose books *The Jesuit Guide to (Almost) Everything*, *A Jesuit Off-Broadway*, and *Jesus: A Pilgrimage* were very helpful in addressing spiritual issues. If there are flaws in my portrayal of vets or in my expression of spirituality, the fault is mine.

Thanks to the many friends who have helped me through the writing of this book and all the other parts of my life: Marcia Menter, Tom and Judy Galligan, Ted Canellas and Bob Roth, Erica Fross, Gene O'Brien, Steve Pitts, Jill Quist, Katie Ryan, Greg Tobin, Sal Vitale, Ted West, and Lindy Sittenfeld.

Special thanks to my son, Greg, who has been an editor (and sometime co-writer) on many of my projects. His creativity and courage inspire me in every part of my life.

Finally, thanks to my wife, Margy. She is a blessing in each and every day of my life.

ABOUT THE AUTHOR

Geoff Loftus is the author of the thrillers *Double Blind, Engaged to Kill*, and *The Dark Saint*.

Murderous Spirit is the first novel in the Jack Tyrrell series.

Loftus is also the author of *Lead Like Ike: Ten Business Strategies from the CEO of D-Day* and was the 2010 Keynote Speaker at the Eisenhower Legacy Dinner at the Eisenhower Presidential Museum and Library.

Like many writers, he once dreamed of writing the great American novel but gave that up in an attempt to write the great American screenplay. The closest he came to that lofty achievement was writing *Hero in the Family* with John Drimmer for *The Wonderful World of Disney*. He has been a member of the Writers Guild of America, East for more than twenty-five years.

He lives in Scarsdale, New York with his wife, Margy; son, Gregory; and the family's wonderful little dog, Heidi.